PRAISE FOR *MY BIGGEST LIE*
BY LUKE BROWN

'A real page-turner. Deeply sensual.'

Gary Shteyngart

'I grabbed this for its mad adventure but came away with a gift for the heart.'

DBC Pierre

'Smart, zingy and extremely funny, this is a real treat.'

Paul Murray

'Its warmth and tenderness are hard to resist.'

Catherine O'Flynn

'Brown's deliciously tricksy novel encourages its reader to pay attention to correspondences between art and life . . . It captures the sun-soaked sexiness of the city . . . and the hazy drug that is desire better than anything I have read in years.'

The Guardian

'Rewarding and ambitious.'

Times Literary Supplement

'An unashamedly literary novel that nonetheless wears its learning lightly and is totally unpretentious: a ludic, drunk, dizzying jaunt.'

Dazed & Confused

'A scintillating, intelligent and uproariously funny trip into the excesses of storytelling.'

Big Issue

THEFT

Luke Brown

SHEFFIELD - LONDON - NEW YORK

First published in the UK by And Other Stories
Sheffield – London – New York
www.andotherstories.org

9 8 7 6 5 4 3 2 1

ISBN 9781911508588
eBook ISBN 9781911508595

Editor: Stefan Tobler; Copy-editor: Gesche Ipsen; Proofreader: Sarah Terry;
Typesetter: Tetragon, London; Typefaces: Linotype Swift Neue and Verlag;
Cover Design: Luke Bird; Printed and bound by TJ International, Padstow,
Cornwall.

And Other Stories gratefully acknowledge that our work is supported using
public funding by Arts Council England.

For Jacquie, Naomi and Rachel

'I never cared one bit about the property. I cared about herself – and always shall do.'

BRANWELL BRONTË TO J. B. LEYLAND, 1846

'. . . theft'

WHAT IS PROPERTY?, 1840

'Verily, what with tainting, plundering and spoiling, Tom has his revenge.'

BLEAK HOUSE, 1853

PART ONE

PART ONE

ONE

What I did to them was terrible, but you have to understand the context. This was London, 2016. My friends and I had lived our adult lives in flats with living rooms made into bedrooms, kitchens into pop-up cocktail bars and gallery spaces; we worked in pubs and shops and schools and clung on to our other lives as artists and musicians and professional skateboarders. For too long I'd suspected that I would have been more successful if I'd spent less time talking to my friends, if I had been more discerning about who they were, if I had put to another use the ten thousand hours in which I had discussed the meaning of love with the lunatics who wouldn't leave my sofa. How much more organised and efficient I thought my mind might be if it had not had so much company. I worried that I had sabotaged myself, ruined myself for both distinction and the humdrum, and I wished I had become another man, a better man, a man who I suppose would feel no sympathy for me, a superior bastard, a loathsome know-it-all, who would replace me, and get away with it, and no one would mourn me. There is little point thinking about what might have been. Character means character.

My name is Paul. I work three days a week in a bookshop and write for a magazine. I am here in my predicament, and it is not so bad. Amy disagrees with me about that. But then

11

we disagree about nearly everything. Or we did until she disappeared.

*

'Do you like the word *property*?' I asked Amy.

My sister, two years younger than me, considers herself the senior.

'Property?' she said.

'You say it a lot. I've seen this great *property*.'

'What word should I use? What word would *you* like me to use?'

'I don't know, something less abstract: house, flat, maisonette, or we could change the subject, talk about, I don't know, music, philosophy, art, love.'

'Something less abstract?'

'Property, property, property – do you know what I hear?'

'What?'

'Mine, mine, mine.'

'Do you know what I hear when you talk about property?'

'What?'

'Whine, whine, whine.'

*

Recently Amy and I have come into some property together, this little terraced house, only three minutes' walk from the sea. Open your mouth and breathe that air in, the freshest air in all of the country. Listen to the seagulls' shrieks. Inside the house you'll see it's very tastefully decorated, with wooden flooring, painted walls, a modern kitchen with a door that leads out to the little garden that catches the sun in the morning. Yes, sun. Such glorious summers you could have here, by the waves. It could make an imaginative person a lovely holiday home. Is 'imaginative' the word? Self-reliant. You wouldn't believe how cheaply things go up here. Mortgage payments would be nothing for someone used to the price of life in London. We'll probably drop the price again soon. It's slow at the moment. Not much movement. Open the door and the freshest air just fills your lungs. The streets, seen from above, ripple out in concentric circles around a man-made hill: a pebble dropped in a pool, a feat of ambitious town planning from Decimus Burton, the Victorian architect who also designed Hyde Park, Green Park, St James's Park. People used to come on the train from miles around for their holidays. The line closed a long time ago, but even though we're surrounded on three sides by the sea we're hardly isolated. It's only forty minutes by tram to the nearest train station, and that's only three hours from London. New trams too, very comfortable. We'd live here ourselves if we could. If it were possible.

*

The magazine I write for is called *White Jesus* – who knows exactly why? The title is composed of words of equal length convenient for cover design, allows for occasional crucifixion photo shoots, appeals to the editor's messiah complex and offends 'civilians', by whom the editor might mean 'Christians', who aren't offended at all, who remain unaware of the magazine, not working in fashion or hairdressing, or living in Dalston.

I write two pages for the magazine, for little more than beer money. I pitched them to the editor, Stev'n – 'rhymes with seven', he insists – when he was going on dates with my sister and briefly listened to what I had to say. Amy, who has been missing ever since our last argument, is sometimes attracted to awful men. (Is there another kind? she says whenever I mention this.)

In one of my pages I write about books. In the other I write about haircuts. I am paid twice the amount to write the haircut page as the books page, though it takes me less than a tenth of the time. I set forth in Hackney and Peckham, approach strangers, and ask if I can snap a picture to feature in the *London Review of Haircuts*. Alongside their picture in the magazine and online I award their hairstyle between one and five pairs of scissors – a system I developed personally and which as far as I know is unique. Hair criticism is not a hard science – it is more akin to the interpretation of dreams. Using the imaginative empathy you might find in an analyst or old-fashioned literary realist, I type a witty summary of what the person attached to the haircut is like, a précis of their secrets and longings, in fifteen to twenty words.

Increasingly, I am under pressure from Stev'n to be cruel. I understand the appeal snark holds to our readers, to our souls. I do my best to resist it. Before I approach the haircut, I have usually decided how many pairs of scissors I am to award; if it's four or above, I will reveal my rating then and there. I have to consciously fight my attraction to women with fringes, whom I usually award four and a half scissors out of five. Technically, of course, that is nine scissors, but this is not a pedantic era, not in the basement discos of Kingsland Road. I never award five pairs of scissors. Perfect hair is impossible, but the quest for perfect hair provides the page with a sense of telos, something the readers of *White Jesus* crave, even if they don't know they do. Hi, my name's Paul and I write for *White Jesus* magazine. I love your hair, it's totally four and a half scissors out of five – would you mind if I put you in the next issue? Sometimes the people I approach giggle and think

I am joking. They are known to sneer and ask me if that is my best chat-up line. But that doesn't happen often. I choose the ones who look friendly.

*

The constant carnivalesque of the night buses, the queues for jerk chicken, the roped-off smoking sections. Contrary to popular stereotype, this *is* a friendly city we live in, often heartbreakingly so. Lack of friends is the least of our worries. There are lots of us out there, looking for each other, who think a new person is the most exciting thing. Not *thing*: don't purposely misconstrue me. Sentient being. Equal. Superior.

'I wish you could be a woman for a year,' said Amy. 'No, like a decade. Three decades. Then you'd see if you like to be constantly harassed and degraded.'

Amy is a serial dater in the American style that Tinder has made standard here too. She sees nothing strange about interviewing three different men a week, for a date to last forty-five minutes and consist of drinking a coffee. It is her experience, she says, that has confirmed her hypothesis that young men in London are the worst men in the world.

She gets no significant argument there from me. I know when I am beaten.

Nevertheless, I don't think it is helpful for Amy to believe in the absolute awfulness of men in this city. 'Don't you think it's dangerous for you to assume the monsters are all on the outside?' I said once to her, only once.

She took her time thinking about which way I had annoyed her most. Neither of us likes the suggestion that we know each other better than ourselves; we worry it is true.

'Is it somehow my fault these men have got wind of the imbalance in our ability to have children? My fault that they're using my greater urgency as leverage to make suggestions about my pubic hair and its removal, or to bring up the subject of my *ideal weight*, or to refuse to make an arrangement for next Saturday, or to answer a text message? I'm talking about men, right, who place wooden shoe trees into their shoes when they take them off at night, men with separate combs and shampoos for their beards, men with Nespresso machines. For these men to want to *take every day as it comes*? For these men to talk about freedom?'

'The thing is, Amy,' I said, 'I don't like men much either.'

But this is even more unfair.

'*You*,' she said, 'don't *need* to.'

*

Every member of the older generation who owns property has the potential to purchase part of the younger who doesn't. Perhaps it has always been this way. The young people dream of collaboration or revenge. Legal documents set out the niceties of the tension. Until recently I owned nothing, and my half-share of an inherited and what appears to be unsellable terrace in a half-alive northern town has not shaken my allegiance with the squatters in this city. These are the people who still talk to me, the ones who live in dilapidated hospitals and office blocks awaiting destruction. I have walked to their bedrooms through dark corridors in decaying horrorscapes like the scariest levels of *Resident Evil*. It's true, perhaps, that except for my sweet nature I don't have much to offer my younger friends. That one day they will decide I have been irresponsible with my opportunities, and judge me for this.

*

The last time I saw Amy before she disappeared was at Christmas, which we spent alone together at Mum's house, ours now, on the Lancashire coast where we grew up, this town from where trawlers used to set out into the North Atlantic, until we were banned from fishing there by the European Economic Community after the Cod Wars in the 1970s. Hard to mourn the end of overfishing. But someone had to.

At the very end of 2015, my sister and I managed three days of peace together before the Argument, and the Argument didn't feel so different from the arguments we had had before, maybe different in scale but not in kind, but then . . . how many more can we have until our desire to avoid them leads us to avoid each other completely? The situation was difficult for both of us. We wandered around, double-jumpered, being as stingy with the heating as Mum had always been, picking up ornaments and putting them back down, finding a quiddity in them that they had never had before. They were ours now. We looked out of the window at the spot where her car wasn't parked.

One evening we started to discuss what we would do with her furniture if we ever managed to sell the house. Amy owns two flats of her own and is always looking for new places to buy, renovate and sell on. This gives her a certain brusqueness when such matters are discussed. I was reluctant to follow her instructions and begin to list things on eBay.

'Don't tell me I'm insensitive,' she said. 'I'm being practical. You're being sentimental. And lazy. When did you even speak to Mum anyway?'

'On Sundays.'

'Sundays? I spoke to her all the time.'

'Does that make you better than me, because you rang her up all the time to moan about your life?'

17

It was not long after this that she threw a wine glass. It wasn't at me, just at the wall that was next to me. But even the little bit of the wine in the glass made quite a mess of that wall, and while I ran off to the pub Amy stayed to scrub the stains off, so that the value of the property wouldn't be diminished. In the morning I heard the front door slam and found she had left for London without me.

*

Mum was never fond of driving, or of teaching, but she drove each day to a secondary school to teach modern languages to depressed children, many of whom would never leave the peninsula where they and their parents had been born.

When the panic attack hit her in the middle of a stretch of dual carriageway, she was two years away from retirement, but at that moment it must have seemed a long way away. Amy and I can only speculate. We both take it as certain that the fact that there was nowhere for her to pull over was a cause of the crash, as well as the reason it was fatal. She had had panic attacks on this same stretch of road before, and usually took a long detour to avoid it. Her head teacher had made her late that night, calling her in to discuss a complaint made by a parent, and she was hurrying to get to a church hall where she had set up a ballroom dancing class, her plan to earn a little bit of money doing something she liked.

Three couples turned up that night, and her dancing partner, Alan. They chatted to each other for a few minutes outside the locked hall, before they decided it was too cold to wait any longer. Alan drove to her house, and then her school, to see if he could find her. The main road out of town was blocked off by the police.

Mum is a cautious driver, she always wears her seat belt. She waits a long time to pull out at junctions. People beeped their horns behind her sometimes, and if I was beside her when they did I would fantasise about smashing their windows.

Because this is what I think happened.

With the steel barrier to her left and the long lorry to her right, the car coming too close from behind and forcing her too close to the car in front, she felt the pressure building and knew it would not subside. The strap seemed to be pulling tighter around her every second, choking off the deep breaths she tried to take. Pushed in on every side, she scrabbled for the button to wind down the window, but she couldn't find it, and the car smelled of hot carpet, the crackle of kindling, bunched newspaper and firelighters, and then her hand alighted on her belt buckle, on the one restraint she could undo, unclipping it just before she blacked out and hit the car in front.

Wherever Amy has gone to, this is one of the few things that she and I can agree upon.

*

The party is about to end but it used to be such fun. We all loved each other. We were all interchangeable, in the best way. We woke up in each other's arms and stumbled out to buy breakfast, past groups of people looking just like us, right down to the same sunglasses and unisex jeans. Someone would always know someone else intimately and we would all embrace each other, breathing in the sweet smell on our necks, something sharp and carnal.

Now I wonder if this city's friendliness is the most dangerous thing about it. There is always someone to inspire new hope in you. There is always a saviour to find.

TWO

When I am not working in the bookshop or reporting on hairstyles I do the work I like the most. This is how I met Emily Nardini. It was quite a coup for me and *White Jesus*: Nardini had not consented to an interview in over ten years, or to a photograph in over twelve, and when I wrote to request my interview I had to insist on a photograph: most of our readers only look at the pictures. I had never seen Nardini in the flesh before, surprising really, as most of the writers who live in London pass through the shop at one point or other. I don't think I would have missed her, despite there being only the one publicity photo in existence, taken when she was twenty-one and her first novel had just been published. It was the kind of photo that made publishers use the words 'highly promotable' in press releases. Dark Italian features bleached into high contrast by the rain and scour of a Scottish shipbuilding city. A formally beautiful face, with pale skin and bright eyes like a starlet in monochrome. Writers don't look like that. They get enough attention for being averagely attractive, competently stylish; her looks are distracting. More distracting for a woman; men don't suffer the same if we are put up on posters. The photo of her shows someone who senses exactly what the camera is taking from her. She looks straight at it, resentful, about to become furious. She is sick of being looked at like this, sick of what we are trying to claim from her. Her seriousness. Her language. So she scowls and becomes someone whom sensitive men want to patronise and cheer up. Someone whom gallants want to rescue.

When she agreed to the interview and photo request it was clear to me there had been a terrible mistake. While *White Jesus* does feature cultural articles, they are often next to photos of girls in their underwear, often just one piece of their underwear. I was concerned about her meeting with our house photographer, due round after my interview, who considered himself to be a boundary-pushing conceptual artist. I hoped he would remember it was a book interview and not try to persuade her to take her clothes off, or pose provocatively on a merry-go-round, or underneath a live swan, or wearing a unicorn horn, or with ice cream on her face, holding an antique pistol, or a serrated blade to a child's throat, or doing a handstand in a loose dress, on rollerblades, or smoking a Cuban cigar in a wheelbarrow, in a short plaid skirt, wrapped in a butcher's apron covered in gore, or attached to a radiator with cable ties, or joke-shop nails, or actual nails, or any other of his signature moves, but I didn't put it past him. I wished I could hang around to keep an eye on him but I had to work in the shop that afternoon.

*

I had not prepared well for the interview with Emily Nardini. On the night before, the magazine had held their January awards ceremony in a warehouse in Bethnal Green. The magazine likes to position itself in strict opposition to the penitent mood of January, the temporary veganism and abstinence. It is catered by the owner's mate who runs a series of Satanic burger joints done out in apocalyptic Gilbert & George-style stained glass. There are mounds of 'murdered yogi' burgers, pitchers of rum cocktails, envelopes full of chisel and big thick Es the size of Scrabble tiles being passed around. Such things once had appeal, but these days I would rather have skipped it – except it was politic to make an appearance. Jonathan, the advertising director, is a man I met in the previous millennium at what was then called the London College of Printing. I would only cautiously describe Jonathan as a friend, for reasons you will come to understand, and last week he had casually mentioned to me that Stev'n was talking about cutting my books page, in favour of a legal highs column. I had not been reassured by Jonathan's reassurance that if this did happen I would be the first choice to write the legal highs column, that Stev'n had a great respect for my ability to enjoy narcotics, and I would probably be paid more money for it. At the party I intended to catch Stev'n when he was flying on a cocktail of empathogens and subtly implant within him an association between my books page and euphoria. But in the end I spent most of the night talking to a woman a few years older than me, the managing director of a clothing company who advertised with us, about who our favourite character in *Middlemarch* was – Dorothea, obviously, not the feckless millennial she ends up with – in between accepting bumps of cocaine from the corner of her credit card and downing martinis from the free bar. You wouldn't know from looking at me, but I've got a real thing about the nineteenth-century novel. I know my freedoms dwarf those of its heroines, but that doesn't stop me identifying with women anxious to see if their saviour will arrive.

The managing director and I were surprised to be having a conversation about Victorian novels in a crowd of 25-year-olds dancing to grime, spilling cocktails and taking dabs of MDMA; and I wondered if she might be interested in me, if she had space in her flat, if she wanted a child, if we could come to a civilised arrangement we could reasonably name 'love'.

I woke up fully clothed, with oily hands. The more vivid details of my journey home struggled to arrange themselves into sequence: falling off my bike repeatedly, making emergency repairs, giving all my money to a homeless man after a bin jumped out at me and I rode up a lamp post. I was due at Emily Nardini's in forty-five minutes. I did not have time to remove the oil from my hands, have a shower or charge my phone – just to pull up the address on my laptop and draw a map on my arm of how to get to her house from the Tube stop. I grabbed my voice recorder, splashed some water on my face and ran out of the house, forgetting to take with me the list of questions I had prepared to ask her.

*

I had been giddy and happy on the Overground; one or two of the many martinis I had poured into myself must have remained active. When I changed to the Tube, however, and started to think about the photographer, I began to feel hot and panicky. I could not work out whether the way the light was flickering in the carriage was a malfunction inside or outside me. I am not a man who drinks in the mornings, but it was clear to me that in this case not drinking was more irresponsible. The only pubs open at this time are Wetherspoons and I didn't like my chances of finding one in Holland Park, so when I rose into daylight I quickly nipped into an off-licence.

Holland Park: that address had thrown me. The protagonists of her novels are always impoverished runaways, cleaners, waitresses, hotel staff, hairdressers, writers or even less employable artists, all roughly the same age as Nardini, living in a room of their own, bed, upright chair, no room for books or bag.

The street I was led to by the map on my arm was a quiet, tree-lined curve of tall white buildings. Outside her door I opened a can of Coke, took a swig and replaced it with an inch of whisky from the little bottle I had just bought. Then I rang the door and waited.

*

I was surprised by how friendly she looked, how cheerfully she held out her hand. More than the intervening years, it was the unexpected range of expression that made her look so different from her photograph. Her beauty was still there, but it was warmer and less intimidating when she smiled. She was only very pretty, terrestrial, made up with eyeliner and mascara.

I held out my hand and she withdrew hers.

'Oh, shit, yes,' I said.

'Have you been fixing cars?' she asked.

'Tinkering with my ute,' I said, in an Australian accent. I make bad jokes when I'm nervous. She didn't smile so I reverted to British English. 'A bike, actually.' I looked at my hands. 'It's very hard to get off.'

'The bike?' she asked.

'It was very hard to stay *on* the bike last night.'

'You are the journalist, aren't you?'

'Um. I am here to do the interview.'

She weighed me up for a few seconds. 'Aha,' she said. 'Well, we're up here.' Her Glaswegian accent was carefully enunciated, like a regional Radio 4 presenter's; I imagined her planing the edges off it, like I had done with mine, sliver by sliver, to wedge between where we had been and where we now wanted admittance. In a dark blue skirt or dress, a grey jumper and black winter tights, Emily was

24

wearing no shoes, and on the balls of her feet she led me to a set of stairs.

'We're right at the top,' she said, turning back to scrutinise me again. Then she headed up and I followed her.

*

On the way up the stairs I tripped on a step and had to grab her arm so I didn't fall over.

'I'm really sorry,' I said, righting myself.

'It's OK,' she said, but she justifiably sounded wary. 'Perhaps you need a cup of tea to go with your Coca-Cola?'

'I just tripped. Yes, a cup of tea would be nice.'

I followed her through the door, which opened into a wide hallway of polished wood with long corridors at right angles to each other. On one side of each corridor fitted mahogany bookshelves stretched to the end.

'There's a camera attached to the front door,' she said. 'What was that I saw you pouring into your Coke? Rum?'

'Oh, shit.' I put the can down on the side. 'Whisky, actually.'

'Are you an alcoholic?' She asked this in the tone she might have used to ask if I came from London. I followed her down the length of a corridor and into a kitchen, shiny, clean, light: a piece with the flat.

'No. That was an emergency drink.'

'That sounds like the sort of thing an alcoholic would say.'

'A minor alcoholic, though. A major alcoholic would accuse you of being a witch and burst into tears before he asked you to pray with him.'

She pressed her lips together to suppress what could have been amusement or irritation. 'Are you drunk now?'

'Not at all. Sorry – I just had to defer a hangover for a couple more hours.'

'Did you consider not getting drunk last night?' she asked calmly, filling the kettle. 'Considering this engagement of ours?'

'It was our awards party, I had to go. They're planning to cut my books page, you see. I'd planned to buttonhole the editor and convince him of the value of it before he replaces it with . . . I don't know . . . a page of weird genitals that look like vegetables, or weird vegetables that look like genitals, I don't know, I can't think like he does.'

I was speaking too quickly. I was pacing back and forth in the kitchen, forcing myself not to pick up the can of Coke.

She watched me walk from one side of the room to the other. 'So, if I understand correctly, you're saying your getting smashed last night was . . . in service of literary journalism?'

'Exactly. I'm very sorry not to turn up completely sober.'

She took two mugs from a cupboard. 'I'm giving you the benefit of the doubt. There have been times too when I haven't turned up completely sober.'

'You're welcome to some whisky, if you'd like.'

'No thanks. Not a whisky girl. Any Italian genes overrode the Scottish ones there. And I'm not an anything girl at the moment.'

'I'm sorry if I seem glib about the booze,' I said. 'I suppose I charged in here like a bull in a china shop.'

'You charged in here *sheepishly*. And then you fell over.'

I laughed, and then she smiled with a little less froideur than before, and for the first time I felt like the interview might be something other than a disaster.

'How come you've invited me over, anyway?' I asked. 'I thought you avoided this stuff.'

*

Desperate times. She'd been too aloof, needed to be more realistic. Said her agent. Said her editor. Said her new agent. Said her new editor. She had to show willing this time. Even though no one cared about novels any more, especially her novels.

I disagreed. She shrugged. The kettle clicked off and she turned to make two mugs of tea. I stepped out of the kitchen back into the hallway.

'Mind if I look at your books?'

'They're mostly my boyfriend's, but yes, feel free. It's mostly art books on this side. All the fiction is round the corner. There's a little room I use to write in which holds the few books that have stuck to me.'

I walked out into the corridor. The art books had been arranged alphabetically, and I noticed the classical taste of the contemporary choices. I looked for Emin, Lucas, the Chapmans – no. Round the corner the fiction began. Whoever she lived with was a big reader with excellent taste. I carried on down the corridor, attracted by the light I could see from the room at the end. It was a long room with two enormous sets of windows that filled it with light and showed the top branches of the tree outside. The walls were covered in paintings, there was a dining table at one side of it, and a living-room area formed by two dark red sofas in an L-shape. Hardbacks were piled in a stack in one corner of the room with spines I recognised as recent arrivals to the shop. There was a photo of a middle-aged woman on the mantelpiece, the sort of woman who belonged in this room. Six of our living room could have fitted inside this one, and I wondered how much the flat had cost when it was bought. I wondered how much it cost now. I observed myself wondering and hated myself for being so dull. A pair of black Chelsea boots faced the corner like a dunce.

'Sugar?' shouted Emily from the kitchen.

I walked back and said no thanks. I watched her remove a teabag from one mug and dunk it in the other. 'Your boyfriend's a big reader too.'

'Oh, yeah. A lot of the books are actually his ex's. She was in the business until – well, that's his business. I've always been too peripatetic until recently to keep hold of my books. I end up buying the same favourites four or five times.' She handed me a tea. 'Probably easiest to do this in my room. The living room's too distracting. You just want to appreciate it. I don't allow myself in there when I have work to do.'

She led me back down the corridor and opened a door. The first thing I saw was a double bed and I thought hopefully that perhaps I had misheard her about the boyfriend, and she was only a lodger.

'It was the guest bedroom before I took it over,' she explained. 'Supposed to be for his daughter but she never stays over, not now I'm here.'

She turned sharply away from me as she said that, and I didn't ask any further.

It was a big enough room for the bed, a wardrobe, a neat desk in one corner and a sofa facing it. A white Ikea Billy bookcase like the three I had crammed into my room was out of keeping with the display furniture of the corridors, and stuffed full of paperbacks, unalphabetised. Two piles of books were stacked next to it, Jenga towers a couple of moves away from collapsing. There was a plastic crate of CDs on the floor next to an integrated stereo of nineties vintage, the type of thing you bought in Argos, and which proudly advertised its Megabass. The contrast between the room and the style of the rest of the flat made it seem like an installation: a young person's room in a shared house, inside the grand surroundings of a public gallery. Outside the window were neat strips of neighbours' gardens, a small and ancient-looking church, a little plot of gravestones. She turned the desk chair around to the sofa and gestured to it.

'Thanks for agreeing to do the interview,' I said, sitting down. 'You may have been surprised to find out we even had a books page.'

'I'm not sure I've seen the magazine.'

'Well, there's no reason why you should have. Perhaps you'd have browsed through a copy waiting in a hairdresser's. There are approximately seventy pages of adverts before you reach the contents page.'

Emily flopped back onto the sofa as if the news had exhausted her. 'My publicist was keen to emphasise the quality of the books coverage. That *did* make me suspicious.'

'That's nice of her. She might have been stressing the contrast. There's a toxic level of irony in much of the content. Though I don't know if that's the word, actually. I don't know if the photos of the models on the toilet are ironic. Or the high-school-massacre fashion shoots. I think they're just corrupt.'

'Why do you write for such awful-sounding people?'

'I haven't had much success offering myself elsewhere.'

'I begin to worry where I fit in here.'

'You're my choice. I'm the magazine's gravitas. Stop raising your eyebrows.'

'I was looking at your wrist. Is that a map?'

'It is, yes.' I pulled my sleeve up further and showed her how to get to her house from the Tube stop. 'If we end up becoming mates, I could have it done as a tattoo as a souvenir of today.'

'That would be original. You probably have a "bad tatts" section in the magazine.'

'Let's not talk about that. It's three times the length of my book section.'

I put the recorder on the table.

'So, shall we begin? Emily, tell me about your body art.'

*

We spoke for about an hour and a half. Her careful vowels serrated at the edges when she became disdainful. There was no getting away from it: she was bitter about the world's indifference to her and the trouble it took to write a book. She knew no one asked her to; she knew she was angry and had no right to be: 'How do we redeem this interview from me moaning on about how crap the world is?'

So I asked her the question I was most interested in, the one I knew to be the most vulgar. 'How much of what has happened to your characters is based on what has happened to you?'

'Perhaps you could be specific,' she said quietly.

*

Emily, are you on the edge? Emily, are your parents dead too? Emily, do you believe love is impossible? Do you believe love is the only hope? Were you married once, for only two weeks? What is it like to live for so long in poverty? What is it about Paris, why do you keep running there? Couldn't you ever have decided to be happier? Is that what you have done now? Or have you always been happy? Have you tricked us? Why did you never mention this flat? Who is this man you live with? Are you writing about him now? Have you chosen comfort over love? Do you think I am an idiot? Am I like the rest of the men in your novels? Are we all so transparently hungry? Are we all so gauche? So vain and inconsequential? Are we the problem? Are we your problem? Are you laughing at me?

Could you ever love someone like me? What has he got that I haven't? Is it money? Or something else?

*

The London Review of Haircuts

An outgrown fringe, half-tied behind, is slipping back across her face. She pushes it back, like the childish thoughts of smoky rooms and loud music we hope lie behind those dark eyes, the same brown as her hair. She doesn't look the way she does entirely by accident, and she would like to test the power and reach of those looks again while they still belong to a young woman.

*

She was laughing by the time she saw me to the door. 'You didn't drink your Coke,' she said, handing it back to me. 'It's full to the top.'

'This should be some kind of epiphany for me. A spur to throw down my crutches and walk unaided.'

I took a swig.

'Stagger unaided,' she said.

'Remember what I said: if the photographer suggests anything unusual, remind him this is for a book interview, lock yourself in the bathroom and ring me on my mobile.'

'I'll handle him. Don't worry.'

I leaned over and kissed her on both cheeks. 'Thanks again. I hope I see you around. If you were serious before about inviting me round for dinner sometime, I'd love to come.'

She looked at me curiously, as if I had nearly tricked her into something unpleasant. She frowned. 'Andrew *is* always encouraging me to invite friends round. I suppose he might like you once he'd got over his disappointment that I'd invited a man and not a woman.'

'I could bring a woman, if you liked.'

'You bragger. No, thanks.'

'Just a bottle of wine, then.'

'And a half-bottle of whisky for the doorstep.'

'I'd turn up sober, I promise.'

'Best not promise. You never know when literature will need you again. Goodbye, Paul.'

'Bye, Emily.'

She shut the door. I stood there for a few seconds and listened for her footsteps on the other side. After about ten seconds I heard her going back up the stairs and I turned away too.

THREE

The bookshop where I work is in Bloomsbury, surrounded by universities and libraries and the British Museum. My colleagues here come from a separate planet from my colleagues at *White Jesus*, being, in the main, graceful, thoughtful people, well read in political philosophy, current affairs, poetry and literary fiction.

'Have you heard about Leo?' asked Helen, as soon as I walked through the door. Helen is the shop's manager, a woman my age from Hull. 'A hundred K,' she said, which is not the kind of thing she usually said, and I wished I were not aware of the context, that my least favourite colleague Leo had been talking to publishers about the novel he had written.

'K?' I said.

'A hundred thousand pounds.'

'That's a lot of M,' I said.

'I know.'

'Is he going to resign?'

'I didn't think of that. Would you resign?'

'No. Or I'd spend half of it in six months and half of it on subsequent rehab.'

'Thank God for you, Paul. I can rely on you not to go anywhere.'

'Particularly if you give me a pay rise.'

'Ah, Paul.'

'Have you spoken to him?'

'Yeah.'

'Is he unbearable?'

'A little bit.'

'You're less bitter than me. That means he's totally unbearable.'

'I'll leave you to judge it. How was Emily Nardini?'

I breathed out. 'If you say something stupid to her – '

'Which you did.'

'Which I did – she looks just like her photo. But on perhaps as many as two separate occasions I actually made her laugh. Then she looks different.'

'You haven't fallen for her, have you? You look like you have.'

'I fall in love with everyone I meet. For a little bit.'

'You're like George Eliot. She used to fall in love with everyone she met.'

'I'm glad someone's finally noticed. That's why I hit it off so well with Emily Nardini.'

Helen bent to look something up on the computer. 'That must be why. Where did this meeting take place?'

'Her flat, in Holland Park. It's huge. She lives with what appears to be a rich man. I thought I'd be meeting her in a rented room somewhere but she has the run of the place.'

'You know *who* she lives with, don't you?'

'No. Who?'

'Andrew Lancaster.'

Andrew Lancaster. I recognised the name, but it was one of those sturdy names anyone could have. There were probably three famous Andrew Lancasters.

'The popular historian. Left-wing, at least to start with. Professor at UCL. Pally for a while with the Blair government. Increasingly right-wing, say his enemies. No fan of the Tories.'

'Oh, yeah. Of course, I've sold hundreds of his books without giving him any thought. He sounds . . .'

'Clever? Accomplished?'

'I was going to use the word "distinguished".'

'Distinguished, yes.'

'And to be called "distinguished", you have to be how old?'

'In general or particular?'

'Of course, in general.'

'I think he's in his late fifties.'

*

My own accommodation was a little different from Emily's.
I lived with a young woman who was not my girlfriend on
the Kingsland Road in Dalston, in a place my friends and
I named 'the château' when we moved in eleven years ago.
It's a two-bedroom flat that during our tenancy has regularly
been a three-bedroom and six-person flat. We didn't need to
have so many people living here to afford the place but it
always felt selfish to have a living room *and* kitchen when a
friend needed somewhere cheap to live. The happiest times
I remember here were those times when we spoke always
about how much we hated living here, when I lived with my
friends Stuart and Lenny and our girlfriends, Monica, Kate
and Anya, queuing in the winter mornings for a shower, the
ceiling paint flaking down like snow, or when we crammed
into the kitchen to try to make dinner, to find space in the
fridge, to locate the milk, Hoover or ironing board, our keys,
our hash, a stash of cocaine lost three years ago during a
party which we still remained optimistic would one day show
up, and one day did, in a secret compartment not one of us
remembered hacking out of *The Line of Beauty* with a razor
blade. Monica was the first to leave, when she took what was

going to be a two-year job in Melbourne. Stuart and Kate left a year ago to buy a house in Margate; and for a while Lenny and I had rooms to ourselves and the rare luxury of a living room (Anya was staying mostly at her parents' by then). We had lived together for nearly ten years, earning what money we needed in ways we found convenient; Lenny made it that long as a musician and professional skateboarder before he was eventually defeated by the idea of a 'career' when the fear of not having one became magnified out of all proportion by marijuana-smoking. He is back in Coventry at his parents' now, working as a teaching assistant. When I speak to him on the phone he is happier than he was during those last years in London, those anticlimactic months when we had what we had always thought we wanted: a TV and a sofa in a room designed for TV-watching. It was not enough. 'For years I was convinced something awful was going to happen to me,' he said. 'Well, it's happened now. It's much better now I know what it is.' I hadn't wanted to replace Lenny in a hurry; it was not urgent on such low rent, and it might have seemed indecent, like marrying again weeks after being widowed; but then I met Mary.

The château is located on the two floors above a branch of inexpensive British patisseries, and though the rent is cheap beyond all proportion for London, there are reasons why it would be offered cheap in a saner world. Waking up in the top bedrooms, the smell of the steak bakes that drifts up through the floorboards is not so pungent, but Stuart and particularly Kate (a vegan), who had what is now the living room downstairs, never quite got used to their closer proximity to the ovens in the shop. It is a mixed blessing to be upstairs: our central heating system is erratic, and our roof porous. In the middle of one memorable dream I woke up choking on dust, looking up at Monica's face as it slowly revealed itself to be the moon seen through a new hole in the roof. I have lived here for over a decade now, moving rooms only once after Monica left me and I switched to the room next door where she wouldn't be quite as absent. While the rest of the area's real-estate value has risen to the extent that it may even rival Emily's W11, I have never had to pay more than the £100 a month I first agreed to in the year after I finished my undergraduate degree. Paying, by this mixture of good fortune and tenaciousness, what might be the cheapest rent in London, I do as little as possible to remind our landlord that we exist – the place has not been decorated or refurbished for at least a decade, and I suspect four. The last time we called him was when the hole appeared in my bedroom's ceiling; mostly, I carry out my own repairs, unskilfully, using a collection of cheap tools and screws we keep in a child's Superman lunch box. Another peculiarity of our château – it has no address. It does not exist, and nor do we – we receive no polling cards, we pay no council tax. Our gas and electricity operate with tokens, and Harpreet, one of the chefs pâtissiers downstairs, has been kind enough to let us share their wi-fi. Arriving *chez nous, vous allez* down the alley and into the backyard before climbing a rickety fire escape into the kitchen, I feel constantly on the verge of being found out. We have our post sent to our places of work, those of us who have places of work, and at the moment that happens to be all of us, including the temporary guest downstairs who I am hoping will sort things out soon with his wife.

*

He was in when I got back, lying on the sofa under a single Postman Pat duvet cover that had belonged to a previous resident. There were childhood remnants in all of our flats which someone had been too sentimental to throw away. Jonathan's boots were peeping out, and he was watching *EastEnders*. 'How do you make Netflix come on?' he asked.

'Our TV isn't well educated enough,' I told him.

He turned it off. 'Fuck it, then. Normal TV is bollocks now.'

'Any news on Julia?'

'Oh, don't mention her. I've had a bad enough day.'

I have known Jonathan since we met on our magazine journalism degree at the London College of Printing, which wasn't such a comic idea in the last year of the last millennium, before they changed its name to sound less archaic. Jonathan has always been an entrepreneurial spirit. He sold Spanish cigarettes and Dutch ecstasy on campus, and by our final year he was wearing Paul Smith suits to seminars and the pub. He had started working for *White Jesus* in the summer of our second year, which was where he met his wife Julia, two years his senior and the only daughter of a surgeon and a psychiatrist. It was at this time he began to insist on being called Jonathan rather than Jonny. She had thrown him out a month ago and he had been living in our living room since. I still hadn't got to the bottom of what he had done that was bad enough to be thrown out by Julia. They'd always been proud of being sexually adventurous; so I didn't think it was infidelity, unless there was some line of etiquette he'd overstepped. According to him, they were just 'working some stuff through'.

He turned up one night with a bottle of Jameson's and a bag of ice. I was touched at the time that he'd chosen me to come to, though I wonder if he had anyone else, or if I was just the softest touch he knew. We barely saw each other outside of work functions these days: Jonathan, the advertising director, is also de facto publisher of *White Jesus* during the frequent absences of the millionaire who owns that title and the magazine. I couldn't afford to go to Jonathan and Julia's wedding, on a Greek island; and Monica preferred to avoid them after that one time when they'd tried to inveigle us into an orgy with them. I never went to the magazine's offices if I could help it.

'Where's Mary?' I asked.

'She's in her room with that little twerp she hangs out with.'

'They're not . . .?'

'They might be.'

*

We are both in love with our housemate Mary, and confused as to whether we love her as another little sister, the mother we miss, or the girlfriend we covet. Probably a mixture of all three: the overdetermined love of man for woman that makes life so full of jeopardy for women.

I first met Mary in the middle of an argument I was having with a cyclist on Theobald's Road. Riding east in the early evening, I was always part of a large peloton: sensible commuters with panniers and fluorescent jackets mingling with posing faux-couriers atop lurid bikes with one gear. I was feeling quite rueful and sensitive about the bike I was riding: the old racer my father had given me was stolen as divine punishment on the night I split up with the woman I went out with too soon after Monica, and the quickest and lightest bike I could buy with the £150 budget I managed to scrabble together looked like something that belonged to a seven-year-old girl, a fixie with rave-orange frame and lipstick-pink tyres. For a brief while the chain had even matched the tyres, until London's filth did its quick work. There were a lot of garish bikes on the road, but I hadn't seen one worse than mine. Even the hipsters had baulked at it, hence the knock-down price I had it for from a Chinese bike shop on Hackney Road. If I shut my eyes, it was an OK ride, quick with narrow handlebars, but shutting one's eyes on London's roads is not sustainable, and observing myself atop this bike in window reflections was inspiring a crisis of identity in me: I am by inclination and prescription an unshaven wearer of thick-rimmed spectacles, and this bike had closed the circle. There was no denying any more that I was a man with beard and glasses wearing a messenger bag and riding his pink and orange bike to Hackney. There was always violence on the roads, but I began to provoke it more often.

On the day I met Mary I judged the space between the curb and a bus too narrow to safely undertake and held my distance. 'Out of the way then,' came a voice from behind me, followed by the sound of a rubber horn. I turned round. There was a man in short shorts and white socks perched on a bicycle like mine, almost identical, except for the rubber horn he had attached.

'Pardon?' I said.

'Just fucking get down there mate,' he said, 'or get out of the fucking way.'

The next thing I knew I was off my bike and had his T-shirt in my hand, shouting about my friend Sam who had died in a bike accident.

Until I was pushed away from him by a young woman who herself then began to shout at him, about her friend Heidi who had been crushed to death on the inside of a lorry that had turned left without indicating.

'Sorry!' he said. 'Sorry!' He must have been twice the weight of the woman who was prodding him in the chest. She backed away from him a step and scowled at him, and he took the opportunity to ride off, looking behind him to check that neither of us were following him. She wandered over to a bike that was lying on the pavement and picked it up, holding a hand over her eyes when I walked up to her.

'Thank you,' I said to her. 'And I'm so sorry about your friend.'

She lowered her hand and squinted at my bike. 'I'm sorry about your friend.'

I have no friend called Sam who died in a bike accident. But it felt like I did when I had the cyclist's T-shirt bunched in my fist.

She was still looking at my bike.

'This isn't my bike I'm riding,' I told her. 'Just so you know, it doesn't belong to me.'

She wiped her eyes and tried to smile. 'It's very colourful,' she said. She had a basket on her bike, containing a handbag and a pair of heels.

'You look shaken up,' I said. 'Let me buy you a drink. Come on. I insist.'

In the pub Mary told me about the interview she had just been to, to work as an intern at a major record label, a job that came with no salary except a ten-pound per diem for a sandwich and bus fare. She had got the 'job'. I asked her how she was going to afford to do her job.

'I work in a bar and I won't eat food.'

'Or sleep.'

'No, I won't do much of that either.'

When she told me about her band, and how she thought they might be about to be offered a record deal, the only philanthropic thing to suggest was that she move into our place. Only above Gregg's can a person be free to dream and create in this city. She was suspicious, but took my number, and said she'd come round the next day to take a look.

The next day there was a knock at the back door. Mary was standing there, smiling, in a dress and trainers, next to a tall young man with lots of hair falling across smooth cheeks. 'This is my friend, Nathan,' she said. 'He's just here in case you turn out to be a pervert.'

'Hi, Nathan,' I said, 'what a sensible precaution,' and I shook his hand.

I showed them the room; dusty and tatty, with a beige carpet coming loose and watercolour peach walls, but room-sized, in a prime location, for one-sixth of her current rent, a rent she paid for the privilege of four or five hours' sleep a night between a bar shift and interning. I did not tell her about some of the things the bed had seen over the last decade.

'Have a think about it,' I said, but of course she moved in. She had artistic ambition. She had no choice.

*

Nathan is the twerp Jonathan referred to. Twerp is unkind. He's a sweet boy, but he'd never been up in Mary's room before.

'It's your fault they're up there,' I said to Jonathan. 'They think this is your bedroom.'

'It is my bedroom!' He held up the Postman Pat quilt as evidence.

'We should discuss that.'

'Just give me a week. I'm working on Julia.'

'What is actually the problem?' I picked up two empty cans and crumpled them noisily.

'Oh, mate. It's too complicated. I'd bore you stupid.'

I took the cans to the recycling box in the kitchen, then went up to my room, just across from Mary's. To my horror, I could hear a man's heavy gasping. The door was ajar and I shouted hello.

'Come in!' she called.

'Are you sure?'

'Come in!'

I went in, where I found her and Nathan sitting up against her headboard, fully clothed, giggling. Between them was one of those shiny chrome contraptions for filling balloons full of nitrous oxide.

'I see,' I said.

'I stole it,' said Mary. 'By accident. From a party last night. I don't remember putting it in my bag. Nathan's been getting aggressive texts all day from the girl whose party it was, accusing him of stealing it. He didn't know I had it. I didn't know I had it until I opened my handbag. When it's late, we're going to sneak around there and try to put it back without them noticing. Reverse burgling.'

'Perverse gurgling,' said Nathan, and he fell over to the side and started laughing silently.

'He's just done a balloon,' explained Mary.

I picked a pile of neatly folded washing off a wooden chair and sat down on it. 'Was that the noise? I thought you were sex-strangling him.'

Nathan sat back up and raised his eyebrows at her.

'Later,' she said. 'Do you want a balloon, Paul?'

'No, thanks. I'm a traditional man. Whisky and heroin. I'm going to sit downstairs and have a beer. You know it's not Jonathan's bedroom, don't you? He's not paying any rent yet.'

'Yeah, I know. Nathan doesn't like the way he looks at him, though.'

'Who does? Come down, will you?' I asked. 'I can't cope with him tonight on my own.'

'Maybe in a bit. We're going to have a couple more balloons first.'

'Fucking millennials,' I said.

'Shut up,' said Mary. 'Go and listen to your Oasis and Blur records downstairs.'

Though we were born either end of the same decade, there is a difference in kind rather than in degree between us and Mary's age-appropriate male friends. We grow old, we grow old, while they, an inch or two taller than us, wear their trousers rolled much higher than we would feel comfortable doing. This superficial difference distracts from their superior ethics. Mary's friends are more earnest, passionate socialists, vegans – what else could you be if you'd ever read a book or used your imagination?

'So why was your day so shit?' I called through to Jonathan from the kitchen.

He shambled through into the room and looked at me. He had a tight white shirt on to set off the Christmas tan he'd acquired on whatever sex tour of South East Asia they'd embarked on before she threw him out. He's a handsome man, with golden hair and a strong jaw he keeps clean-shaven.

'Money,' he said.

'Are you all right?'

'Not my money. Magazine money. There isn't enough of it. Advertising's down. Which is your fault.'

'My fault!'

'Editorial's fault. Stev'n's fault, really. The brand's not as edgy as it used to be. We're losing clients.'

'What are you going to do?'

'We were discussing again whether we should bin your book column and replace it with a legal highs column.'

'Are you joking?'

He looked at me and I saw him make some calculations. 'Yeah, I'm joking.'

'You didn't sound like you were joking.'

'We'll have to assess all the regular features, Paul, work out what's working and what isn't.'

'So you're not joking.'

'Course I'm joking. What's going on upstairs then?'

'They're inhaling nitrous oxide.'

'Fucking millennials.'

'That's what I said.'

'I'm going to go and ask them for some.'

'Yes, do. Nathan would love to see you.'

He gave me a hungry grin and disappeared.

*

Two hours later we were all watching *Question Time* in the living room. Nigel Farage was shouting about small businesses spending half of their working week complying with EU regulations. Trade will continue with Europe whether or not we're part of the EU.

'Turn him off,' said Jonathan.

'Turn him off,' said Nathan.

'No, I'm interested,' said Mary. 'I want to see how convincing he is.'

'He's not convincing at all,' said Nathan.

'Not to men like you, but other men exist.'

'And they wouldn't like you, Nathan,' said Jonathan.

'I don't expect they'd like you either,' said Mary.

The crowd cheered, or half of it did.

'Where did you two meet again?' asked Jonathan.

'My band were supporting Mary's,' said Nathan.

'What's your band like?' I asked.

He looked at Mary. 'Er. . .'

'Sort of bouncy Steely Dan post-feminist pop rock,' she said.

'Post-feminist?'

'Yeah, we do songs about not cheating on our girlfriends, imagining things from her perspective, that sort of thing,' he said.

'Ironically or in earnest?' asked Jonathan.

'Well, it's a bit of a joke, an antidote to all the clichéd rock bullshit. But it's not just a joke: we don't cheat on our girl-friends. I mean, I wouldn't cheat on my girlfriend if I *had* one.'

He turned to look at Mary.

'How do you know you wouldn't cheat on your girlfriend if you don't have one?' I said.

'Well, I just think she'd be enough for me.'

'How conventional,' said Jonathan.

'Jonathan,' said Mary. 'Paul.'

'I mean, you might *not* cheat on your girlfriend,' I said, 'but it might be a bit complacent to assume a monogamous happy ever after. Have neither of you read that book about how women are naturally far less monogamous than men? This myth that men have higher sex drives derives from the counter-fact that women are so quickly bored by just one part-ner that sex in a traditional one-to-one relationship becomes almost immediately a chore to them.'

'Wow,' said Nathan.

'Wow,' said Jonathan. 'Did Monica write this book, Paul?'

I ignored this remark and continued. 'Women find chimps desirable in tests. Men don't find chimps desirable, not in the main. We're really boring like that – it's no wonder women stop fancying us.'

'And that's what you think, Paul? That I desire chimps?' said Mary.

'I think you desire chimps,' said Jonathan.

'I don't care what you think.'

'It's a hypothesis,' I said. 'Women are wilder, sexually, than men. Men are very conventional. I've no idea whether it's accurate or not. You might be atypical. Of course no one's saying you want to fuck chimps.'

'I'm saying she wants to fuck chimps,' said Jonathan.

'See. He's saying I want to fuck chimps,' she said.

'That's called projection,' I said. 'He wants to fuck chimps so he can't stop saying you want to fuck chimps.'

'Do you think that's it?' said Jonathan. 'Where do I *find* a chimp to fuck?'

'I'll lend you the book, Mary.'

'I don't want to read the book,' said Mary.

'All of this doesn't really correspond with my observation of life, Paul,' said Nathan.

Jonathan turned to him and put his hand on his shoulder. 'Nathan, I thought like you when I was your age. But the things you believe when you're young and in love, they're romantic. Like, if you were going to be a real feminist, perhaps your songs should be more about how your girlfriend sleeps around all the time and you don't mind, because you know it's what she wants and needs – and deserves! – and you know *you* personally can't satisfy her on your own.'

'Wow.'

'Don't listen to him, Nathan.'

'It's quite a good idea for a song, though,' said Nathan.

'It's not,' I said. 'Don't listen to Jonathan. He doesn't know anything about love.'

'Fuck you,' said Jonathan.

'Fuck you. And don't fucking joke about Monica, all right? No wonder your wife threw you out.'

'Don't take out your failures on me,' said Jonathan, calmly, looking away from me. Mary was looking at me with an expression that wasn't quite pity, or without tenderness.

'I'm going to go and get some beers,' I said. I didn't want any beers but I headed out down the fire escape and bought some from the corner shop. When I came back in I didn't open one but just walked straight up to my room and lay on my bed.

I woke up alone. From the window came the rolling traffic of Kingsland Road, a car horn, a muffled shout. It was half one in the morning. There might have been somewhere still open where I could have gone to have a conversation with a stranger, to buy a beer and perhaps get offered a bit of something and an invite to carry on drinking back at someone else's, the opportunity to wake up next to whoever this was. This had once felt like research, like a cartography project, a search for something that I would only recognise when I saw it. I wanted to be in constant motion, constant communication, until I received my vision. Or perhaps I just meant person. Somewhere close by there was someone I would love even more than Monica.

I went downstairs and filled a pint glass full of water. The living-room door was shut and the lights were off. Back upstairs, I noticed Mary's door was still open. I looked through to where her bed was lit by a street light shining through a crack in the curtain. She wasn't there. I walked in and stood there for a second, looking at the shapes around me and smelling the smell that was her in this house: fabric softener, perfume, damp and exhausts. Things are all right, I told myself. I have books on the shelves, food in the fridge, a roof over my head and clothes to wear, and in Mary's room there were those memories I avoided, Monica crying on a mattress, my hand on her stomach, my face against her hair doing my best to calm her down. Dark nights when she filled the room with her heat, when I felt mad and afraid of her, afraid she would go, afraid she would stay, afraid there was no going back.

FOUR

Andrew Lancaster came into the shop the other day. By now I had googled him extensively. I looked hard at his face on book flaps, trying to work out which photo was the most honest, the most recent, which was the oldest man and how much older he might have become since the photo was taken. I watched videos of him calling out audience members at book festivals: 'Stand up and call me a racist! Have the courage and decency to call me a racist, if you think you can justify it!'; that kind of thing. One of his recurring targets in recent interviews was 'the infantilised metropolitan Left' who saw everything in terms of good and evil, and were far too confident of their own virtue. He denied vehemently that he was just an ageing man getting comfy. 'Have I travelled to the right? No. Have many of the Left travelled towards the stupid, away from the critical, away from nuance and the thorny and the difficult? Certainly.'

'I didn't know you were so interested in politics and history,' said Helen, as I put through a pile of books for me on my discount, which included an old book by Lancaster in which he justified the invasion of Iraq. 'I hope this new political consciousness isn't a sign that you're going to go alt-right on us.'

I resented this comment. And so the next day I didn't use my staff discount to purchase Lancaster's quick history of the Russian Revolution, but simply transferred it from the shelves to my bag.

And the next day, there he was, in a beige detective's trench coat, as if he had got wind of the crime and arrived to investigate. I watched him dart a glance towards the history section, where a gap remained that would not be filled automatically, since no record of the book's sale existed. I noticed him notice and tried not to give myself away by smiling too hard.

Frustratingly, he looked younger if anything IRL than in the photos. He was a broad-shouldered man, shorter than me, but then I am six foot two; he might have been six foot himself, and he walked tall, pushing his shoulders back and rolling them as he browsed the fiction table, as though he was working out the knots in his back from a hard morning's word-processing. I had already picked up that he was a good-looking man from my trawl through his headshots. A touch of the dandy too – a pink shirt and suede boots. Light-brown hair that might have been dyed, I suppose, but looked natural, thick enough to be swept back in a floppy parting. There was a sighing brutality to him; he held up a book and seemed to look through it into some disgraceful scene from his past; he grimaced and I thought he might tear the thing in two; but he placed it back on the pile and glanced around the shop, as though he was looking for someone.

I was distracted from him then by a customer who couldn't find the philosophy section downstairs. When I came back up Andrew was embracing his daughter. I knew it was his daughter, illogically, because she looked a little like Emily, with the same straight dark hair and pale cheeks. She was so blemishless that you could have described her as plain, not that there was anything unattractive about her face; it was fresh out of the box, unmarked. She may have had the same blue eyes as he did, I don't know, because I was only concentrating on how she put her hands on his shoulders and reached up to kiss his cheek, like well-bred girls did to Daddy to thank him for what his money did for them. I looked at her quite arrogantly, I suppose, confident of my ability to see the transparency of things, as though the soul was something that could be peered at through a closed window, like a puppy in a back seat waiting for its owner to come back.

*

Helen came to relieve me for my lunch break. I was reluctant to stop observing Andrew and daughter, so I took my time leaving until Andrew went to pay for a book by the till. While he was doing that I left the shop through the front door, stopping to smile at his daughter, who was flicking through the magazine section. Out on the street I crossed the road and leaned against a shop front, lighting a cigarette I didn't want. After a couple of minutes they came out together. They didn't spot me. I was typical, a poseur, an extra, who started to follow them as they walked together down the road. Andrew leaned down to say something right by her ear and she moved her head so it brushed against his chin, and when she did this he put his hand on the back of her head and ran it down between her shoulders towards her waist.

Incest! I thought, and then worried I had been too harsh, for the daughters of the intelligentsia raised in London are so European they may as well be French and they grow up used to kissing their parents, kissing strangers, dealing with propositions from adults on buses. Andrew turned around and scanned the street, looking past me, before he rested his hand on her shoulder for a second, put it back by his side, and carried on walking down the road. It was possible, I realised then, that they were not father and daughter.

When they reached the Hoxton Hotel, she held his arm and pointed towards the door. He shrugged, and they went in. I waited a minute, then followed.

*

Inside I sat at the bar and ordered a beer. They had taken a booth at the quiet end of the long bar room, sitting side by side and facing me. She pulled out a laptop and opened it, but they only looked at each other and after five minutes she pushed the lid shut. From my stool at the bar I was too far away to hear what they were saying, but it meant I could stare in their direction without it seeming like I was singling them out. The way they talked seemed intimate to me, weary, as though they'd exhausted all their best anecdotes already. Did I detect accurately that he was managing her in some way, meeting her more to prove that he cared for her than for the pleasure of her company? A situation which could just as easily have applied to daughter as to lover. As a lecturer he would have to forge close professional relationships with young people every year. Of course these relationships would mean more to the students than they did to him. Of course they would want as much as they could get from him. If they were ambitious they would have to. There was something sorrowful in his face. Whoever she was, he seemed to care for her and be pained by her presence. She was inconvenient. She had a woman-sized body: all its movement, all its weight. He had to care so that she didn't destroy him. I was running away with my own fictions at the bar.

Perhaps I had been staring too intently in their direction; I realised Andrew Lancaster was returning my interest. I looked down at my book; prompted by Helen's comment, I was reading a biography of George Eliot to find out if there were really any ways in which I resembled her, and so far it was not at all obvious. When I looked up again he was striding towards me. I looked down at my book again as he leaned into the bar next to me.

'Good book?' he asked.

I showed him the cover.

'Ah, the *little moralistic female*, as Nietzsche called her – stupidly, in that instance, of course. What excellent taste you have . . . I knew *you* weren't stupid, just by looking at you. Do I know you from somewhere? I thought I saw you looking quite intensely at me before. I haven't annoyed you? Given you a bad mark? My memory isn't what it was.'

'No, no. I recognised you, that's all. I've read your short history of the Russian Revolution. And your book about how the Left betrayed its principles.'

'Ah, I see – well, thank you. Or is it that book that's annoyed you? Everyone younger than me hates that book.'

'I'm not annoyed. Honestly.'

'I must be paranoid. I was worried I'd wronged you somehow. Or that you knew my companion and she'd wronged you instead.'

'No, sorry, I was just looking over. I was wondering if she was your daughter, actually.'

'God, no – what makes you say that?'

'Oh, I thought I caught a resemblance.'

We both turned and stared at her. She looked quizzical and turned away from our scrutiny.

'She's not my daughter, but you're accurate in one sense: it's a relationship of formal obligation. I'm her PhD supervisor. What are you having?'

He got me a pint, himself a half and a bowl of nuts, and then he shook my hand and wished me luck. When he returned to the booth he sat opposite her this time, so I could only see her face. His exchange with me seemed to have annoyed her. She was frowning and kept looking up at me, and I was forced to become a better spy, to pay less attention to them. I caught him shaking his head at her at one point. She looked at him incredulously and then seemed to change character completely. She pulled her laptop back in front of her, a barrier between them, and looked down at the screen every time she spoke to him. I couldn't see his face to ascertain what his reaction was. Eventually, she stopped asking him questions and stayed quiet for a while, studying the surface of the table. This lasted for a few more minutes until he stood up. She got up too, and they made their way back through the bar together, both smiling at me when I glanced up at them. I had half of my pint left so couldn't leap up and follow them without being obvious. Nevertheless, I downed it quickly and looked to see if they walked past the window back in the direction they'd come from. When they didn't, I hopped down from my stool and headed out. I couldn't see them in any direction. I looked back into the reception for the hotel and wandered over to the receptionist.

'Excuse me,' I said. 'Do you know if Andrew Lancaster has checked in yet?'

He looked down at his screen. 'What's your relationship to him?'

'I'm just meeting him for a drink and he's late.'

He looked again. 'No one of that name has checked in,' he said.

'Thanks,' I said, and left.

FIVE

Carl and I had grown up at different ends of the same street. The houses were a bit smaller at his end. Instead of gardens they had yards with back gates through to the alley where we played football together. I would call for him every morning, where I'd stand in the hall while his mum and he tried to dress his younger sister Leia and two little brothers before we shepherded them along the road to school. Before Carl's dad lost the fingers on his right hand he would have been away working on a rig, or still in bed if he was home. Sometimes he would take us sea-fishing when the tide was up, showing us how to whip the line out into the churning waves while the wind drilled into our ears. We preferred playing Subbuteo on my kitchen table but it was hard to tell Carl's dad that. Carl would often knock on my door. It was quieter in our house – if my parents weren't fighting. When we got older we didn't want quiet. Carl's parents didn't find anything strange about us drinking at fifteen and so we began our nights in the living room with his mum, slurping cans, shouting at soap operas, singing along to Abba and Queen with her if there was nothing on TV, pestering Leia to bring her friends out to the beach with her later.

Now Carl was dead, Leia wrote in a Facebook post, from an accidental overdose of prescription drugs.

This analysis began to be disputed.

What drugs? asked Tracey.

Accidental? wrote Lee.

And then, from Wozza, who had once held me upside down to shake the change from my school trousers: *I'm not being funny but everyone knows that family likes their smack.*

*

I hadn't gone for a drink with Carl for years now, over a decade. He'd worked in the big supermarket that Mum went to every day. Perhaps I felt guilty that he saw my mother more than I did.

'Some of us have more ambition, you know, Mum?' I said once, when she'd told me again how polite and friendly he always was.

'More ambition than to be polite?' she asked. 'Grow up, Paul.'

I'd run into him there, wearing his bright green shirt, and we'd talk for a minute or two, as he looked around as if he were about to be told off for skiving, or was looking for a good excuse to leave, even though, as Mum had told me several times, he was an assistant manager by then.

'What's it like down there now?' he'd ask.

Carl had visited me just once in London, at the end of my first year. We went to a house party in Deptford and when we were scoring he asked for five Es, so he could take some home with him. I left him talking to a girl on the sofa, came back and heard him talking about being the manager of the fish-processing factory where he worked, how the money was really good, how they might be sending him to work in the head office in New York. I handed him a beer without contradicting him. The woman got up and left the room and didn't come back. Half an hour later Carl was staggering from room to room, white-faced and gurning. I dragged him out. Propped him up as we walked back to get the train into town. He was apologising. He'd taken all his drugs. His comedown was going to be awful. He could barely respond to a question the next day. He had a specific ticket booked for the day after but said he had to go home early. Said he'd be all right on the train, hide from the conductor, feign ignorance. I let him go, didn't argue hard that he should stay. The next evening I forced myself to call him, to reassure him that the visit had not been a disaster. He told me that the train conductor threw him off in Milton Keynes when he couldn't afford to buy himself a new ticket. There he went to the pub where he was befriended by a beautiful woman who then took him back to her house for a party with her twin sister, with whom he had a epic threesome. When they woke up he was able to get on the train for which he had a valid ticket. Great, I'd said. That's brilliant. I'm glad everything worked out for you.

What was London like now? he'd ask, in the supermarket. I'd say, oh, busy, expensive, dirty. It didn't occur to me to try to describe the place accurately to him, how it had changed me, how I had loved being changed, how I knew there might come a point when I would not be able to afford to live here but could not imagine how to live back there. The supermarket we were standing in sometimes felt like the only place left in the town with any bustle to it. Each time I came home another pub was boarded up, another shop on the high street. They had recently found a huge cannabis farm above the old Woolworths, with thirty million pounds' worth of plants maintained by two Vietnamese slaves who had never set foot outside in the town, who had never even known for sure if they were in England. I didn't want to talk about my life as if I were bragging to him, even this fabulous life I lived in my crumbling flat on one of London's most polluted roads. 'Sorry.

Better get off.' 'Sorry. Say hello to your mum.' 'Yeah. Say hello to yours too. Ta-ra.'

*

Don't stick your nose in when you don't know shit! wrote Leia. *Carl was never into that. Me? That was TEN fucking years ago! We're fucking GRIEVING here you prick.*

I am a real voyeur of this type of conflict, which flares up all the time between Facebook friends from my old school. The cars they have failed to protect adequately. The construction machinery they haven't locked up 'when you know what pikey scum are like'. The husbands who have left their wives because their wives drink and eat too much and have got ugly, aren't raising their kids proper. These things were pointed out. It looked malicious but it wasn't just cruelty. We wanted disaster to be our own fault. To believe that catastrophe was preventable. A matter of right choices enforced with vigilant criticism. You *had* to be cruel to be kind. The alternative was bleaker.

Carl's dad Mike lost three fingers from his right hand after catching them in a chain that wasn't supposed to be moving. 'You can barely hear each other out there,' he told me and Carl. 'The twat who turned it on said he'd shouted to me. I don't think he did, but it's fucking windy out there and the noise of the machines . . . You two need to pay attention at school, right?' By the time the helicopter dropped him on the mainland it was too late. His colleagues had had to get straight back to work. They'd seen similar injuries before.

Mike must have been about my age now when he had his accident. I suppose he got compensation. He'd walk the little ones to school when we went to high school, smoking Superkings, singing songs, the Bee Gees, Phil Collins; we'd watch him from the bus stop. Something restless about his good humour, something I found awful.

*

Amy had deleted her Facebook account after our last argument. I wondered if she knew about Carl's death; she was in Leia's year at school and they'd kept in better touch than I had with Carl.

I was glad to have this excuse to find Amy, something to say if she didn't want to speak to me, to offer her beyond an apology, a subject to discuss that wasn't our own disagreements; a tragedy, a dead body. Her disappearance from Facebook was nothing unusual: Amy's always taking her profile down and putting it back up again, much busier than me in trying to fix her life through industry and decisive measures. She takes her profile offline when she disgusts herself with the time she wastes looking at pictures of ex-boyfriends plummeting into blue lagoons, surveying natural landscapes from on high, wanderers exploring Eastern temples with strong-jawed girls, the type you saw in Chelsea. We both have adventuring conquistadorial ambitions based on appealing to our betters – something we have only ever been good at realising briefly. Amy takes the failure of these liaisons more politically than me. 'This country is still like a fucking Jane Austen novel. It's not just that money marries money, but that these people think that this is the moral place for the story to end.' I didn't make the mistake of pointing out that this is only really an accurate description of *Emma*. It's unwise to quibble with Amy when she is regretting all those minutes she has wasted watching ex-lovers brag about their happiness when she could have been making something or reading a book or cleaning the flat or writing an application to the council for a lease on some disused public toilets that would make the perfect waffle café – all those hours viewing babies with Edwardian names, looking at weddings held in the homes of fading aristocrats, reading discussions in which friends referred to themselves in the third person as *Mummy*. Oh, she knew she was becoming bitter and that mummies needed to buy into the role they found themselves in, but when she had a child – and now she really meant *if*, she had to be realistic given her predicament, a single woman in a city that pitied single women in their thirties with the same abstract compassion with which they pitied the animals they ate on their Tinder dates, certified to have been treated kindly right up to the moment they were executed – *if* she had a child, she would not surrender her subjectivity to the omniscient god of a wipe-clean picture book about an elephant's trip to an art museum. She would not be so guileless in posting her passive aggression towards the women who were still photographing cocktails on a regular basis, wearing bikinis under turquoise skies, proselytising for the single life, the childless life, heroic women who neglected to take selfies of themselves making the morning commute the wrong way round in smudged make-up and heels but should really have been proud to, and would have been if the world didn't know men for what they were, which was big fucking pervert babies. One huge benefit of closing her Facebook profile was the way it stopped Tinder from working, and denied her addiction to shopping for men, for the worst men in the world, of whom there must have been hundreds of thousands still left for her to meet in this ugly safari of a city.

*

After work I jumped on my bike and headed over to see if I could find her at home. I got out of my saddle to pump my way over an overpass on to the Old Kent Road, a street like a Benson & Hedges lit from the end of a Lambert & Butler lit from a burning tub of paint – as English as it gets, with the megastores full of white goods, and the African churches with great names: Behold He Cometh!, the Everlasting Arms Ministry. A white van with a Millwall FC sticker on the back shaved my arm by a couple of centimetres and I swore at the driver as I overtook him a minute later when the traffic had stopped again. 'Get out of the fucking road, you mug,' he shouted, but I was way ahead of him. A bus blew a plume of carcinogens into my face. I held my breath and turned right to Peckham.

In the ten years I've been working in the shop Amy has had so many jobs and engaged in so many money-making schemes it's hard to keep count. She studied Fine Art at Goldsmiths, having arrived in London three years after I did, after she spent an extra year at home doing an art foundation. I had suggested to her that from my own experience it might be more fun to do a degree in a regional city, where rent was less than half the price, where university campuses were leafy, tranquil spaces set away from huge traffic islands and exhaust-blackened concrete. She paid no attention, thinking as she always does, perhaps correctly, that I was patronising her.

She had less fun on her degree than on her foundation; the teachers discouraged her from painting; she thought the theory animating many of her fellow students was bullshit. It was easy to anatomise the problems of capitalism when you had money; the first practical thing she needed to do was get some, so she learned how to use design software and made flyers for other students' club nights, then she put on club nights with her friends in Peckham and New Cross. She printed T-shirts and sweaters to sell on stalls. She became interested in furniture design – wished she had done a more practical degree. She argued with her tutors, took rejection hard and dropped courses in retaliation. By the time she had her degree she had given up on the art world; it was fraudulent and childish, 'rich people pretending to be revolutionary'.

'Are you sure you're not characterising it in the way that's easiest to allow you to give up on it?' I asked – and we had to avoid each other for a month or two after that argument.

Amy's flat – the one she lives in herself – is on a small street of Victorian terraces separated by floor into flats and rented (or sold off) by the council. I tried her doorbell: no answer, but Clive came to the window and peered at me.

'Hey, Clive – it's Paul, remember?'

Clive is retired and lives as a council tenant in the flat underneath Amy's. I had once answered the door to him when Amy was having a party. We were being quite civilised, in our opinion, but he was worried that the number of people we had in the living room was going to make the ceiling collapse. When Clive complained we moved everyone out to the pub. I hoped he remembered me fondly.

'Paul? Yeah. I remember. Not so old I forget a face yet.'

'Have you seen Amy?'

'I was hoping *you'd* tell *me* where she is. She's got people staying upstairs again. Airbnb, what have you. She knows she's not allowed to do that. Council regulation. I don't know who these people are I see coming in through the front door. I get nervous. And they loud too. I understand if girl needs money. I understand that! But can you tell her to tell them girls to nah do so much clomping on the damn floor. Sounds like they stabling horses up there.'

'I'll tell her. Haven't you seen her for a while?'

'I don't know. Two months ago, more?'

'Was she all right then?' I asked, thinking about what kind of a brother it was who allowed his sister to go missing for two whole months.

'I don't know. I asked her if she'd had a nice Christmas. She just shook her head. "I know that feeling," I said to her. I never seen her again. She in trouble?'

'I hope not.'

'What about her job?'

'She doesn't work there any more. They won't tell me any more than that.'

'Sounds like she ran away. Well, she's still taking those bookings.' He pointed down to a little key safe at the foot of the door. 'Look at this thing! I've a good mind to take a hammer to it. You need to find her and get her to talk to those upstairs. Or I'll have to call the council.'

'I'll find her,' I told him. 'I will.'

The connecting train was cancelled and I got stuck in Preston, the nearest city to home, though it only won its city status in the years after I had moved to London. It was an exotic, cultured place to me as a teenager. There was a university a few of my older friends commuted to. The novelty of seeing Asians in large numbers. A place to watch bands in the union. The nearest bookshop. Dickens called the place Coketown. A rainy, Catholic cotton town – which now always made me melancholic, though that was not its fault but mine, my mood always coloured by the fact of travelling towards or away from my town.

While I waited for the next train I wrote an email to Emily to ask if she would like to meet up when I got back to London.

*

Outside the wooden door I listened to the familiar rhythms of the prayers. The wind was up and the sky was washed-out cotton in all directions, so much of it, broken only by the church spire.

Opposite was the church hall, my classroom for a year in primary school, where I accomplished my greatest ever achievement, the completion of the Italia 90 sticker book. And here, inside the church, through the door I opened carefully, was the cold stone basin for the holy water. In the name of the father. The first third of the church was filled up; I couldn't see past to the family on the front bench. And of the son. Who probably hadn't been inside the building for twenty years, but had been stamped with the sacraments same as me. He lay in a dark-wood coffin under Christ on the cross in his golden robes. And the holy spirit. The incense from the censer the Nigerian priest was swinging on his punishment posting. The lemon wood polish. The stained-glass Peter and Andrew, the fishers of men. I put my knee to the floor. Amen.

None of the congregation noticed me come in, and I took a seat at the back, looking around to see if I could spot any old school friends, wondering what the girls I had fantasised about in school Masses now looked like. I could only see the back of people's heads.

When the congregation stood to leave, I stood on my tip-toes, and there she was, her hand on Leia's shoulder. Thank God. A miracle. It was Amy.

*

The wake was in the Cons club down the road. We began the walk in a group but as the conversation went on Amy's friends strode ahead.

'Seriously, where the fuck have you been?'

'Thailand. We've just established that. I told you.'

It had only been two months since I last saw her, but there was something different about her. It wasn't the tan, too natural-looking to fit in with the other tans in the room, but something in the way she stood up, in the measure of her words, and I feared this was a new distance between us – a declared dislike – which we would struggle to cross.

'But this text you sent me doesn't exist,' I said. 'Why didn't you get in touch when you didn't hear from me?'

'I thought you were pissed off with me. I sent you a text from my new phone.'

'I thought you'd disowned me. The way you ran off like that. I thought you were dead or you'd disowned me. Jesus, I'm so pleased to see you.'

'You don't seem pleased.'

'I'm furiously pleased. How long have you been here?'

'Two days.'

I was looking at her profile while she stared straight ahead. She was doing her best to seem nonchalant, but I could see something else shaking beneath her straight face.

'And have you quit your job? I called them too. They said you weren't working for them any more.'

'Yeah. Sort of.'

'Sort of?'

'I just – I just swore at my boss and stormed out of the office and haven't been back.'

I looked at her and didn't say anything.

'Don't look at me like that,' she said. 'You're just as bad as me.'

'I've had the same job for the last ten years.'

'Exactly,' she said.

*

It had been stupid of her to burn her bridges there. The job had been administrative, it had been stupefying and enraging whenever there was an away-day, or a lecture addressed as if to children on digital innovation, but there were many more boring and more difficult jobs she could have done – and thank God the organisation existed. Nowhere that had to employ people was perfect. She looked after the public-funding relationships with a few art galleries, advised artists who were looking for money for their next projects. It was silly to wish she was sitting on the other side of the table, when she had happily retired from creating 'art'. What nonsense it was to waste time thinking about the galleries, when you could just make things and sell them on the street, when any idiot with enough working capital could make fifty thousand pounds a go in exchange for a few intense weeks' work doing up and selling a decrepit flat to some lazy twenty-something whose parents were buying it for them. That was satire, that was art.

Admittedly, not all the people who came to look round the properties she bought and sold were very privileged. It was harder to enjoy the performance when it was an anxious couple trying to find somewhere their savings would stretch to a deposit. She feared then that she was part of the problem, not the resistance, but there was no solution that could be effected by her on her own. She had to take what she needed while she could get it.

As a single woman she could only get her buy-to-flip mortgages with a regular salary to show the lenders. Her job had been perfect for the way she made real money: no one kept track of where she was; she worked from home whenever she could, answering the occasional email but mostly pursuing her own schemes, scouring through the estate-agent sites for promising properties in east and south-east London. She wasn't going to keep on with the property-renovating forever, just until she had enough money for a little house of her own with a garden, just until the money wasn't there begging. It was better that she picked up the profits than someone who had been to private school. Mum was gone, and with the brother she had she couldn't rely on anyone else to look after her if things went wrong.

Which was why the argument at work had been so shaming and stupid.

Not all her colleagues were awful, just the ones who made the most noise and did the least work. She had liked her manager, Hannah, who had looked after the art team, which was made mostly of people doing exactly the same job as Amy while claiming expertise in a certain niche (with less plausibility, the louder they were). When Hannah announced she was leaving she had taken Amy aside and said, 'You'd be good at this. You should apply.'

'Thanks,' said Amy. 'Are you pleased not to be doing it any more?'

'Um . . .' her boss said.

'Yeah, I thought so,' said Amy.

But she thought about it, and about working under the colleagues who did want the job, and she decided that she would apply, even if she'd have to work harder and care more about what she was doing. Perhaps she did care, after all.

The interview was with a panel of three people: a senior manager, the new CEO, and an HR manager. It went well. She knew what she was talking about. When they asked the diversity question she knew they were going to ask she made the standard sensible points and then spoke about coming from a place without much ethnic diversity, which was 98 per cent white and with hardly any art funding, and how important she thought it was to include these places, to remember that there were lots of places that weren't at all *diverse* in the way people in London used the word because no one who hadn't been planted there for generations would ever want to go there. The CEO had nodded along, and Amy had decided that was more promising than the slight worry that crossed the HR manager's face.

It was very difficult to decide, said the HR manager the next morning, but I'm afraid we've gone with Matthew. He was just that little bit stronger than you on certain questions.

'Which questions?'

'Well, say, the diversity question.'

'How so?'

'He stuck to our priorities. We worried you weren't quite as familiar with them.'

'Was it because I said that thing about there being places where white isn't really anything like a synonym for privilege?'

'Of course not, of course not. An interesting nuance but of course class isn't a protected characteristic and so it's a much more difficult metric to assess.'

'Right.'

'I am sorry, Amy.'

Matthew wasn't a bad man, probably. A little man from Hertfordshire, he enjoyed his job, and the conferences, and saying 'strategic' in meetings. He kept a neat beard, wore black turtlenecks, and looked fifteen years older than her but was two months younger. The argument came at the end of a team meeting. Matthew asked her to stay behind, because of certain things she was saying that weren't in tune with agreed priorities, and because she was making her points in meetings too aggressively.

'I care about this,' she said.

'Now, Amy. It's great that you care. I just wonder . . . We've never spoken about the fact you went for the job I'm doing.'

'Well . . . That's not relevant. I wasn't disappointed.'

'OK. Fine. You weren't disappointed.' He nodded sagely, as if he understood her in ways she did not understand herself, and she recoiled at the way he half-shut his eyes.

'Look, Matthew, this job isn't my life. I know it's your life and so it must be hard to imagine it isn't everyone's, it must be hard to have thoughts that haven't arrived in a PowerPoint presentation, but I *don't care*.'

'Now, you're being aggressive and *rude* now. Please lower your voice.'

'I'm not being fucking aggressive, *we're having a conversation.*'

All of this time Matthew kept his voice in a soft mellifluous measure. 'And please don't swear like that. It's totally unnecessary.'

It's one of the most enraging things a man can do to a woman, to place himself on the pedestal of logic and reason while refusing to listen to a word she's saying.

'We're grown-ups, Matthew! We can talk like grown-ups!'

'I am now going to warn you that I will be having a conversation with HR about your interpersonal skills, to seek advice about training that might be able to help you develop them.'

'You know you look like you're going to a fancy dress party dressed as a beatnik? Go and seek some fucking advice on that,' she said. And she walked back through to the office to pick her bag up from her desk, and caught the lift downstairs to the basement where she kept her bike, and she rode it home and made her flat available on Airbnb and booked a flight to Thailand.

*

'Wow,' I said.

We'd reached the Cons club by now and walked in through a foyer I remembered from the long-ago weddings of school friends who'd married in their teens, in the summers I still spent at home.

'It's one of the reasons I changed my number when I lost my phone,' she said. 'I thought it would clear away the repercussions, get rid of some of the other rubbish in my life at the same time.'

'Anyone else in particular?'

She waved her hand. 'Where to start?'

I gave her a meaningful look.

'Not you,' she said.

'Good. What do you want?'

'Just a lime and soda, please.'

'Very restrained for a funeral round here.'

'I'm on a diet.'

'Why?'

'Lime and soda, please.'

I got myself a pint of Guinness, looking over at Carl's parents, Mike and Janine, in the corner of the pub. People were coming over to hug Janine, while Mike studied the table surface in front of him.

'Do you understand how he went?' I whispered to Amy. She'd been to see Leia the night before.

'Pills. Opiates. Not the kind of thing you usually get round here but someone had a big bag of them. Leia thinks he didn't know how strong they were and did a handful, thinking they were just like Valium or something. Or that he stepped up a dose and got it wrong. That's her theory. Not suicide, just an accident. She knew he'd been taking Xanax and Valium: that's how he relaxed in the evening, how he slept. He got at least one of them on prescription. I've been wondering if it might have been something in-between. Let's see what happens if I do this. You know: would it be so bad if I went all the way over?'

'Right.' I was thinking of the way he had necked all those pills on his one trip to see me in London. 'Did she think he was unhappy?'

'He was looking anxious,' she said.

'He always looked anxious.'

'Yeah, I know.'

'What about his girlfriend? Which one's she?'

'Her over there. The redhead.'

I looked. A woman of about forty was sitting with another woman her age, and two teenage boys arguing over an iPad. She didn't look devastated, but most people don't look devastated at funerals. We've spent a long time hardening our faces for these occasions.

'Poor woman,' said Amy.

*

Mum had mentioned her when I last saw her. 'Carl's got a new girlfriend,' she'd said. 'Two grown boys of her own. Do you think they'll want one together?'

I don't know what I said in reply but I suspect it was petulant. Mum was always bringing up the subject of children with us. She wanted the impetus to retire, to do so selflessly, so she could take long trips to London to see us and help us look after her grandchildren. She had discovered a love for London in her last years. As Amy got into her swing of renovating flats there were often places for her to stay for free on her half-term holidays, free if you count the implied painting-and-decorating labour that is the only real way to spend any time with Amy when she is the middle of one of these frenzies. It was a stressful, exhausting, lucrative hobby they did together.

I'd provide the cultural tourism side of Mum's holiday, taking her sightseeing while Amy was at work.

'It must be great having all this on your doorstep,' she said, the last time I saw her, as we were coming out of a gallery.

'You forget it's there. Forget to enjoy what the tourists come here for. I used to get dragged to all the exhibitions when Monica was here. She'd get us in everywhere for free.'

'I don't mind paying for you, Paul.'

'Oh, I don't mean that. I love being a tourist with you.'

And I did. I liked standing with her there in front of the Thames, with new places I could take her to in all directions, an update on our old routine. When I visited her at home in the summer we would walk along the beach to watch the sunset go down, standing at the limit of things, the tide out and the sun aflame in the little puddles left in the sand. You could trick yourself there that endings were beautiful and reversible.

'How is Monica?' she asked. 'Do you ever hear from her?'

'Oh. She's – did you not read about it in the papers? She was the first person ever to give birth in an Uber cab.'

'What?'

'Here. Look.' I pulled up the story on my phone, and handed it over to her. '*Melbourne woman gives birth in an Uber.* She's not from Melbourne, she's from Portsmouth.'

'Oh. Oh, I'm sorry Paul. You weren't still hoping . . .?'

'I was. Stupid me. We'd always spoken of having kids ourselves. It just wasn't the right time.'

'It never is. You just work it out as you go along. I didn't think I wanted to be pregnant with you but I couldn't have been happier when you came along.'

'You didn't want to be pregnant with me?'

I was joking but she took me seriously.

'We were enjoying being young, living in Manchester, having friends. Teaching wasn't so bad then, it was a challenge, it was getting easier, I thought it would get easier forever.'

'I'm sorry I ruined that for you.'

'Don't be daft. I'm glad. It wouldn't have been you if we'd waited, it would have been someone else.'

'I'm even more sorry about that. You might have given birth to a doctor or a lawyer.'

'Stop it. I'm proud of you, Paul,' she said.

'What for?'

'For everything.'

'But specifically.'

'Don't be daft. Well . . . you're funny.'

'That's it? I'm funny? Jesus Christ.'

She tutted. The Lord's name in vain. It would have been cruel to upset her by letting her know that Monica had been pregnant with our child a few years ago. She was twenty-seven, I was twenty-eight; after years of being exploited as an assistant her career was just beginning to get moving.

We were both very tentative and considerate; we would do what the other wanted. I like to think I would have been delighted if she'd said she wanted the baby. And now I always wonder if she would have been delighted if I'd said I wanted it, her, him. But we both shied away from that. We were living in the château and earning very little money. We had this idea that if we just waited three years, 'three years' was the magic number we had in our head, then we'd be in a position to give our child a proper home. The Tories had just got in; what eager bourgeois we were. I don't blame us for our conventional desire for a place to live, but I wonder if it was cowardice that I'd dressed up as feminism: it was her body and I had not wanted the responsibility of voicing an opinion about her body, for being responsible for the way her body and our lives would change forever if she had decided differently. We were both relieved to use the other as our excuse to prolong our freedom and decadence for another few years.

The first show she put on was a success and she was offered a job on a three-year project in Melbourne, though she'd be able to get out after two, she said. We discussed it and agreed she should go. There was no absolute reason not to, not if we believed in our magical three years. I think we were punishing ourselves for a decision that we couldn't admit to each other we regretted. It was a penance. Or I used the idea of a penance to justify my baser instincts. Two years wasn't that long. It was long enough that we shouldn't kill ourselves over faithfulness in the strictest sense, but it wasn't that long, it was survivable. We took a holiday from the weight of being in love, from its limitations, and we behaved like we had done in the years after we'd just met each other, when we'd been waiting for the inevitability of us coming together. We had joyful reunions, spaced far apart. We lived two lives. The halves grew unequal. We lived on Skype at different ends of the day. The Monica who loved me grew smaller. The bigger half of her is sitting exams for citizenship now, bringing up an infamous baby with a colleague from the gallery. The part of her that loves me, if it is anywhere, is still there too, far too far from me to be of any use to either of us.

'Well, at least I'm funny,' I said to my mum, the last time I saw her.

'You're not that funny,' she said. 'You can work on your other qualities too.'

*

In the Conservative club I looked over again at Carl's parents. Mike was sitting down now and staring through his pint, rubbing the knuckles of his right hand. Janine was busier – talking to other mourners, giving Leia instructions to see about the sandwiches. Carl's little brothers weren't little any more – they came in for pints of lager and took them outside to smoke. One of them smiled at Amy and came over to say hello. Mike caught me looking at him and waved, so I walked over to sit next to him.

We had stopped going fishing with him when we became teenagers but when we were drinking on the beach at night we'd see him sometimes, sitting silently on a camping stool at the tide's edge, just visible in the dark, with his line cast out into the sea as it drifted out.

'I'm sorry for your loss,' I said.

He nodded. 'Silly bugger,' he said. I felt the stubs of his fingers as they woke up to the handshake and began to squeeze my hand. 'Are you working, Paul?' he said.

'Yeah.'

'Yeah?'

'In a shop.'

'What kind of a shop?'

'Bookshop.'

'They still have them?' He managed a little grin. 'In a shop? You were top of the class. Still . . . work's work.'

'It is.'

'Carl was doing all right, you know? People think you work in a supermarket you're just a shelf-stacker or a till girl but there's more to it than that. He was a shift manager.'

'That's what my mum used to tell me. He was great to her, always said hello, asked how she was. Mum thought I should be more like him. More settled, more realistic about things.'

Mike snorted and looked away from me. 'Realistic? I suppose she thought that were the best he could have got.'

'She wasn't saying that.'

'And you too.'

'You just said it was a good job.'

'It was a bollocks job! He was a fucking shelf-stacker.'

'Assistant manager.'

'Fucking arse manager.' He took a sip of his pint and shook his head. 'Paid a fucking pittance. I'd earn near what he earned a month in a week out on the rigs. I should have encouraged him more with the books. Like your dad did with you. I've been thinking about where he might have gone if I'd made more effort with him.'

'You're being too hard on yourself.'

He snorted. 'Have I even spoken to you since your mum passed away?'

'Maybe not. It's OK.'

'I was there, you know. In church. At the back. When you and your sister spoke about her. It's not OK, is it? It was a nasty way to go.'

'A horrible way to go.'

'You're angry too, aren't you?'

'Of course I am. The fucking people round here.'

'The fucking *people*?'

'Not you. Whoever it was who complained about her at school.'

'What did they complain about?'

'That she wasn't in control of the class. And that's her fault, is it? Those fucking little shits she had to teach. Those fucking scumbags round here.'

Mike shook his head. 'You are angry. You might be talking about my grandkids.'

'Yeah, well, I'm not saying your grandkids are scumbags.'

'They're not scumbags,' said Mike. 'Not yet. Who knows what they'll turn into? But, Paul. I know you didn't know Carl as well as you used to, but what do you reckon? Do you think he could've done it? Killed himself on purpose?'

'No way,' I said. 'Of course not.'

He shook his head again. 'How do you do your workings out with that? I wish you were right.'

'I've been gone a while, I know.'

'You were never here like he was.'

'I wasn't anywhere else.'

'Ah. Yeah. Maybe I'm talking crap.'

I put my hand on his shoulder. 'I'll get you a Guinness,' I said.

*

Carl used to lie all the time. His dad's fingers had been bitten off by a shark when he went for his morning swim off the oil rig. Joanne O'Reilly had shown him her fanny and asked him to touch it. An Olympic trainer had offered him a running contract paying exactly four hundred pounds a week if he'd stop smoking and would travel to Manchester four times a week. It occurs to me now that this sum, more than we'd ever considered in our lives, wasn't that outlandish, and Carl *was* the fastest 100-metre runner in the district. Still . . . He did not travel to Manchester or stop smoking. He lied to us when he failed his GCSEs and pretended he was doing A levels at the sixth-form college when he was actually doing resits. There was no pleasure in catching him out in a lie. We'd always regret it, listening to the long implausible counter-facts we had not considered before we nodded and agreed with him: yes, we hadn't thought of that. He looked so anxious as he tried to convince us. The fact that we would lie to him to save his face might have been doubly humiliating. He dropped out of the resits too, and took a job working at the fish-processing factory, which had outlasted the fishing.

Joanne O'Reilly was the prettiest girl in our year, or I thought so; she seemed to like Carl more than me but neither of us stood a chance back then. We would watch her in Maths class as she wrote the names of older boys on her pencil cases, on the text books we had to cover with wallpaper, and it wouldn't have been much more painful if she had scratched their names on our arms with a compass needle. The older boys would never understand our girls like we did, our comrades, solvers of maths problems, destroyers of iambic pentameter, recipients of the same cruel humiliations at the hands of vicious Madames and Fräuleins. We thought about our girls sexually all the time, but secretly, and imprecisely; we knew the older boys would not know the things that were so alluring about them apart from their looks; the tapes they listened to, the band names they also wrote on their text books; the older boys would not know the difference between them except in the most trivial way; they could not identify them blindfolded by the sound of their laughter and the smell of their shampoo and chewing gum.

The older boys who we hated and became.

I wandered over to say hello to Joanne.

*

Amy was still in bed when I got back to the house the next morning. Everything was just where Mum had left it. I took my shoes off before I walked on the white carpet in the living room, lifted the lid of the piano and played a few chords. The remote control for the TV in the corner rested on the arm of the sofa, as though Mum had just popped out to the shops.

In the kitchen I turned the kettle on, opened the cupboard where the cups were kept, took the cosy off the pot and opened the ceramic jar full of teabags that she must have filled up before the crash. When the tea had brewed I poured two cups and carried them upstairs.

'Do you want a brew?' I called through.

'Yes, green, please,' she called back.

'I've made you a normal one.'

'That'll do. Do you want to come in?'

I pushed the door open slowly. She was sitting up in bed, rubbing her eyes. 'You're still wearing your suit. Oh, God. You've just got in.'

'Yeah.'

'I was feeling quite impressed with you when I heard the door. I thought you'd gone to get the paper or out for some breakfast.'

'Yes. Don't be impressed.'

'Where were you?'

'Joanne's?'

'Right. I saw she had her hand on your back towards the end. Isn't she married?'

'We didn't talk about that,' I said.

'Did she have a ring on?'

'I didn't notice.'

'My God, Paul.'

'It's . . . I know. What time did you get back?'

'Eight o'clock. It wasn't much fun sober. Not that funerals are supposed to be fun.'

'I don't know. They normally are. People are at their best.'

'Their drunkest.'

'Apart from you. What's with that? Did you go on some super-bender in Thailand you're compensating for now? Did your liver explode?'

'No. Nothing like that.'

'Good.'

'Except . . . Prepare for a surprise.'

'Yeah?'

'I did get pregnant.'

'Ha!'

'No, Paul. I got pregnant.'

'Are you still pregnant?'

'Yes, I'm still pregnant. Two months pregnant. That's why I came home.'

'Are you really pregnant?'

'Yes.'

'And you're staying pregnant?'

'Not forever. About seven months more.'

'No, really? You're pregnant?'

'Yes.'

'I don't believe you.'

'This is very dull.'

'You *are* pregnant?'

'Yes.'

'Who's the dad?'

'I think a guy I met from Bristol.'

'You think?'

'I'm certain.'

'Right. Who is he?'

'He's an acupuncturist.'

'An acupuncturist. No way.'

'Who promotes jungle nights too.'

'Who promotes . . .?'

'Stop smiling!'

'Does he know?'

He did not know. Not yet.

'And you're sure you're keeping it?' I asked.

'I've been going through it for weeks now. I thought I'd have an abortion. But I don't want to. Not after Mum going. It just feels – it shouldn't only be us two left. I have this awful feeling that somehow it might . . .'

'What?'

'It's stupid. Like what if she was trying to come back and I prevented it.'

I looked away from her, at the little bookcase filled with children's novels about ballerinas. I left the room and came back with some tissues.

'Sorry,' she said.

'There's nothing to be sorry about. Will you tell the dad?'

'Do you think I should? Do you think he has a right to know?'

'I don't know. It depends. Is he a wanker?'

'Why would I sleep with a wanker?'

'For sex?'

'*You* would sleep with a wanker for sex. He was nice. It just wasn't the sort of relationship either of us were intending a lifelong connection to result from.'

'And are you excited? About having a child?'

'I'm terrified. It's going to be hard. But yeah. I did want to have one at some point. In theory.'

'Congratulations, then.'

'It's so sad too, without Mum. Who am I going to ring up when I don't know what I'm doing? Who's going to help me out?'

'That's what I was thinking. Your friends?'

'I keep imagining what she'd have said when I told her. Our conversations. Remember her stories about how easy it is to give birth? About what a fuss modern mums make of it. She'd have driven me crazy with shit like that.'

'She was only twenty-five, wasn't she?'

'With you.'

'With me,' I said.

'Imagine.'

'Weird to grow up so much earlier than our generation.'

'No wonder she thought we were whingers.'

'She hardly thought you were a whinger, Amy. She was in awe of you, how tough and effective you are.'

'I feel very far from tough. I feel like I've been whacked with a hammer all over. God, it would have been so much easier with her here.'

She reached down to take a sip of her tea and put her other hand to her eyes.

'But look,' I said. 'I'll come to the hospital, for the scans, for the birth, for whatever. I'll come and stay with you if you want. I'll do everything I can, I'll be there all the way . . .'

She turned away from me and put her head in the pillow, and I knew then what small consolation I could be, how my good intentions were only a little more use to her than indifference. I put my hand on her shoulder anyway, all I could do to let her know I was there with her.

SEVEN

The new *White Jesus* was back from the printers, and Jerry's photos did not seem to document an atrocity. Emily had given in just a little. She wasn't wearing antlers, or high-waisted PVC hot pants and bikini top, but she'd put a different dress on, and the photo they'd used had caught her turning round to hear something Jerry had said – something ambiguously offensive rather than outright – her facial expression incredulous but amused, at least in that split second, though she might have become angry in the next seconds. But this at least captured something of her brusque charisma.

I followed up the email Emily never replied to by sending her a copy of the magazine in the post with a note, saying I hoped she liked it.

And I asked again if she might like to meet me for a coffee one day, or a Coca-Cola. In the first week after I'd sent it I kept checking my emails, but when I didn't hear back again I didn't give much more thought to the matter. And that might have been that.

*

But towards the end of one shift in early spring, when I was digesting some particularly bitter news about my books page,

Leo asked me if I wanted to go with him to a public debate about the dangers of Brexit.

'Are you mad?' I said. 'Don't we breathe in enough of that without having to seek it out?'

'Your man Lancaster is speaking.'

'He's not my man.'

'You've been reading his books.'

He gave me a look and I worried that he suspected me of stealing Lancaster's short history of the Russian Revolution. 'All right, I'll come.'

It was round the corner in Senate House, a building of such imposing grandeur that Hitler was supposed to have earmarked it for his headquarters upon his successful invasion.

'Yes, I know that,' I said to Leo.

'But did you know this?' he said, and talked some more while I let my thoughts drift elsewhere. Something, something, terrible curators. Something, something, Georgian terraces. Something, something, knock it all down and start again, don't you think?

'How do you have so many opinions?' I asked.

'I think about things. Have you ever thought of doing the same?'

'About which buildings to tear down?'

'Yes.'

'For aesthetic purposes?'

'Yes!'

'No.'

We entered the foyer and I read the poster advertising the event. What the history of British isolationism should teach us about the impact of leaving the EU. Andrew Lancaster was arguing the case for disaster against another historian who was in favour of us leaving. There were wine glasses on a long table but no wine in them yet. You had to do the time to earn the wine. We were five minutes late and a man on the door to the hall beckoned us over, just as a door opened at the other end of the foyer and three late-middle-aged men walked in, one of whom was Andrew Lancaster. I waved in his direction. He gave me a puzzled look and nodded; he hadn't recognised me.

The seats were nearly all taken, so Leo and I had to sit separately. I squeezed past people's knees to find an empty chair in the middle of an aisle, and as I did I looked up and caught sight of Emily a few rows behind me. She raised her hand and smiled at me, just as the man who had accompanied the speakers spoke into the microphone on the stage to start proceedings.

*

Lancaster was as impressive as you may have seen from the YouTube clips people post on Facebook. He took ten min-utes to neatly sum up his position. British isolationism has always been associated with Continental disintegration. Not to mention the harm we would do to ourselves in terms of trade. Furthermore, its focus on stopping immigrants from the EU will do little to slow the changes to our society that the anti-immigration voters are justified in wanting to be acknowledged, even if they're wrong about what to do about it, easily manipulated by nostalgic rhetoric. Looking up at him from the front row was the student I suspected he was sleeping with, the one who looked a bit like Emily, the one I had assumed was his daughter. She wrote something every so often in a little notebook, and I kept myself interested by imagining this was a list of all the delicious transgressive fanta-sies that had occurred to her while watching his commanding performance, which she would later push under his office door along with instructions to come round to her flat in Kentish

Town as soon as he was able, so she could submit to the force of his powerful arguments. I was too distracted by thinking about what I was going to say to Emily to fully follow the man arguing against Lancaster, though when I remembered to listen to him I found that what he was saying about the interests of those on low incomes, people who might claim reasonably that the worst thing that could happen to them would be that things stayed the same – all of this sounded plausible enough to be worth further thought, even though Leo, a little to the front and right of me, was screwing his face up while listening to him.

Lancaster set about explaining why what had sounded plausible was not plausible, and I resisted the urge to turn around again to look at Emily, resisted it again, and again, and wondered if she was looking at me, at the back of my head, and then the audience was applauding and I did look round, curious to observe Emily's style of clapping, which from where I was sitting seemed only to be delicate and dutiful and not rapturous, unlike the student in the front row, one of a number of people there who had let out a mini-whoop, who was still bashing her hands together and flapping her elbows as if she were trying to take off.

When we had finished applauding we were invited to have a glass of wine and have books signed by the historians. I would have waited in my seat but the man next to me had stood up and was looming, so I stood up and loomed over the woman to my left, who did the same, and we all queued on our feet to be among the first out, as though we were very keen to escape or be first to meet the historians. I turned to Emily again. She was looking past me, to the front of the room, where I turned to see that Andrew's mistress had approached him and put her hand on his arm. She was speaking quickly and touching her hair with one hand, and he nodded then looked up to the back of the room to see Emily looking back at him. He smiled. I turned back to look at Emily. She was looking at me now. I put an imaginary glass to my lips. She nodded and got up, and we met in the aisle, awkwardly, not knowing if we should shake hands or kiss, doing neither.

'What did you think?' she said. 'That's, er, Andrew, did you know he was my . . .?'

'Uncle. Yes.'

'*Boyfriend.*'

'Yes, I knew.'

'"Boyfriend" is too childish a word, isn't it? "Partner" is such a legalistic word. We need something in the middle.'

'Fucktoy.'

'That's not it. Anyway, that was my man on stage, holding forth.'

'You sound like Tammy Wynette now.'

'I give up. That was my Andrew.'

'Holding back the tide of nationalism.'

'Doing his best. I didn't have this down as your scene.'

'I was dragged along by a colleague.'

'It's not really my vibe either. Perfectly engaging though, I thought.'

'Perfectly. Very educational. Like live Radio 4. Here, what colour do you want?'

'Red.'

I passed her a glass and looked down at the floor. I had never seen her in shoes before, and so I was momentarily fascinated by those she chose to wear, the black patent-leather heels with a delicate strap to fasten across the light-brown nylon that covered her feet.

'Thanks for sending the magazine, by the way,' she said. 'Sorry I didn't get back. Andrew tells me the interview was good, so thanks for that.'

'It's a pleasure.'

'I didn't read it myself, I'm sorry to say.'

'No?'

'Too embarrassed to. I can't imagine what stupid things I said.'

'You weren't stupid.'

'Our opinions might differ about that.'

'Are you saying we have different standards of intelligence?'

'No!'

'Liar.'

'Well, we probably do,' she said, 'but that's not what I meant.'

'Thanks.'

'I didn't mean mine were superior.'

'Just *different*.'

'You probably have a much more intelligent idea of how to live and be happy than I do.'

'Do you think? Christ, how miserable are you?'

She put her head to one side and seemed to think about this.

'Do you go to these things with him much?' I said.

'No. I'm making an effort to get out more.'

'For what reason?'

'I ask myself the same question. The usual reasons, though. Other humans. The hope of stimulation.'

'Stimulation?'

'Stop it.'

'Stop what?'

'That grin.'

Leo strode towards us. 'Hello, hello, hello! Aren't you Emily Nardini?'

'I am,' she said.

'Leo,' he said. 'I'm a big fan. I have my own novel coming out next year, actually.'

She shook his hand. 'What do you mean, actually? Did I imply the contrary?'

'We're colleagues,' I said.

'I brought him down here, actually,' said Leo.

'Actually?' she said.

'Literally,' I said.

Leo scratched his bald spot. 'Did you enjoy the debate?' he asked Emily, not me.

'Yes, I did. But do you mind giving us a moment? I was just discussing something personal with Paul.'

'Oh! Yes, of course. Ha ha! I'll just join the queue to talk to the speakers.'

'See you later,' she said.

He went and stood in the queue and tried not to look at us.

'I can't stand men like that,' she said.

'I love you,' I said.

'Thank you.'

'I really do.'

'That's your prerogative.'

'You can do what I want to do,' I sang.

'That's your prerogative,' she sang back.

We looked at each other and grinned. We were from the same era with the same bad songs clogging up our memory.

'I'm sorry I didn't get back to your note,' she said.

'What note?'

'The one you sent with the magazine.'

'I'd forgotten I even sent one,' I lied.

'The photo came out well. I was too vain not to look at that. I couldn't go any further but, like I say, Andrew says it was fine.'

'Do you trust him to be honest about things like that?' I said, and looked over to the table where his admirer was watching him sign books and talk to his fans.

'Oh, yes,' she said, following my eyes. 'He's very articulate about the things he considers stupid. It's what I like most about him.'

'Well, that's reassuring. What are you doing now?'

'I don't know. Something. Drinks, dinner. His publisher Susannah is here; they're old friends; we're going on somewhere. Why? Do you want to come?'

'I'm, er –'

'You could come. It would be nice to have someone to talk to who isn't here to worship Andrew. I'll introduce you to him in a bit.'

We waited for the queue to run down and found a sofa to sit on. 'This is my first glass of wine this year,' she said to me.

'It's nearly not your first glass of wine any more. I'm going to get another.'

'Go on then,' she said, holding out her glass to me.

We'd drunk two by the time the queue had died down. The historians were keeping up an amicable disagreement throughout the signing, as those queuing directed further questions at them. Leo had reached the front and was opinionating about something, and while Andrew's attention was occupied his student mistress had retreated a few paces to talk to a younger man I took for a fellow PhD student, or a disgruntled boyfriend. She was doing most of the talking, gesticulating and constantly twitching back to face the signing tables; he nodded, covered his mouth with his hand when he spoke.

'It looks like she enjoyed Andrew's performance.'

'Chloe. Yes, she would have. His brightest student, apparently.'

'I think that boy she's with is worried she's in love with him.'

'With Andrew? Hmm.'

'How's the wine?'

'Vicious.'

'If you ever want to drink wine with me again, I can tell you that I'm pretty much always available.'

She had been watching Andrew but now turned to me. 'Why is that, Paul?'

'Are you asking what's wrong with me?'

'Precisely.'

'I have stringent taste in other humans.'

'I don't believe that at all.'

'Why?'

'I imagine you'd knock about with just about anyone.'

'Well, you're insulting yourself there as well as me. Here, give me your number.'

I passed her my notebook and she studied it for a second before writing in it. She'd just finished and handed it back to me when we became aware of Andrew Lancaster standing over us.

'Oh!' she said, and stood up. 'Andrew, this is Paul.'

He held out his hand, which I took after putting my book in my bag and standing up.

'How do you do?' he said.

'Hi, Andrew.'

'Did you just take my beloved's phone number?'

'He did,' said Emily.

'I shall keep my eye on you.'

'You'll remember: Paul came to interview me.'

'*White Jesus*! You know, you're very familiar-looking. I haven't taught you?'

'No, no. I wish. I went to the London College of Calligraphy. But Emily says you thought the profile was OK. Was she being polite?'

'Not at all. If it was shit, I'd happily tell you. You asked some interesting questions. And printed a nice photo too. She looks as beautiful in it as she does in real life.'

'Flatterer. I invited Paul to dinner with us,' said Emily. 'Is that OK?'

'More than! Will you come?'

Leo was standing in earshot on his own, and looked up hopefully at me. I turned away from him and said, 'Yes, thank you, I'd like to.'

*

There were eight of us. Emily, Andrew, his publisher Susannah, the event organiser and his wife, and Chloe and her grumpy companion. Emily and I took one end of the table, with Emily sitting next to Andrew and Susannah sitting next to me. Chloe got in next to Andrew on his other side, and her companion was wedged out on the end, talking to the event organiser's wife, whose husband spent the meal facing in Andrew's direction.

I watched Andrew, trying to get the measure of him. He cared about his appearance, that was clear – you'd have to if you had a girlfriend more than twenty years your junior. You wondered how the pontificating old Jeremies of this world could bear the photos that were taken with them and their young women. The contrast was too great to be explained by charm and intelligence, even if you didn't already know that the men concerned had been punished by the moral universe with exactly the faces they deserved. Did they revel in the contrast or look away from the snapshots? The photos of these older men and younger women together looked like they belonged in plastic evidence bags, documents of the continuing crimes against women. It disappointed me that I could see no similar crime when I framed Emily and Andrew together. The suit and tie he was wearing for the occasion sat well on him, and if it made him look a bit formal, I imagined how that itself could be cool in the world of academia, adopting style and convention against a culture of sloppy iconoclasm. It irritated me that I could see what she saw in him. What they all saw in him.

I found myself talking a lot to Susannah, who ran a division of one of the big publishing houses. She interrogated me about which books were selling in the shop; which I thought were good and which were awful, telling me which she'd been involved with or had tried to buy and lost out on. She had published Andrew for years, and been friends with him for even longer.

Emily left at one point to use the toilet, and during this time Andrew turned his attention towards me.

'Emily says you showed up drunk to interview her. Is this true?'

'It was the magazine's annual party the night before. It can't be done sober.'

'Oh, you write for a magazine! Which one?' said Susannah. I told her.

'Isn't that a fashion magazine?'

'He does the books page,' said Andrew. 'That's how he met Emily.'

'Oh, that's over now. The books page.' I explained to them that they had axed the page last week, replaced it with a legal highs column, and tried to persuade me to write it.

'It's not that funny, you know,' I said when faced with their amused reaction.

'Are you sure you couldn't have written the drugs column?' Susannah asked me. 'It might be great fun.'

'I'm quite sure,' I said. 'I did some research into the matter.'

*

On the day I conducted this research I had been summoned for an emergency meeting at the office. The magazine was not doing well, of course it wasn't doing well, no one bought style magazines any more apart from hairdressers, and it was only a matter of time before we worked out how to stick our head in a machine and download our haircuts.

I have always avoided the offices of *White Jesus* as much as possible. They're just off Broadway Market on the edge of London Fields, the epicentre of newly rich Hackney, the street with the highest percentage of beautiful young people in all of London. The receptionist is a thirteen-year-old boy with the face of a torturer who we all call Macaulay Culkin. He was wearing a baseball cap backwards, an XS vest that was baggy on him and a thick gold chain that was either a joke or not a joke, either gold or fake gold, just like he was either a teenage rent boy or a diminutive adult journalist – blurred lines were the magazine's aesthetic and the modus operandi with which it conducted its crimes. He gave me a complicated handshake and sent me off through the messy arrangements of desks to my meeting.

Jonathan shares an office in the basement of the building, the 'bunker', with Stev'n. I took the steps down and they both looked up from the table they were sitting round.

Stev'n is a mournful-looking man, with a shaved head and glasses, who looks like he has never seen sunlight. He was wearing one of his expensive shirts with intricate patterns involving skulls and bones. Jonathan, in contrast, has the year-round look of a man at a summer wedding in Italy; he is comfortable in the casual smartness of the wealthy class – he has mimicked their gestures to perfection.

Jonathan stood to shake my hand, the gesture of someone interviewing me rather than a man who currently lived on my sofa. 'How are you, Paul? Thanks so much for coming in.'

Stev'n was still looking at the papers on the table. He spoke quietly. 'We've got customer surveys, traffic figures from the site, feedback from advertisers. I'm annoyed with you, Paul. Why on earth do we have a books page? No one reads the thing. People who read books don't know it exists. People who read the magazine don't read books. Oh, it's not even that. Some of them do read books. But every fucking magazine under the sun that doesn't know how to fill a back page sticks a few book reviews on it, some cunt who aspires to be a literary critic. No offence, Paul.'

'You can't just say something really offensive and then take it back with three words at the end of the sentence.'

'Now, Jonathan, didn't I say? I worried he would be like this,' said Stev'n.

'We need to focus on what makes us original is what Stev'n's saying,' said Jonathan. 'We need clickbait. The hair reviews, everyone loves the hair reviews. They're funny. People want to be in them. That's what we do that no one else does. But you on Norwegian literature? Get real, mate.'

'If you feel so strongly about it, write a review on Amazon,' said Stev'n.

'Or don't,' said Jonathan.

'We had an idea.'

'We think you might like it.'

'I doubt it.'

'Paul,' said Jonathan. 'I know you're upset about losing your book column. But let's make something clear. This isn't a negotiation. This isn't your chance to win us over with a passionate speech. The books page has only lasted as long as it has because half of us didn't even know it was there.'

'It's like the human eye has evolved not to register short reviews of literary fiction,' drawled Stev'n.

'If there's a teenage girl with her legs open on the facing page.'

'Exactly,' said Stev'n. 'We could have a teenage girl with her legs open on both pages. When you shut the magazine, it's like they're scissoring each other. And right underneath them, a big fuck-off advert for Uniqlo.'

'So you see,' said Jonathan, 'that you will need to find another venue for your literary criticism. Or alternatively, you may decide to write something else for us instead. We'd even give you a small raise.' Jonathan reached under his desk and slid a large Jiffy bag across the table towards me. 'These might be the last days of legal highs,' he said. 'Don't you think we need to document that? We can be the first mainstream publication to regularly review them, you know, with a bit of gonzo humour, the stuff you're good at.'

'We have a great respect for your ability to consume narcotics,' said Stev'n.

'Look,' I said. 'I don't want to tell either of you your job. But aren't the people who travel to work every day on the Tube more interesting to advertisers than nerds who stay at home inhaling Chinese chemicals?'

'They don't read the magazine, they don't go on the site,' said Jonathan. 'Anyway, the brands aren't targeting the people who take the Chinese chemicals, they're targeting the people who get a thrill from reading about *you* taking the Chinese chemicals. It's edginess that attracts the brands we want.'

'Exactly,' said Stev'n. 'Now, we don't want to tell you your job. But you're the guy who takes the Chinese chemicals.'

I didn't even argue. I had suddenly realised that all I had been doing for the last few years was writing an expensively produced blog. A blog might have had more readers.

'Think about it,' said Stev'n. 'For five minutes. You'll still have your haircut review, whether you take it or not.'

'I don't need to think about it,' I said. 'I'll see you later, Jonathan, will I? Or has your wife taken you back?'

Jonathan looked away from me and said nothing. I turned around and started to walk back up the stairs.

'Paul?' said Stev'n. I turned back and caught the Jiffy bag he underarmed towards me. 'Take it away and think about it.' It was as heavy as an average-sized human's ashes. I put it in my satchel and left.

Later that evening Jonathan knocked on my door and asked if I'd thought more about the package, if he could have a look at it. I pulled it out of my bag and tossed it to him, and he poured the contents onto my bed, sachets of capsules and pills, fake cocaine, weird herbs, lurid spice, all with garish packaging, connotations of radiation and supervillains, of the origin stories of mythical monsters.

'I did consider it,' I admitted. 'I was thinking perhaps I don't need to *do* the drugs, I could just imagine what they're like from the packaging and the press release. I mean, drugs can only have so many effects, don't you think? I can just describe them all in terms of what I've done before. I could actually become the great drug critic – I could supply the critical vocabulary by which all drugs are subsequently judged.'

'You would have to do *some* first.'

He was shaking out a white powder now, onto my bedside table.

'Man, if you want to be a lab rat, do it in your own bedroom. The living room, I mean.'

'This is just a zingy alternative to the Bolivian marching powder.'

'I bet it's one molecule away from hillbilly bathtub crank.'

Jonathan rolled up the note he had pulled from his wallet and held the thin tube out to me. 'You try,' he said. 'It's *your* job.'

'No. I am sacrificing my payday for the good of others.'

'It would only be the people who read the legal high reviews in *White Jesus* who would suffer. You could argue they were asking for it. It's not like anyone who really needed to live would die.'

'You're not making me feel better about my book column.'

'Have you written the *London Review of Haircuts* yet?'

'No.'

'Well, why don't we go out and do it together? Mary's on at the bar. We can do it gonzo style.'

'Absolutely not. And anyway, I always do it gonzo style. You don't think I approach women and ask to take pictures of their hair when I'm sober, do you? I'm not a monster.'

*

The drugs were as bad as I'd imagined. But we were still sober-ish when we arrived at the bar to surprise Mary.

'Wow, what a treat,' she said.

'You don't mean that,' I said.

'I don't not mean it yet.'

This was a bar called Catch down at the bottom of Kingsland Road. It's a pitch-black dive bar with an upstairs room for dance nights and a little dance floor at the back on the ground floor too. Many of my briefest and nicest friendships have been initiated in the roped-off smoking area in the street.

Mary was wearing what looked like a vest of iridescent chain mail.

'No one's ever called it that before,' she said.

'It doesn't look like it would provide you much protection,' said Jonathan.

'What need have I of protection with you two besides me?'

'You really are delightfully naive,' said Jonathan and placed his hand over hers on the counter.

She snatched it away, gave him a look and walked down to the other end of the bar to serve someone else.

'You and her, you're not – ?' I said.

'No, no. Just flirting. Making sure I still know how to do it.'

'It's like riding a bike,' I said. 'No, it's not like riding a bike. Yes, actually it is like riding a bike. It's like riding a bike while you're really drunk so you keep smashing into lamp posts, and other pedestrians, but not hurting yourself or them badly, just annoying them, and hardly ever killing anyone or yourself, unless you're really unlucky, that is.'

'Christ, are the Chinese chemicals taking hold?'

'The not-drugs are not working.'

'We better do some more then.'

'Which ones?'

'I don't think it makes a difference. More is the key.'

Five minutes after we did some more the first doses began to work and it became clear we had made a terrible mistake. The rest of the night melted into a garish puddle. There was a visual effect to the combination of drugs I had taken which made me keep turning my head to catch the sun rising behind me, but I could never catch it in time. Women's faces were lit by morning dawn that quickly turned into night. I felt as if I was in a time-lapse video, watching myself fast-forward through every night I had left on earth. We continued to talk to the faces that appeared before us, but we made less sense than usual, and the shiny green ants that crawled across them were distracting and counterproductive to good repartee. The fake MDMA we had taken had none of the warmth of real MDMA, no feeling of empathy, of love; and at the same time there was none of the devilish humour and euphoria of acid or mushrooms. There was only visual disorder and vicious energy. If I had taken these drugs on my own, they would perhaps have broken me, had me clinging to a lamp post in terror outside, but at least with Jonathan around we could try to make light of them, revel in their awful indignity and pretend the experience was comic. Mary had gone from being amused to being appalled by us, but consented to our request for quadruple gin and tonics for the price of singles; it was the only thing, we said, that might cure us, and she must have hoped we would knock ourselves out before she finished her shift and had to return to the flat.

'These must be the worst drugs I've ever tried,' I said, or he said, it was hard to tell.

'They are really, really bad. But do you remember when we went to that weekend party in Cornwall with the Scottish philatelist?'

'He had a medicine bag full of liquids . . . and pipettes . . . and penny farthings.'

'All his drugs were just numbers. 2ci, 2cb, i c deadpeople.'

'They're beckoning to me too.'

When we got back to the flat everything was much harder. Jonathan found a single Valium, took it and conked out. For a long time I leaned out of my bedroom window smoking, looking down on the people below like a vampire about to swoop on them. For a moment I understood what it was like to be truly evil, the loneliness of it, the thrill of exclusion. There was some kind of creature climbing up the wall of the kebab shop across the road, an angel, or something crueller than that. A tower block in the distance had the square jaw of Elvis and the sideburns to match. When he opened his eyes I turned away and took to my bed.

*

'So you will understand why I decided that opportunity was not for me,' I concluded, while a waiter in a starched white shirt, bow tie and waistcoat topped up my glass of wine.

Susannah and Andrew were still laughing at me.

'They're drugs for feral kids who have been deranged by porn. They're not for us.'

'Oh, that's nice that you said *us*.' Susannah reached over and squeezed my arm.

Andrew then began to tell a long story about his time working as an advisor for the Secretary of State for Education. Chloe kept touching his shoulder and throwing her head right back to laugh.

Emily came back from the toilet and yawned. She was drinking water now and refused a refill of her wine glass.

Before Andrew could finish his story his phone began to ring. 'Sorry, let me just see if this is serious. Hello.' The person on the other end spoke and Andrew let out a quick breath, stood up and left the table.

The table was quiet for a few seconds as we watched him stride off with his phone pressed to his cheek, stopping at one point to give it a good shake before he put it back to his ear and disappeared round a corner.

'And how are the signs with your book?' Susannah asked Emily.

'Sorry, give me a second,' said Emily. 'I'm just going to check what's happening.'

Emily and Andrew were gone for a while. The food arrived, and Susannah declared that we should all start eating; half my plate was gone by the time they arrived back.

'I'm very sorry. I'm afraid I have to leave. Something's come up with my daughter.'

'Oh, Andrew, nothing serious?' said Susannah.

'Nothing very serious, no. Just irritating.' He looked down at his brill. 'What a waste. I'll tell you about it another time. Can I leave something for the bill?'

'Certainly not,' said Susannah.

'I might go too,' said Emily.

'Stay,' I said.

'Yes, you must,' said Andrew.

'You must,' said everyone.

'OK,' she said, and sat down in her old seat, leaving the gap between her and Chloe. Susannah, sensing the awkwardness, turned and began to ask Chloe questions.

'Is everything all right?' I asked Emily, quietly. She filled a glass with wine now and took a swig.

'Oh, that's nice,' she said. 'That really is nice.'

*

I was distracted from Emily for a time by Susannah, who continued to show sympathy for my cancelled column and general despondency, and asked if I might be interested in a career in publishing. There were often entry-level jobs in sales or marketing, she said, where bookselling experience came in very useful. She gave me her card and told me I should come and talk to her. I said I would.

When I turned back, Emily was looking furious. 'I'm going to go,' she said.

'Are you OK?'

'I'm fine. Sorry, I'm not in a good mood.' She looked up at the grand ceiling of the room we were in, at the waiters gliding past us in their bow ties. 'This isn't my sort of place at all.'

'We could go somewhere else. Let's go somewhere else.'

'I'm not sure. Oh, OK. As long as we go right away.'

*

It was hard to find a pub in Mayfair that wasn't full of loud men in suits sucking the marrow from platefuls of hacked-up bones, and we gave up. I walked Emily home along the top of the park, against her insistence, wheeling my ghastly bike beside her and feeling like a boy talking to one of his friend's older sisters.

Andrew's daughter Sophie had been caught shoplifting in Selfridges; that was the crisis. Sophie had called Andrew because she didn't want her mother to know about it, and she hoped he could help.

'Can he help?'

'He has enough lawyers and barristers as friends. One of them will go along with him and throw her weight around.'

'I imagine Andrew himself can be pretty fierce.'

'Yes.'

'To his daughter?'

'He's quite indulgent of her. He feels he owes her for leaving home when she was a kid.'

'What's she like?'

'She's difficult. Young. Superior. Doesn't smile much, or not when I'm around. She's just submitted a PhD and has started writing these opinion pieces on being a Marxist activist for the *Guardian*. Dinner talk with her is what I imagine it was like to have a tutorial at Balliol. Which she knows all about, and perhaps it's just the style you learn there but she certainly takes on the role of the tutor in our conversations. I sometimes wonder if she believes I wrote my books myself. The egalitarianism she professes is abstract rather than intuitive. She'll have a book out herself before we know it. It will sell in one week more copies than all my books have ever sold. In interviews she'll outline utopian plans to end sexism, famine and war. I can see it. It's the future. I'm sorry, listen to me. I'm ranting. I'm hateable. Fucking kill me, please.'

I made my fingers into the shape of a gun and pressed them against her temple. 'Bang,' I said, though I had not yet had a single murderous thought towards her.

'I didn't know she was a shoplifter,' she said, 'but it's one of those details that make perfect sense.'

'Why's that?'

While she tried to penetrate the remaining mystery of Sophie's personality, I looked out at all the darkness to our left as we walked down the road. It had rained earlier and the air smelled green. The gates to the park were all locked by now. I wondered how we would get in.

'Because,' said Emily, 'she thinks she's invincible and fascinating and at the same time worries that she's not. Worries she might only be well educated, connected and a little boring. For example, she plays the violin very well. I know this because she told me she does. She said, "I play the violin very well."'

We didn't say anything for a few seconds.

'Did you ever go shoplifting?' I asked her.

'Make-up. Sweets. Nothing serious. You?'

'Similar. Only ever on a whim. Just to test my courage.'

'Sophie wasn't stealing on a whim. She had lined a bag with tinfoil. Come on,' she said. 'This is a nice pub coming up. One for the road.'

*

'Do you think he's back?' I asked.

It was an hour later and we were standing outside her flat.

'I doubt it.'

The street was so quiet. If I woke to this sort of peace in my place, it could only be because everyone in the city had been massacred. A church spire rose behind the fenced-off square at the end of the road. The English pastoral in the heart of the city. Serious money.

'Goodnight, Paul,' she said, and leaned in to kiss me on

the cheek. 'I'll see you in a couple of weeks at the launch, if you can make it.'

'Goodnight, Emily.'

She shut the door and I looked up to the top of the building, to where I thought her living room was. I watched the darkened glass and imagined her climbing the stairs and that I was behind her again, following her to the top. After a few moments, I gave up looking for a light to come on. She would be in the kitchen, or in her study, on the other side of the building, or she would be standing upstairs in the darkness, watching me as I turned around and walked away.

EIGHT

Ever since Boris Johnson came out in favour of leaving the EU there has been a febrile atmosphere in the shop. The customers are all, naturally, in favour of remaining – it is the standard position among everyone we know; we are Europeans and friends with Europeans, who do not threaten our jobs. We use our English language with the written precision that comes with having lived here for so long, we trade on our articulacy; we employ Eastern Europeans to do the labour we don't know how to or don't want to do ourselves. We like the Eastern Europeans especially and it is not simply because we are good people, though we *are* good, but because such people are useful to us, and being friendly with them gives us a sense of our magnanimous power. Our time is money, better money than scrubbing surfaces or knocking down non-supporting walls with a sledgehammer; and we do not like to overpay for things; we have money precisely because we know we aren't made of money. By *we* I refer to our customers, our milieu, not to me and my friends, who paint our own walls, theoretically, hoover our own floors, no longer theoretically due to the feminine influence of Mary. Even so, we do not feel the distance we probably should from our wealthier associates. We have grown used to their presence. We secretly hope that we are down-at-heel members of the same group; we suspect our interests are aligned; we may become like them one day. We. Me. Who am I kidding?

Though tense, the atmosphere in the shop has even become a bit happier than usual. People are animated. They sense the approach of something they won't like; it's exciting.

Leo, emboldened by his notices in the *Bookseller*, by his newly full bank account, by my betrayal at the lecture, has decided I'm a little too flippant in my lack of focus on the world historic and has begun to lecture me on the subject to amend my flaws. I'm a sponge for this sort of oration; men and women are always explaining things to me.

He's saying something about Israel. I know I'll agree with him, but not enough for his liking. He is so certain about everything. You're all so certain.

That morning the rain had come down suddenly when I was cycling through Farringdon. I don't have a mudguard on my back wheel, and it spun a steady jet of water just over my belt and down into the seat of my jeans. I spent every spare break leaning against a radiator in the staff room, trying to dry myself out, but I was still clammy, and I felt myself turning into a desperate character, becoming angrier, Gordon Comstock, the impoverished bookseller from Orwell's *Keep the Aspidistra Flying*. I remember arguing about this novel once with a woman at a party who hated it. Why didn't he lighten up? Money, presumably, was a matter of maintaining a positive attitude. There may be some truth to this, a minuscule amount of truth. I had maintained a positive attitude for the last ten years and it had kept me afloat. But no longer. I could feel myself shifting to a new way of seeing things.

*

A few mornings earlier there had come a knock on the back door of the flat – a rare occurrence. It was eight o'clock and I was still in bed, and I could hear the shower going in the bathroom. I pulled on some jeans and a T-shirt, and there at the door was our landlord.

'Hello, Paul,' he said. 'It's been a while.'

It's OK, I thought. We could handle a small increase in rent.

In the end I offered to pay triple, but it still wasn't enough. They could make more selling the whole property than keeping the shop open. It had all been decided. We had three months' notice.

I saw him to the door and let him out. I walked into the kitchen and put the kettle on. Always I had been waiting for this to happen, but I had grown used to the fear and called it something else. Now I would have to change my life.

*

But change to what? I have always worried that I am destined to become my father. I am like him a white male from the north of England, small town, moribund, working class-cum-middle class, with books on the shelves, schooled in low aspiration in lessons and high aspiration at home, a reader, an autodidact, a would-be escapee.

There is a list somewhere of secondary-school English teachers with my name waiting to be added. If my father's hadn't been there already, if I hadn't seen two graves filled, that's exactly where I would be, and my life might have been all the better for it. That would be the way the moral fable of my life (TV version) closes, with me accepting the pleasure of sacrifice and embracing my duty as a tutor of the young, a facilitator of their escape attempts, a decision taken under the calming influence of a sensible woman, pretty in a red jacket in autumn, the season that would dominate my life from then on, the back-to-school, the evanescent glory of summer, the sharp, cold air of the mornings. She was always there for her friends and knew how to talk to small children and stop them crying. We would marry and move into a house we would certainly not be able to afford in London; the story would take place in Oldham or some other benighted town of the north, somewhere with some regional colour, redbrick terraces and new-built mosques and the skeletons of manufacturing. That was one thing about teaching – you could do it in the north. And nursing. I am from a family of teachers and nurses and I am ashamed and proud that I am not like them. But the woman will make me good. I will teach a class of hopeless children from families with no purpose in a landscape devoid of industry, and the children will hate me while I try to love them and to love myself in a town of pound shops and book-makers, the Wetherspoons the only pub with custom, serving fish and chips and a pint for a fiver on a Friday, as busy in the afternoon as it ever is in the evening, and I will try for as long as I can and then I will cheat on the good woman, I will cheat on her every chance I get, regardless of my children, who will be of the town and not of it, who will move away and leave me there and feel superior to me.

*

I heard the shower stop and called through to Mary to ask her if she wanted a cup of tea. I made two mugs. She came into the kitchen wearing a towel, her hair dripping down her shoulders. I handed her her tea. She saw me look at her and held my gaze briefly. Her eyes the colour of a swimming pool. She could save me, I thought. I wanted to step forwards and hold her.

'We've got to move out,' I said.

'I heard you talking to him. I was worried it might be something like that. How long?'

'Three months minimum. Maybe a bit longer. He wants to give us as long as possible. He was quite nice about it. He even said there might be another property above another shop we could have – but far out. Zone 6 or something.'

'I don't want to move there.'

'I don't want to move there either, wherever *there* is.'

'Oh, well. It was never going to last forever.'

'No.'

'What are you going to do?'

'I suppose I will have to transform myself. Get a sensible job. Marry a sensible woman from the Home Counties. Produce babies. Get a pension. Buy a motorbike in ten years to let off some steam. Take prescription pills for my anxiety.'

'Where are you going to find this sensible woman from the Home Counties?'

'There's this thing called *Guardian* Soulmates?'

That stopped her up short. 'You sound almost serious. But will they like *you*?'

'It's not impossible.'

'Would a sensible woman want to go out with a man who thinks the word *sensible* carries such a terrible burden?'

'Oh, I know what you mean, but I like sensible people, I like sanity. I meant a boring woman from the middle classes.'

'Now you're being boring.'

'I know.' I sat down on the sofa. 'I know.'

'Your problems will not be solved by a woman.'

'My problematic lack of a woman would be.'

'Your housing problem. Your aimlessness.'

'What's so good about having an aim? What's great about trajectory? That's how people impale people with things. I just want to live quietly.'

'Stop sleeping with everyone then.'

'Sleeping with who? It's they who've stopped sleeping with me.'

'Stop trying to sleep with everyone.'

'Have I ever tried it on with you?'

'No. But I have been very careful to project a consistent *don't try it on with me* aura.'

'I've noticed it.'

'Good.'

'So what are you going to do next?' I asked. 'Where are you going to go?'

'I'll get another houseshare. It'll be fine. Nathan's housemate is always talking about moving to Berlin – maybe he'll actually get his arse in gear.'

'Yeah?'

'And if Jonathan gets a new place he said I could stay there for a bit.'

'Jonathan?'

She looked away. 'What?'

'Jonathan?'

'What?' She stood up.

'Jonathan?'

'None of your business, Paul. You know his wife has left him for an Old Etonian banker?'

'He told you that?'

'Last night. They've known each other since they were children or something.'

'Right. But why hasn't he told me?'

'I guess he's . . . embarrassed? Ashamed?'

'I'll become a teacher if you marry me,' I said.

'Don't you need a clean criminal record to be a teacher?' she asked. She laid a hand on my shoulder. 'I'm going to get dressed.'

NINE

My glasses steamed up as I entered the shop where Emily's launch party was being held. I unzipped my parka to wipe them with my T-shirt. When I put them back on, Susannah was standing in front of me.

'Paul! How nice to see you again. You didn't write to me like you said you would.'

'I was just thinking how I should. I'm quite desperate for a career now.'

The room was busy already. A group of men in their twenties with side partings and retro glasses stood by the wine table, trying to look like they were attending a cocktail party sixty years ago on the Upper West Side. I could see Emily behind them, talking to the literary editor of a newspaper. She had her hair up and was wearing a white dress that showed off her shoulders. He said something and she laughed. Her new editor, James Cockburn, whom I knew well from his visits to our shop, was standing beside them, beaming, dressed in tight black jeans and a leather biker jacket, pointy boots. He must be knocking on for fifty, but he's tall, not detectably fat while wearing clothes, and his long hair comes down in curls over his shoulders.

He was waving at me and so it was hard to focus on what Susannah was saying to me.

'. . . my treat, what do you say?'

'Yes, please.'

'Great.'

'Thank you!'

'Are you going to write it down?'

'Yes, I am,' I said. I took my phone out. 'Now, remind me . . .'

She gave me the details again and I wrote them down.

*

Amy was due to arrive too. I was keeping my eye on her, scared she would vanish again if I didn't keep in regular contact. While she was back up north she had changed our estate agent and reduced the price of the house slightly, and now she was back in Peckham. She had devoured the proof of Emily's book I gave her. 'This is really miserable!' she said, smiling and turning over the pages.

*

A mother is dying in hospital in a Scottish town and receiving visits from her two daughters, Ella and Ailsa. It is the first time the daughters have seen each other in several years. Ella tells the story. The conversations she has with her mother and sister bring back memories of her childhood. At first there is a hole in the novel where the father might be. So the reader might surmise that there is no father, that the daughters have never known him. Or a reader might surmise that he is a subject so momentous that he has to be avoided. The reader knows that there is a reason why these women have found it so hard to speak to each other, why Ella has not spoken to either of them for so long. But the reader does not know the precise details. The contrivance is either a realistic imitation of repression or an elegant device to keep the pages turning, with neither interpretation cancelled by the other. The father, we discover, is dead, though he has only been dead for four years, and this is no time at all. Ella still fears sudden phone calls from him in the middle of the night. Death alone seems too slight a thing to have freed them from his dominion, from his violence. Ailsa thinks Ella exaggerates. She doesn't want to talk about her father. Their mother is dying. What good will it do at this stage to accuse their mother of cowardice, of failing to protect her daughters? Doesn't Ella think she tried? Why should she have been so much stronger than her daughters? Ella needs to get on with her life. Like you? asks Ella. With the two husbands you've had? The ones just like Dad?

I got rid of them, didn't I? Ailsa yells at Ella. I got rid of them! I stayed here with Mum. Men in this town: that's what they're like.

That's why I left, says Ella. And then she leaves again.

*

While keeping my eye out for Amy I made my way over to Emily, who was surrounded by men and women wearing dark or eccentric clothes. When she saw me she excused herself from a conversation with a man with a floppy fringe, a hooped earring and a cravat – and came over to give me a brief hug.

'He's a bit intense,' she whispered in my ear. 'A pen pal from a while ago.'

I looked at her in her white dress. 'You look great. Like you're getting married.'

She reeled backwards with convincing horror.

The man with the cravat was hovering closer. A woman in a trouser suit shouldered him into the cookery section. 'Emily,' she said. 'Do you know Peter from *The Times*?'

'I'll leave you to it,' I said, and stepped away and into Andrew.

'Pushed out of the inner circle too, I see,' he said.

'I know. I feel like such a pleb.'

'Join the club.'

'I keep trying to. No one will nominate me.'

'I'd offer to help you, Paul, but I've never been a member of a club in my life.'

'The first rule of the club is there is no club.'

He laughed. 'I'm in the Illuminati. I thought you meant the Groucho.'

Behind him I saw Amy arrive in the front of the shop and look around. I waved at her and she came over and hugged me.

'Andrew, this is my sister, Amy. Amy, this is my new friend, Andrew Lancaster, a serious intellectual and historian.'

'Delighted to meet you, Amy. And historian. What an intro.'

'It's nice to meet you too,' she said.

'Amy's an intellectual too, of course,' I said. 'She's a big fan of Emily's novel. Amy, this is Emily's boyfriend.'

'Oh! That's nice. I'm actually a failed artist who sells T-shirts at Brick Lane market.'

'That's exactly what a real intellectual would say,' said Andrew. 'You should never trust a self-declared intellectual.'

'Seriously, though, Amy's very clever. She's a property guru too.'

'Paul likes to patronise me, when he's not accusing me of being a greedy landlord.'

'I'm sorry to hear that, Amy,' said Andrew. 'It sounds like you have the same unfortunate dynamic with him that I have with my daughter. She's supposed to be here but I can't see her yet. Of course, she's thirty-three years younger than me, and Paul's . . .?'

'Over two years *older* than me.'

'Let me get you a glass of wine,' Andrew said.

'Oh, go on, I'll have an extremely small glass of white, if you're offering.'

'I am,' he said and went to get it.

'What's the deal there?' she asked me.

'What do you mean?'

'Are you two really friends?'

'No. I'm friends with his girlfriend. I don't mind him, though.'

'He seems very charming.'

'He seems fond of younger women. How are you, anyway? Have you decided whether to tell the Bristolian?'

We looked down at her stomach.

'Not yet. I think I will. I was just . . . I wondered if . . . I'm just, oh, let's talk about it later. This is too hectic.'

A bearish man brushed past us and we watched him lumber towards Emily. She raised her hands in surprise and rushed over to him. I watched her cling on to him in a way she had never clung to me.

'Who's he?' said Andrew, returning with glasses of wine.

'I don't know, but he's very tall and rugged,' said Amy.

'You'll make me jealous,' he said, handing her a glass.

We continued to watch this man crush Emily against his chest. 'Do you want to come outside for a bit?' I asked Amy. 'I need a cigarette.'

'No, thanks,' she said. 'I'll stay here and mingle.'

'Good,' said Andrew. 'If you stand next to me Emily might feel as jealous as I do.'

'Do you expect me to be charmed by that?' asked Amy. 'That you want me to reduce me to a sort of status symbol for you to stand next to in order to manipulate your partner?'

'Was that not charming?' he asked. 'Let me try harder then.'

I left them to it, turning back to see Amy tilting her head and grinning while he spoke to her, as though she was looking forward to challenging him.

*

I borrowed a lighter outside from one of two women who were talking politics.

'Do they have any idea how much worse it's going to be for them if it's a Leave vote?'

'I know.'

'All these white men – let's be honest, all these *racists* – throwing their toys out of the pram because they can't face up to the fact that they've had their time.'

I thought of Carl. I thought of his brothers and sisters, his mum and dad.

'Thank you,' I said, and gave the lighter back to her. I smiled at her and her friend. There was an awkward silence. 'Would you mind if I asked something?' I said.

'Yes?'

'I wondered whether you thought that white women aren't also going to vote for Brexit? Black men and women? Asian men and women too?'

Her friend was Asian herself. Indian, mixed-race, maybe. She was tall with dramatic glossy hair, and she had an amused expression hovering on the edge of annoyance. 'Are you going to vote for Brexit?' she asked.

'No. Course not. Oh, look, ignore me – I'm sorry for interrupting.'

'He thinks we're unfairly maligning white men,' said the woman whose lighter I'd borrowed. 'Is that what you're saying?'

'I suppose I think you may as well malign them for their unique faults rather than their shared ones. There are probably enough specific faults to keep you busy.'

'*Sorry*. Men suffer terribly at the hands of women assigning imaginary faults to them.'

'I'm regretting this. I'll shut up and leave you alone.'

'No, no, we can address your point. Who are you, anyway?'

'I'm no one. My name's Paul.'

'Sophie.'

'Rochi.'

'Let me leave you two alone.'

'No, come on,' said Sophie. 'Do I think women will vote to leave in the same numbers as men? I have no evidence but I don't think they will. I think we're more likely to reflect on things than act with some primitive self-assured sense of right-eousness. We can't be as nostalgic about the good old days.'

I thought about that. 'So you think it's male arrogance and aggressiveness that will make us more likely to vote to leave?'

'Male entitlement. Male complacency.'

'What about the men who don't have much of a sense of entitlement?'

'Oh, come on. Sexism goes on from the top to the bottom.'

And then I made the mistake of continuing. Of trying to accept the truth of what she said only in part, of arguing the case of men who were killing themselves in increasing numbers because of what little there was left for them. Of suggesting that not everyone who votes for Farage is a malevo-lent racist.

'Really?' said Rochi.

'I know it might seem – '

'What's interesting to me is the way you want to sideline any discussion of gender privilege,' said Sophie. 'We see men do this all the time.'

'Just like I see expensively educated women and people of . . . God, listen to me.'

'Wow,' said Rochi.

'Who do you think has it worse among the poor white people you think I'm unaware of? The men or the women?' said Sophie. 'Do you know that's where the gender pay gap is most pronounced?'

'I believe it.' I took a deep breath. It didn't work. 'Though sometimes it's danger money for the men. My friend's dad lost the fingers on one of his hands working on a rig.'

'You've got an exception for everything. Why aren't women allowed to do those dangerous jobs? What about male on female violence being statistically high in poor communities?'

'And then his son, my friend, died of an overdose.'

'Oh, look, I'm sorry, that sounds awful. Where is this place, anyway?'

'It doesn't matter. I'm not saying that – '

'It really *does* matter. If you're going to refer to individual cases you should state the circum – '

*

I threw my cigarette out into the street and rushed back into the shop. Amy was explaining something to Andrew, who had his hands raised in surrender. I asked a bookseller if I could use their toilet and she showed me to the back of the shop. In the little plywood cubicle, I took off my glasses and put them on the cistern, and I let myself break down. It happened from time to time. A wave crashing down, delicious and terrible. Nothing profound, I thought, just indulgent. I'd invoked Carl to make me more authentic, more miserable, than them. This wasn't suffering as much as congestion and once I'd blown my nose I felt steadier. I washed my face, dried it with my

T-shirt when I couldn't find a towel, put my glasses back on and went downstairs.

Amy was on her own now. 'Are you OK?' she asked. 'Your eyes are red and your T-shirt's wet.'

'Hay fever.'

'Do you want an antihistamine?'

'I've just taken one. Do you have anything stronger?'

'Are you serious?' She patted her stomach.

'Good point.'

'How's the job search going?'

She told me then that she'd given up applying for new jobs and was hoping she could get her old one back. She'd apologised to her old boss for the way she'd left, citing 'delayed grief for which she was seeking advice', and a panel had been convened for tomorrow to discuss what had happened. She was keeping the pregnancy to herself, as was her right under employment law.

'How pregnant do I look to you?' she asked.

'If I didn't know you, I'd just think that you were having a baggy fashion moment. I'd be more concerned with working out how you are going to prevent yourself from losing your temper.'

'I've been practising mindfulness techniques; perhaps they'll help.'

'Just think of the money.'

'That will probably help more.'

*

Andrew came over with Emily and Cockburn and we all introduced each other. Cockburn began to tell a story about a restaurant he'd been to round the corner where you ate in confession booths, and Andrew and I inched backwards from him while Amy and Emily looked at him in amazement. 'Do you need another drink?' I asked Andrew.

'I'll come with you,' he said, smiling. 'Are you all right?' he asked. 'Your face looked thunderous before.'

I told him about the argument I'd had outside.

'Do you want my advice, Paul? Don't be one of those people, even if you're right. It's like writing below the line of a newspaper article.'

'I know. But what else can I do? We're not relics. Not even you, at your age.'

'Very funny, Paul.'

He didn't look amused and nor will I if I ever reach his age and have to deal with the ebullient and barely hidden disdain of some little shit who thinks himself superior to me because he hasn't lived long enough to make as many compromises and take responsibility for someone other than himself.

'I'm sorry,' I said. 'I really am. When I admire someone I get nervous and insult them.'

'Thank you for admiring me enough to be rude to me. Is that why you're so miserable today? You think you're being made obsolete?'

But before I could explain, we were interrupted by the arrival of the two women I'd argued with outside.

'Sophie! Rochi!' said Andrew, kissing them each in turn. 'This is my new friend, Paul. Paul, this is my daughter Sophie and her friend Rochi.'

'We've already met,' said Sophie, 'and had our first disagreement.'

'Oh, it's you! Of course! Paul was just regretting your argument. We've agreed between us that the great white male is a specimen only fit for zoos.'

'That's right,' I said.

'It's funny,' Andrew continued, 'because he writes for a magazine called *White Jesus*. Reviews books *and* haircuts.'

'Oh, really,' said Rochi.

'He's been asked to review *legal highs* for them,' said Andrew.

'I turned down the legal highs column,' I said. 'Stop looking so amused. I'm just a bookseller.'

'Selling books is an honourable job,' said Sophie.

'Maybe. It's more honourable than stealing them.'

Sophie stared at me, and suddenly laughed. It transformed her face. We looked at each other with complicity for a second.

'I know your hair reviews, actually,' said Rochi. 'Everyone loves them.'

'What is she talking about?' said Sophie, taking her phone out of her bag and looking at it.

'She's a Marxist commentator,' said Rochi.

'Stop finding that funny. I am, actually,' said Sophie.

'Whereas I am a scholar of Marx and his influence on world history,' said Andrew. 'Shall we rescue Emily from her editor?'

'You do that, Dad. We'll stay and get to know Paul.'

While Rochi explained the *London Review of Haircuts* to Sophie, I watched Andrew walk towards Emily and Amy, then suddenly veer off towards the door, where his PhD student Chloe was coming through, looking around her with an expression of amused despair on her face, like an Austen heroine making the most of the bad company that she would be stuck with for the entire rest of her life. Andrew held his arms up as if he were delighted to see her, and they walked out of the shop together. Sophie had looked up from her phone to notice this performance too and our eyes met again.

'Are you on duty?' asked Rochi.

'What?' I said.

'Are you out looking for people with terrific hair?' She shook her hair like a shampoo model.

'That was impressive,' I said.

'Put her in the magazine,' said Sophie.

'Put us both in the magazine,' said Rochi.

'I don't mind being trivialised in this instance,' said Sophie.

'Fine,' I said and pulled out my phone. 'Can I do you together?'

'What an impertinent question,' said Rochi, mussing her hair.

'We're not a pornographic fantasy,' said Sophie.

'I'm resisting the urge to say "I'll be the judge of that"' I said.

'You are precisely not resisting that urge,' said Rochi.

'You're exactly the problem,' said Sophie. 'It's lucky for you that the patriarchy has conditioned us to be forgiving of reprehensible creatures like you.' She was looking back into her phone and adjusting her fringe.

I caught them in my screen and loved them both. Sophie's dress was loose enough just to skim her hips, to turn her silhouette into a pair of straight lines, an easily drawn icon of a woman, the two-dimensional version many of us preferred to see instead of the complicated actuality. There was no hiding the actuality of Rochi. Everything about her was big, her mouth, her eyes, her hips.

I took the picture. I took another. Posters for platonic female friendship, for the irrelevance of men. Bookshelves were clearly visible around them. Stev'n would probably want to photoshop some caged dwarfs in leather behind them if he used the photo.

I felt a hand on my back. 'Hello,' said Amy. 'You keep leaving me with the lunatics.'

I put my phone away. 'This is my sister,' I said, and made introductions.

'I didn't expect you to have a sister,' said Sophie.

'He does,' said Amy.

'I thought you might be one of those men who hadn't been round women much,' Sophie continued, without looking at Amy.

'We've been disagreeing about whether if Brexit happens it will be the fault of men,' I explained to Amy. 'I expect Sophie and Rochi went to girls' schools and base their opinion of men on men who went to boys' schools.'

'Is there much difference?' said Rochi.

'The ones who go to boys' schools are even worse,' said Amy. 'From my experience.'

'At least they aren't talking over girls like they do in the mixed schools and getting in the way of their education,' said Sophie.

'Is that what they do?' said Amy.

'It's statistically proven,' said Sophie.

'I must have had an inferior education to you, then. Don't mixed schools tend to have poorer pupils than the all-girl schools?' asked Amy.

'You're like your brother,' said Sophie. 'Exceptions don't disprove general rules.'

'And what should we do with those boys I went to school with and who ruined my education?' asked Amy. 'Should we just execute them at birth? Or would sending them to the Gulag suffice?'

Sophie considered this silently. 'I'm sure we can find something more compassionate to do with them,' she said, glancing at me.

'We're just jealous you got to hang around with boys at all,' said Rochi, stepping between Sophie and Amy, and she winked at me as a glass began to ting. I looked up to see Emily casting around the room for Andrew, and then Cockburn started speaking.

*

After Cockburn had finished, Emily made the briefest of thank yous to her agent and editor. 'I was going to thank my partner but I can't see him – oh, here he is. Thank you to Andrew too for all his support during the writing of this book. Thank you all for coming.'

Andrew had returned alone, and made his way over to kiss her. The crowd began to buzz again.

I looked for Amy. She was browsing in the Latin America section.

'You're not plotting another escape, are you?'

'Yes, I thought if my trial at work goes against me, I might hide out in Argentina for a while, like a Nazi.'

'I'm glad to see you're keeping things in perspective here, Amy.'

'Yes, well. I've realised I do want that job back. How depressing. I spent years earning my public-sector maternity benefits and get pregnant the second I storm out.'

'Your body must have bloomed at the freedom.'

'Probably.'

'Just stay calm. Say sorry.'

'I know. But it's they who should be apologising to – '

'BAAAAH. Wrong answer.'

'But seriously, they're such mor – '

'BAAAAH. To be kidnapped by Mossad and tried as a war criminal.'

'Will you let me talk, Paul?'

'Sorry.'

'It shouldn't all be one-way traffic.'

'I'm just trying to suggest you bury your anger for the purpose of your meeting.'

'I spend my whole life burying my anger. What's that fucking look on your face about?'

'Sympathy. Would you like to get out of here and get something to eat? It can't be much fun here without booze.'

She looked around the room. 'It's OK. I liked Emily. But I'll just head off in a bit. Need to prepare for tomorrow's showdown. You're probably right. I need a script.'

'I could help you work on one.'

'Don't you want to stay with your new mates?'

'They're not exactly my mates. Sophie seems to actively dislike me.'

'Not as much as she dislikes me.'

'Or you hate her.'

'What a stuck-up bitch. Did you hear the way she spoke to me?'

'I think that's just the way she talks to everyone. The other one, Rochi, she's OK, isn't she?'

'She's a lot less rude. And she must be absolutely minted. Have you seen her bag? That's about two thousand quid's worth of handbag.'

'Maybe it's a knock-off.'

'Women like her don't carry knock-offs.'

'I didn't notice.'

'I think you do notice. You're always going for women like those.'

'I wish. I don't come into contact with them.'

'You love those North London girls.'

'Monica wasn't posh. Or from North London.'

'Wasn't she?'

'No! She was from Portsmouth. That's not the same as posh.'

'You're not *still* thinking about her?'

'Sometimes.'

'Oh, Paul. She's gone.'

'Let me buy you dinner.'

'Nah. You belong here. This is your scene. I'm getting my book signed then heading off for a pizza on the sofa with Netflix.'

'When will I see you again?'

'Don't worry. I'm not going to disappear.'

'Please don't.'

'Chance would be a fine thing. Were you crying earlier? I know you said you had hay fever but you looked like – '

'It was just hay fever. If I looked miserable it was just because they got me thinking about Dad and Carl.'

'Yeah?'

'Oh, I'm being oversensitive. I thought they were saying Dad and Carl were . . . insignificant, but all they were probably saying is that women have it harder. Which is true, isn't it? Look at Mum.'

'We need to talk about Mum. About what happened, about what we do next.'

'Oh, I know. Let's. But let's not now.'

'That's what you always say. *Not now. Not here.* Call me, OK? We should come up with a plan to do something to remember her in the autumn.'

'Yeah, yeah,' I said. I was finding it harder to forget her, not the other way around.

'*Yeah, yeah?* For fuck's sake, Paul.'

She shook her head and walked away. I nearly watched her go but I was scared of not seeing her again for months and so I ran after her to apologise.

*

Emily was still talking to the big bear of a man when I got back to the shop. I approached her with my book open at the title page.

'This is an old friend, Richard,' she said, 'from when I lived in Leeds; Richard, this is a new friend, Paul.'

'Nice to meet you,' he said.

'You too. Do you live round here?'

'No, no. In Leeds. Just down to surprise Emily and get my own signed copy.'

Emily signed her name in my book with five kisses, a girlish and endearingly out-of-character gesture, then she turned them into scissors by adding handles to them.

'Very cute,' I said. 'Have you had a good time?'

'Reasonably. He was a nice surprise,' she said, putting her hand on Richard's shoulder.

'So how do you two know each other?' I asked.

'Emily used to come and see my band,' he said. 'Before I got a real job and became a teacher.'

'They were a good band,' said Emily.

'We were OK,' he said.

'Are we going out afterwards?' he asked, turning to Emily.

'Yeah, yeah. Andrew has a plan. Food somewhere.'

They turned back to look at me and my invitation never arrived so I volunteered my own information. 'I thought I might go for a drink with some women I just met. Rochi and her friend Sophie. Andrew's Sophie, I think.'

'Oh,' said Emily. She looked up to where Sophie and Rochi were talking. Sophie saw her and waved. 'Yes, that's her,' said Emily. 'Well, good luck with *that*.' She put her hand on Richard's shoulder and leaned slightly into him.

'We're only having a drink.'

She nodded, then realised where her hand was and removed it from Richard. 'I'd better talk to Andrew and see what's happening. If I don't see you, Paul, thanks for coming.'

She walked away, and I smiled at Richard. 'So, how are you doing?' I asked.

'All right,' he said. 'You're new friends, you and Emily?'

'Yeah. And you two go way back,' I said.

'Way back.'

'So, you're a teacher? My parents were teachers.'

'Were?'

'Were.'

'Well, very sensible of them to get out, I'm sure. Actually, do you mind? I'm just going to have a quick cigarette,' he said, and he left me alone, turning back to glance at me when he was near the door.

*

I lingered for another few minutes, talking to Rochi, Sophie and James Cockburn. By now I'd drunk a few glasses of white wine. I poured myself one last glass, meeting Andrew at the table as he was putting an empty down.

'Did I see you leaving the shop with that young woman who came to dinner with us that time?' I asked.

'I hope your tone isn't insinuating anything,' he snapped.

'I didn't mean to insinuate anything at all.'

'I'm sorry,' he said. 'Yes, you did. Chloe. She's a demanding PhD student.'

'Right. She's probably infatuated with you.'

'No, no. Not like that. Let's please not talk about her. She's interfered with the evening already.'

'Fine by me. So what's next? I think I'm going to go for a drink with Sophie and Rochi, if you fancy joining.'

'Oh, we have a table booked. Do come along if you want. Emily's already added one other new guest so I can't see why we can't add another. Did you want to come?'

'I did say I'd go for –'

'Yes, good. You go and have fun. And look after Sophie for me, won't you? Keep her out of trouble?'

*

Meanwhile Cockburn was stepping up his friendship with Sophie and Rochi.

'What a marvellous party this is,' he said, turning to me as I walked over. 'Aren't Sophie and Rochi wonderful?'

'Yes,' I said.

'Paul hates us really,' said Sophie. 'He thinks we're champagne feminists.'

'Well, Jesus, what's wrong with that?' said Cockburn. 'I'm a huge fan of champagne and feminism. Paul, you know Sophie's writing a book about how to change the world?'

'Can I be of any assistance?' I asked.

'To write my book? Very generous of you, but I'm not sure we'd see eye to eye on everything.'

'I meant, do you need any help to change the world?'

'You can stop trying to deny the existence of the patriarchy.'

'Or you can buy us drinks,' said Rochi.

'How about I stop denying the existence of the patriarchy and he buys us drinks?'

'Works for me,' said Cockburn. 'Let me just see if I can get out of this dinner plan,' and he walked off towards Emily, who was talking with Richard and Andrew.

'I am sorry about before,' I said. 'I'm really not trying to deny the effects of sexism and racism.'

'It's OK. We believe you,' said Sophie. 'It's grim up north! Did I annoy your sister earlier with my comments about mixed education? Rochi's right: at least you had people of the opposite sex at your place.'

'What I was most conscious of at the time was of the lack of contact with members of the opposite sex.'

'You do surprise me,' said Rochi.

'Not as conscious as we were,' said Sophie. 'We were boy crazy.'

'Boy mad,' said Rochi.

'We chased them round shopping centres at the weekends.'

'What did you do when you caught them?' I asked.

'Educated them,' said Sophie.

*

Sophie wanted to take us to a place on Portobello Road that was 'so grotesque it was barely believable'.

Cockburn was going to have a starter with Emily and the rest and join us as soon as possible afterwards.

We turned past the florists and delis into Ladbroke Grove, walking past houses painted in delicate pastels. In their tall window panes we could see through long rooms to more tall window panes and flowering gardens behind them. Then we turned onto a road of terraces like the one Emily and Andrew lived in, a long cream stretch of pillars and railings and sash windows looking over a locked park.

'In the 1980s I think Philip Roth used to have his writing studio somewhere around here,' I said.

'I knew you'd like Philip Roth,' said Sophie.

'Did you grow up in one of these places?' I asked her, trying to avoid starting our argument up again.

'No,' she said. 'I don't know what impression you've reached of me, but I didn't grow up rich.'

'I was wondering, you see, because your dad lives close by.'

'Yes, he does.' She looked more interested and put her hand on my arm. 'Have you been round?'

'Yes, I interviewed Emily there.'

'I see.'

'You have to be stupidly rich to have one of these,' said Rochi.

'You do now. I grew up in Clapham,' said Sophie. 'I'm staying there at the moment with my mum. It's Rochi who's from round here.'

'I'm not really from round here. I'm from Kilburn.'

'Your parents' house is *not* in Kilburn.'

'It's not like this. Where are you from, then?' asked Rochi. 'More specifically than *oop north*?'

I did my routine, the bleak beauty of the peninsula, almost an island, the psychological effect of the isolating landscape. They listened politely.

'I don't want you to think I was saying there's no such thing as regional inequality,' said Sophie.

'If you're not careful we'll start agreeing on things,' I said. 'Then we'll have nothing to say to each other.'

'Conversation doesn't have to be a battle, you know?' said Rochi.

'Next thing you'll be telling me that history isn't the record of the struggle between classes,' I said.

'Oh, God. You two are almost perfect for each other,' she said in disgust.

*

'I'm not saying it's a good place,' said Sophie as we arrived at the tapas bar. 'There's part of me that thinks it might have been a dream. You're here really to corroborate my story.'

Sophie pushed forwards into the bar and we followed. Inside she hugged a young woman, and introduced her as Frankie, her friend from school, the restaurant manager. They talked about the man who had set the restaurant up, one of a small chain in London, and Frankie's voice went up to emphasise the importance of the name I didn't recognise.

'Is the bishop in?' asked Sophie.

'The bishop's always in,' said Frankie, with a knowing nod and smile. We were told to go downstairs and say hi.

Rochi and I followed Sophie down the stairs to what looked

like the toilets. But just beside those doors Sophie stopped in front of a full-length mirror and reached her nails behind its right side, pulling it open like a door to reveal a dim corridor, lined on each side by thick velvet curtains in sacristal purple. We stepped through and there we were greeted by a good-looking young man in a cassock. I could see his Converse trainers peeking under the hem. He had tousled indie-music hair and wore an iron cross over a black cassock.

'Where's your hat?' asked Sophie.

'It's called a mitre,' I said.

The bishop disappeared into an alcove and came back with the correct headgear.

'Do you want a booth?' he asked, before he led us along to the end of the corridor and pulled one of the curtains back to reveal a small table with church pews either side of it. There was a buzzer in the middle of the table. 'Anything you need, just ring and I'll bring it for you.'

'This is sacrilegious,' I said.

'Isn't it?' said Sophie. 'Look at this.' She pulled the house rules off their hook on the wall.

WE GUARANTEE EVERYONE'S PRIVACY IN THIS PLACE
OF REPENTANCE.
STRICTLY NO APPROACHING GUESTS IN NEIGHBOURING
BOOTHS.
WE WILL NOT ENTER UNLESS YOU BUZZ.
TAKING DRUGS IS ILLEGAL AND A SIN.
WHAT GOES ON IN YOUR CONFESSIONAL IS BETWEEN
YOU AND YOUR GOD.

Sophie turned the rules over to reveal that the reverse side of the sign was a mirror, tracked with the faint scratches a razor blade had made on its surface.

I didn't do as much coke then as I used to when I was younger, and I've resolved never to touch it again. It's not that I ever enjoyed the effects of the drug on its own so much as the intimacy of consumption, the pockets of time alone with a friend to do something quiet and secret and then return, altered and better prepared for the busy room and brand-new people we had temporarily escaped. The appeal of cigarettes had increased enormously for me when you had to go outside for them.

None of us had any coke, but we were in a place designed for making lines and so we yearned for some.

'Ask Cockburn if he has any,' I suggested.

Sophie texted. The phone buzzed back immediately. 'He's getting some,' she told me.

In the meantime we sipped gin and tonics and waited.

*

It is no wonder that places that are unbearable without drugs are so popular: they provide such a good reason to do drugs, to ring a number and prove our ingenious ability to satisfy our needs. So we can remove the awkwardness of our boundaries; so it feels natural to reach over and put our hands in each other's hair and draw our mouths together.

Cockburn had arrived with what we wanted and we had been talking for what might have been hours now.

'You need to be careful,' Sophie was telling him. 'My generation are going to want to burn your houses down.'

'No they won't. They'll be too worried about not inheriting them.'

'There won't be anything left,' she said. 'You'll have mortgaged them all to pay Harley Street doctors who say they can make you immortal. You'll have spunked it all on Viagra and opioid sleeping tablets.'

'And security guards,' said Cockburn. 'With big guns.'

I was enjoying talking to Rochi on my side of the table. She was a TV development executive who spent her Saturdays scrubbing scales and removing guts at a fishmonger's in Hackney. 'Why?' I asked. 'It's a skill,' she said. 'I like having a real skill.'

We got in the habit of going out in pairs to smoke, she and I, Cockburn and Sophie.

'Do you think they're getting off with each other when we're out smoking?' Rochi asked.

'He's too old for her, isn't he?'

'She doesn't mind old guys. It annoys her dad. That's why I thought maybe you and her were going to hit it off.'

'He is significantly older than me, you know?'

'You all look the same to me.'

Next time we were in the booth alone I asked, 'Do you think they're out there wondering if we're getting off with each other?'

'Definitely,' she said, and we looked at each other for a moment before we leaned in.

TEN

And for nearly a month I was redeemed. I liked nothing more than hearing Rochi tease me. She had taken all the good things from her good school, she was so confident and curious, kind and unembarrassed. When I was next to her I believed that the rich were better than the poor. They hadn't been deformed by envy and bitterness. They had been free to think and express themselves, to study under the guidance of the world's best teachers. They were so good-looking and healthy. They had experienced the best of British cultural life. When they married each other it was more than wealth marrying wealth – it was beauty and intelligence marrying beauty and intelligence. You couldn't blame them for it.

On those light spring evenings I'd walk over to London Fields to the flat Rochi shared with a friend in Broadway Market. She was taking meetings with publishers and production companies about writing her own book and hosting her own TV series about preparing and cooking fish. She was going to be famous.

It was her skill at slicing into fish that left me completely helpless, that she could do something so practical and unsqueamish. She made me think of home, and she liked hearing about home, or tolerated it at least, that blankness at the edge of things, the white noise of the sea, the smell of life fizzing up and going off. I began to imagine taking her there, walking down the street with her and watching people look at her, watching people hate her.

'This is just a bit of fun, yeah?' she said one morning when I walked her to the Overground station.

'I know. Of course!' I said, but I was too enthusiastic.

'Oh, Paul,' she said. 'We need to talk.'

ELEVEN

My hairdresser and I were discussing his brother, Tony. I played football with Tony every week, Tony who had taken to posting videos about the problem with Islam and feminists and Jeremy Corbyn and the *Guardian*. He was all in favour of Brexit, and Donald Trump's election campaign, and this was regarded by some people as such a strange look for a black man that he was frequently accused online of being a white supremacist, hiding behind the profile photo of a black man. This did not make Tony less angry or more liberal, and now he had started wearing a Make America Great Again cap to our weekly five-a-side game, which, as we played in Whitechapel, most people thought was ironic, or just Tony's quirky style. There was no reason, of course, why a black man should not have the same right as the rest of us to post videos of Tommy Robinson talking about Islamic fascists who ran paedophile gangs, these Muslims who got away with it because of people like me who read the *Guardian* and hated the working people and refused to condemn their enemies. But we wished he wouldn't.

'I try not to get into it with him,' said Michael, snipping away. 'He's still the same guy when we talk about music and Arsenal, still a great uncle to the kids. What do I know anyway? I haven't read half as much as he has.'

Tony is a handsome and stylish man. He wears his hair in an Afro, wears long coats and colourful scarves, a natty funk-musician from the 1970s. When I was looking for a new football game after university, Michael had introduced me to Tony. He was one of my first London mates who I hadn't met through university or the bookshop. We'd go for pints after the game and talk about music, go to gigs at Cafe Oto or Village Underground. He worked as a train inspector back and forth into Essex from Liverpool Street every day. And he had become so angry. I watched the videos he posted on Facebook of Tommy Robinson charging into the offices of think tanks to confront people who had labelled him racist, flustered men who would refuse to back up their statements with evidence. I could see how someone could be convinced if this was all they saw of him: how effective a tactic it was to find and confront people who had condemned him on received opinion, who couldn't precisely point out the incidents in which he'd proved himself to be racist. (Any who *could* would have been cut from the edit.) People who liked him might have liked him more because of the middle-class people he embarrassed than because of the Muslims he hated. Trails of thumbs-up and lovehearts moved across the videos in animated graphics from left to right across the screen, like immigrants heading back to their own countries.

'Hey, look, Tony,' I said, a few days later, while we were walking back to the bike rack in our replica shirts, Arsenal and Fleetwood, swigging from our water bottles.

'Yeah?'

'I've been following those links you've been posting on Facebook.'

'Good.'

'But, you know, you don't really believe that all Muslims support terrorism and want to take over the country, do you?'

'Bruv. Don't patronise me. It's more complicated than that. That's not what we're saying. Course not all of them. Not most. But are they doing enough to condemn it? Nah, they're not doing that either. We're funding their schools for them to teach children what's wrong with our society. It's *our* society, man.'

'And Corbyn being a terrorist too? He's not a terrorist.'

'The IRA, man! He supports the IRA!'

'That was ages ago. Why do you care so much about it?'

'Bruv, bruv, I can't do this with you. You're a nice guy but you're blind to what's going on here. Which is you people living miles away from the problem and telling people like me who have to deal with it that there is no problem.'

'You people? That's me, is it?'

'Not all the way, man. Not *all* the way. But I know where you live. I don't see you down in Forest Gate, man, do I? I don't see you all the way down where I am.'

'Come off it. I live in Dalston. Right by the market.'

'You live in Dalston now. Not Dalston fifteen years ago, when people could afford to live there.'

'Well, what about feminism? Equal rights for women? Why's that a problem?'

'Oh, bruv. I love women. Equal rights is fine. But that's not what it is, is it? It's an agenda that has no interest in a man like me. You know, I'm not doing this with you. We play football together. I like it like that. Let's keep it that way.'

But shortly after that he stopped coming to football. I followed him for a while on Facebook. He kept getting banned for arguing with the people who accused him of being a white supremacist, and then he was gone for good. And now I don't know where or how he is.

*

Friday in the local. After months of working for free, Mary was offered a wage at the record company doing their online marketing and PR. We were celebrating: Nathan, me and Jonathan, who was still 'a week away' from moving out, as he had been for months now. Although he was always still in a crisp white shirt (he took a bag of them to the cleaners every week and kept them hanging up in his office), he was becoming shabbier in other ways. He seemed torn one week to the next between being clean-shaven and having designer stubble. I saw him going to work one day wearing a pair of new white trainers with one of his suits, a combination he had pointed out to me scathingly in the past: web designer getting married, he called it, or wake at the indie disco. Without Julia he had lost the strength of his certainties. And because of his downfall I'd lost the will to kick him out. We'd all be forced out soon enough.

Nathan must have been wondering why so many of the nights he now spent with Mary were in the company of her two older housemates. He got quieter as we got louder, and abruptly stood up and said he was going.

'Don't! Stay!' said Mary. 'Let's carry on back at mine.'

'No thanks,' he said, and walked out.

'I better go after him,' she said.

'Leave him alone,' said Jonathan, but she went anyway.

We could see them through the pub's open door. She had her hands on Nathan's shoulders but he was looking away from her. He put his hand on her chest to keep her from hugging him and spoke slowly to her, then turned and walked away. She followed in the same direction and that was all we could see from where we were sitting. I had thought that we had all been having a good time that night.

'I'm rooting for him,' I said. 'He's a nice boy.'

I looked at Jonathan. He was staring down into his pint. 'You don't see many of them around,' he said.

Though he was still sleeping in the living room I wasn't seeing all that much of him. He was distracting himself from his marital problems by going out most weeknights. There was always some gig or opening to go to – and Jonathan's misery had been good for business: he'd found a heap of new clients on his nights out. He was getting into fights too. On one occasion I noticed grazed knuckles on him and a swollen lip.

'I'm sort of a nice boy,' I said to Jonathan.

'You're thirty-five!' he said.

'I'm thirty-three!'

'You look thirty-five.'

'You look forty-six.'

'You don't look like a nice *boy* is all I'm saying,' said Jonathan. 'Most women don't want nice. They want men.'

'That's not true at all. And if it is, it's just Stockholm syndrome. Do you and Mary have something going on?'

'No, course not. I haven't given up on Julia.'

'Good.'

'Mary and I are going out next week, though.'

'What?'

'Not a date. I'm borrowing her. Not borrowing her, exactly – that sounds wrong. I'm taking her to party where she'll meet lots of cool people and have a good time, and where Julia will probably be.'

'And she knows this?'

'I didn't mention Julia. She might think that was a bit weird.'

'Have you considered that you might be better off without Julia?'

'What? No.' He pulled his phone out and unlocked it, looked at it and put it down again. He had been doing this every couple of minutes. He was waiting for something. I wasn't sure if it was Julia or drugs.

*

On the following Friday I went to Soho for lunch. The dining room in the club was busy and Susannah seemed to know everyone there.

Her role in the company, she told me, was unfortunately not as important as it once was – without demoting her they had hired someone above her. She had to make sure he didn't take over the relationships with her bestselling authors or she'd become replaceable.

'Replaceable,' she sighed. She was fifty-four and her husband had just left her a year ago for 'a fucking 35-year-old. Well, of course, at that age and childless, if you haven't found someone you can be attracted to anyone. The bloody fool. He thinks he's escaping into some youthful *vita nuova*; he'll be changing nappies in a year or two, mark my words, and pretending to be happy about it.'

She laughed, and then her face fell.

'The awful thing is that she works in the same industry. I'll see them together at book fairs and launch parties – until she has the babies and her career falls on its arse while she's waiting for them to grow up. God knows how I managed. It was better then, I think, or perhaps it was more acceptable to farm your kids off on someone else. My kids, by the way, are absolutely fine, they're delightful young people.'

She told me about her kids and after a while I realised I had not listened, distracted by thoughts of what my own imaginary child would be like, and I tried to correct this by earnestly nodding along with a story about her daughter which I didn't understand.

'So, what are you going to do with your life?' she asked suddenly. 'I don't want to assume that you're a bit lost. But you seem a bit lost.'

She cut me off as I became vague and uncomfortable.

'You strike me as a bright young man, full of creative ideas. And you're right, the editor positions are full of confident Oxbridge graduates who are used to arguing forcefully and articulately, but there are other ways of getting in the door, particularly for people with years of experience selling books and . . .'

She told me to apply for a marketing assistant position, that it was possible to progress quickly. I nodded my head and took out my notebook and made notes on what she thought I should say in my application. Do anything you want to me, I wanted to say to her. Tell me to do whatever you like.

'That's very kind,' I said. 'I'll definitely apply.'

I wanted to succumb to a powerful change.

She didn't go back to the office that afternoon. We sipped glasses of wine until we were drunk enough to move on to cocktails and she introduced me to entertainment lawyers, literary agents and novelists, and Jude Law, who seemed to be wearing a denim jacket without anything underneath, though I was so drunk I suppose it might have been a denim shirt, or Benedict Cumberbatch.

At twelve we decided to go home.

'Walk me to a cab,' she said.

As we were getting in I leaned forwards to kiss her, as I assumed she wanted me to. She put her hand between us and laughed. 'Oh, Paul. That has cheered me up. How funny! Make sure you send in that application.' And then she got in the car and it drove away, leaving me feeling quite foolish and drunk, disappointed even, but not unhappy, not ashamed. I reeled away to the bus stop, looking for someone else to talk to.

*

I got to the hospital before Amy. A young man in a green hospital gown and socks was sitting on the ground and asking people hopelessly if they could spare a cigarette. I walked over and lit one for him, wondering if I was doing something awful to his health.

I had spoken to Amy on the phone the night before, and she had told me that she had accepted an offer for her flat and had an offer accepted for another, larger flat, in a quieter part of town, the sort of place where young middle-class parents lived. She also told me that the interview to get her job back had gone OK, but they were making her wait for a verdict until a series of other meetings had been conducted. She was due to hear from them first thing in the morning, just before her twelve-week scan, 'the same morning I'll discover if my baby is still alive or deformed or – '

'I'm coming with you,' I said. 'I'll get someone to cover me in the morning.'

'Really?' she said. 'OK. Thanks.'

When she arrived I hugged her, carefully. We were running late so we hurried through to the maternity section and checked in at the reception, looking around us at the various couples waiting quietly next to the plastic children's toys and colourful picture books.

'Did you hear about the job?' I asked, when we sat down in a far corner of the waiting room.

'Yeah, they gave it me back, on probation.'

'Hooray!'

'Hooray.'

'That's good, isn't it?'

'They're such caring people, they couldn't bear to think that they weren't caring people. I went to the doctor and got a note to say I'm suffering from depression and am seeing a psychologist for resulting anger-management issues. I think that clinched it.'

'And they believed you?'

'Well, yeah. Because I am actually doing that.'

'Are you? You're depressed?'

'Yeah, I mean, yeah. I need the job.'

'Is it helpful? The therapy?'

'I've only just started it. She says I show the classic behaviour of a rageaholic.'

'Rage*aholic*? Does that make sense etymologically? It's like saying people are gamblingaholics, heroinaholics, wankaholics.'

'Does it matter?'

'No. Sorry.'

'I like the woman I speak to.'

'Are you really depressed? I didn't know you were depressed.'

'I'm sad, Paul. Really sad. Aren't you?'

We were speaking quietly now, not wanting our bad vibes to carry over to the other pregnant women.

'I haven't thought about it.'

'I think you have.'

'About Mum, well of course. And yeah, I'm worried about what's become of my life, how I've wasted so much time and don't know what the hell I'm going to do next. I still miss Monica. I still wince when I imagine the life I could have had if I'd been more careful. But I'm not *depressed*. I'm appropriately sad. I distract myself. There's still a good chance I can fix my problems.'

'How do you stay so optimistic all the time? Do you really feel like that?'

'We have to believe that. Life isn't all sad.'

'But aren't you lonely now? Like a hundred times more lonely?'

'I don't know. If I'm lonely I go out and look for someone.'

'Someone? To do what?'

147

'Connect. Talk.'

'Yeah, talk. I don't think that's what you mean. And that just makes me more lonely.'

'What about your friends?'

'It's not the same, is it? They're busy. They're having babies. I see them occasionally, then I come home and I'm still lonely.'

'That's just . . . circumstantial.'

'I don't care if it's circumstantial or integral. It's how I feel.'

A woman walked quickly from the consulting rooms holding a hand over her eyes. A man came out a few seconds later, looking around for her.

'You know you can rely on me completely when the baby's born,' I said. 'And before. I could even move in if you want.'

She smiled with her mouth shut, and we looked around the room at all the hushed couples, the men studying their phones, the women more alert, looking up whenever a name was called. These hopeful alliances we formed to continue the species.

'No, thanks,' she said. 'It's good of you to come here, but let's be real. I want to get a housemate. Maybe you're right about friends being the answer. Hannah might move in with her one-year-old. We need new structures. Why can't two single mothers live together and help each other out?'

'You're right.'

'I might meet a man who isn't a dickhead if I'm not in such a rush.'

'It takes time to find men of sensibility.'

'And you and me living together? With a baby? We'd kill each other.'

'Maybe. So what's the therapist like? Do you talk about me with her?'

'She thinks you should probably see someone.'

'She does? Right. Nah. I'm fine.'

'I don't think you are.'

'Honestly, I am. Leave it alone.'

'You don't get angry?'

'Of course I get angry. There are infuriating dickheads everywhere I go. They should make me angry.'

'Are they definitely as infuriating as you find them?'

'Yes, they are. They're really fucking infuriating.'

'If you say so.'

'I do, thanks. What else do you talk about with this woman?'

'Mum. Dad. Tactics for not getting pissed off with people. That's the bit I like least. It's sort of linguistic reprogramming. I'm not allowed to say "People always do this" or "You all do this".'

'I've been saying that to you for ages.'

'But when you say it you're usually denying my right to be angry about the behaviour of certain men because you think I'm attacking you.'

'That's what you think I'm doing, but what I'm trying to do is say I agree with you that these men are awful but don't lose hope in all men. Because if you lose hope there's no hope.'

'Well, it comes across as you telling me there's something wrong with me that makes men treat me like that. Because I'm not sufficiently upbeat for them.'

'That's not what I mean. You should know that.'

'Should. You're not supposed to say people "should" do things either.'

'This woman sounds a bit basic to me.'

'Don't belittle her. She's a reason to be optimistic. You should think about why you want to belittle her.'

'Because she's a woman and I'm a man?'

'That's not what I meant. What a stupid thing to say. Have you noticed how you're getting angry now?'

'I'm not getting angry.'

'Then why's your voice getting louder?'

149

I looked up and realised the couple nearest to us were looking at us.

'Because,' I said, in a hushed voice, 'you're talking in that soft way like a meditation instructor and it's fucking provoking.'

'You should go to something like meditation.'

'I'd rather relax doing something intelligent, thank you.'

'Fuck you, thank you,' she whispered. 'You're full of rage.'

'So are you.'

'So what are you going to do with it?'

'No offence, Amy, but you've been to two sessions with a psychologist and now you're Melanie Klein? Give me a break.'

'I'm saying I'm worried about you. Stop being so angry. Try to calm down. Focus on the present.'

'Fuck living in the present. I want to take revenge for what's been done to us.'

'And you want to come and live with me and help me raise a happy baby?'

I looked away. 'If you wanted me to.'

'You tell yourself that. Now try breathing out slowly. That's what I do now. You take more in-breaths when you're angry than when you're relaxed.'

I tried breathing out slowly, thinking all the time that if I could just get this breathing over with, I could get on with something important. 'Do you think there are therapists to treat people who don't get angry enough? Telling them they need to breathe in more and not out.'

'If there are such people, I don't think therapists bother with them. I think those are the people who make society work.'

'In that wonderful way it does. Do you really want to become one of them?'

'Breathe out. And pause. Now breathe in deeply, then out slowly.'

'I can't. We need joss sticks. The ambience is wrong.'

'And pause. Now breathe in deeply.'

'What if being angry is the only thing that keeps me going?'

'Breathe out slowly. Then you'd better find something else to keep you going.'

*

'Wright?' called a Spanish voice. 'Amy Wright?'

We followed the nurse through to meet the sonographer, a kind, reassuring woman with technical expertise and an Italian accent. It took some doing to cast her as the enemy.

I looked away and towards the screen as she squirted lubricant over Amy's belly and went to work with her machine.

And there it was. A blur at first, an untuned TV, and there was its head, the length of its body.

'Yes,' she said. 'There's definitely a baby there.'

The baby was moving. Jiggling around.

'You've got a busy one,' the sonographer said.

Amy and I looked at each other. It took the sonographer a while to get the head measurement she needed.

'You've wound the baby up,' said Amy. 'I'm coming with someone else next time.'

The sonographer switched something and suddenly the room was filled with noise – a hard, squelching beating, like something they'd play downstairs at Berghain.

'Jesus,' I said.

'I think that's unlikely,' said the sonographer. 'Unless you're a virgin?' she said, looking at Amy. 'What that is is a healthy heartbeat. Congratulations.'

Amy was shaking her head at me and smiling. We listened to its heartbeat, furious already: one of us.

PART TWO

TWELVE

Your office is a white room in a house, with two low armchairs and a small coffee table between us, and a box of tissues ready for when you make me break down. Good luck with that. There is a fireplace to my right with a tasteful arrangement of dried flowers in it. The room is neutrally prepped, the way a real-estate developer might deck out a show flat. Ikea art on the walls. Nothing as messy as a book in here. A clock is angled towards me so I won't be surprised when you ask me to leave.

'Why do you think you're here?' you say in an American accent, after we've said hello and sat down.

Because I can't afford a psychoanalyst, I'm tempted to say.

But, disgraced as I am, I still pretend to have some manners, and would be happy to be proved wrong about the futility of this process, and so I say what I have tried to rehearse myself into believing on my way over.

'I'd like some help to learn how to confront my difficulties rather than repress them through anger and desire.'

'OK,' you say and begin to write something down. 'And you said on the phone that there was a particular incident after which you recog – '

'Yes.'

'In which you behaved in a way that shocked yourself?'

'Yes, I suppose.'

'And going back to your words, was this an act of anger or desire?'

'Anger. Desire. Angry desire.'

You write something down and look at me like you're assessing me, and so I assess you too. You're about my age, straight hair with highlights, and I think you might be trying not to let a little bit of boredom or disappointment creep into your expression. It's that word, *desire*, isn't it? I know men's desire is boring. Disappointing. People are disappointing. But bear with me. We're not all disappointing in the simple ways. It's not all lust. There are other reasons to decide to love someone.

*

One Sunday in June, I spent an unprecedented twelve pounds on a bottle of wine from a Tesco Metro, walked down to Dalston Central and made my way west on the Overground for lunch with Emily, Andrew and Sophie.

I had enjoyed Sophie's recent opinion piece: I WAS CAUGHT SHOPLIFTING AND LEARNED THE DISGUSTING TRUTH OF MIDDLE-CLASS PRIVILEGE. In it she explained how she had been apprehended leaving Selfridges with a £500 dress in a foil-lined handbag, before being handed over to the police, who, eventually, 'shamefully' believed her story that she was researching a novel and let her off with a warning – 'though how did they know to trust me? Would they have believed me if I'd been a person of colour or spoke with a strong South London accent?'

I hadn't had the opportunity yet to ask Emily what Andrew thought of that.

*

I had been meeting Emily regularly for lunch now it was summer. She was getting up then at first light to write, and would have worked for five or six hours before she took a walk into town through the park to the shop. She never arranged things in advance. I would get a text in the morning to ask if I was working, and if I wasn't I'd ride over to meet her anyway. We would buy sandwiches and sit in Bloomsbury Square, with the students and tourists and yoga extroverts. The pollen made her sneezy and interrupted her sentences. I learned how she had met Andrew, twelve years ago at a literary festival when she was promoting her first novel, and how they might not even have thought of getting together then, if it hadn't been for a woman who insisted on inviting herself to lunch with them and who had warned Emily, when he went to the toilet, that he wasn't only attracted to her talent. 'I should hope not,' said Emily. 'I don't think he was thinking of me like that at the time but I was quite pretty then.'

I always took the opportunities she gave me to compliment her. She would leave little spaces for me to contradict her self-criticism, then wince when I did.

I was discovering that there were limits to her renunciation. She dressed differently every time I saw her, in styles that were from different eras, with the feminine clearly demarcated – there was rarely any androgyny, or even jeans, nearly always a dress or skirt, shoes and tights, her face made up. I rarely saw her in the same outfit twice but when I did I felt I had gained a notch of intimacy with her. I didn't flatter myself that she was dressing up for me. It was in keeping with her correctness, her old manners, a formality that suited the way she handled her emotions – when, for example, I asked her about her parents, she exhaled sharply, and changed the subject. The way she presented herself was also simply the outward signs of someone who appreciated style in and outside of the sentence, who knew her body and how to make an effect with it. Her decision to avoid being assessed by her photograph may have been taken with mixed feelings. Sitting on a park bench with her, I imprinted my memory with the shape of her calves, the angle of her nose; and I learned how to make her laugh. I came to know her frustrations too. She lived off meagre advances and grants and Andrew's charity. She had to think hard if she wanted to buy a new frock. 'It should be me out shoplifting, not his pretty little daughter.'

'She is pretty, isn't she?'

'I thought you'd think so. Yes, she is. You can see her dad in her.'

'That wasn't the thing I appreciated most about her.'

'From the photos I've seen, the mother's not bad either.'

'You've never met her?'

'No.'

Jean had been Andrew's teenage sweetheart; they both went to Oxford at the same time from the same town; he became an academic, she became a head teacher.

'The brightest kids from their grammar schools. The shining hope of an egalitarian future. Who rose through their talent from industrial Nottingham. Their union betrayed by lechery.'

'You have to cut Sophie a bit of slack. Why would she like the woman who took her dad from her mum?'

'But that wasn't me! Is that what you thought?'

She corrected me. Andrew had left his first wife for his literary agent. They had lived together for four years before she was diagnosed with cancer. They had married the summer before she received the diagnosis. And the next summer his new wife had died.

'It's their flat we're living in. I've suggested he might be happier somewhere else, but he won't hear of it. Her books everywhere. I wonder if he'd sacrifice me for her in the blink of an eye.'

'Come on,' I said.

'Best to be real about these things. If he could redeem all that suffering and grief for the price of one small life like mine? No one would miss me but him. I've disconnected myself sufficiently to be disposable. My carbon footprint is tiny.'

'I don't believe you. About having disconnected yourself. Who was that man at the launch?' I said. 'The giant. You were very pleased to see him.'

'Oh. Richard. He's got a wife now, and children. We were together in our twenties. It wasn't serious – even if it felt so then.'

London summers felt like they got hotter and longer every year. Even at the centre of the square, covered by trees, we were never unaware of the hum of traffic, the grit and petrol in the air.

'I need to get out of here,' she said. 'Go somewhere to work that's quiet, with clean air. Fields and hills, or the sea breeze – '

'Do it.'

'I've no money to.'

'Stay at my mum's place,' I said. 'The air's clean. It's quiet. It's free. It's extremely breezy. We'll sell it soon, I hope, but it would be great if it could be useful to someone before we do.'

I had thought about moving back there myself until it sold, if it ever sold. I wondered sometimes whether the boredom would be so crushing there that I would have to create something of my own.

'I mean it seriously,' I said. 'It might be perfect. There's nothing else to do there.'

'Maybe a couple of weeks?' she said.

'I'd love that. I'll ask my sister. Andrew wouldn't mind you going?'

'He'll be fine. He won't have to feel guilty leaving me at home to accept dinner invitations from his ex-girlfriends.'

'Does he have that many?'

'I'm exaggerating. One or two before me.'

'Why do you think Sophie dislikes you?' I asked. 'Are you sure she does dislike you?'

'Perhaps she hoped her mum and him might get back together.'

A woman a few metres in front of us leaned back from a kneeling position and stretched herself into a perfect O.

Emily and I blinked at each other, and she spoke. 'But then who ever needed a good reason to hate someone else?'

*

Andrew answered the door in his Sunday wear: jeans and casual shirt with just the top button undone, a pair of sandals. We squeezed each other's hands as hard as we could and he gestured for me to walk up the stairs.

'Are you drunk, Paul?' he asked cheerfully.

'What kind of question is that? Are you?'

'You were drunk last time you arrived here, weren't you?'

'It's two o'clock on Sunday afternoon.'

'I never know with you. You might have been out since Thursday.'

'I've been working in the shop for the last two days. I went to the cinema last night with my flatmate.'

'How disappointing. You mustn't stay sober this afternoon, Paul. I doubt I'll manage it.'

'Is Sophie here yet?'

'No, she's on her way. You hit it off, did you, at the launch?'

'We had a nice time drinking in an ersatz confessional booth.'

'Sounds sacrilegious.'

'That's what I said. And, oh! I read Sophie's article about shoplifting. Did you see it?'

He gave me a long assessing look before he spoke. 'I did, and that is a subject I have been advised by Emily not to bring up over lunch. I say *advised*, but what I mean is *commanded*.'

In their hallway I stood again at the intersection of two book-lined corridors. Emily stood barefooted at the end of one, wearing an apron; she beckoned me towards her. There was a smell of bread baking. It was a dreamy vision, like one might have before being jolted back into life with a defibrillator. The wooden floorboards looked like they had been recently polished, though that may just have been my heightened sensitivity to our different environments. The carpets in my place had frayed through in patches to show the lack of under-lay. I sometimes found myself wandering through streets of Edwardian terraces in Dalston, looking into living-room windows with lustful thoughts about alphabetising my books there.

'I brought a bottle,' I said.

'Thanks very much.' Without looking at the label, he put it on the floor next to an umbrella stand. Then he ushered me into the kitchen.

*

In the centre of the kitchen there was a round table, where we sat while Emily sliced and whizzed and put things in the oven. Andrew and I shared a bottle of white wine, while he interrogated me about my childhood.

'That must have been hard,' he said.

'Which? When he walked out or when he died?'

'Both. But I meant when he walked out. And refused to see you. God knows I haven't lived a perfect life but I've always seen Sophie regularly.'

I looked up to see if Emily would look at me, but she kept facing the other way, stirring something in a pot.

'He still saw me occasionally. It was my sister he stopped talking to for a while.'

'How was that for her?'

'I mean, she got over it. Did she? We both grew up quite quickly after it happened. Don't let me go on about it. It's nothing remarkable.'

'And your mother?' he said.

'She . . .'

'You needn't go on if you don't want to.'

'No, it's fine. She was a teacher too, like her brother and two sisters. The other two sisters were nurses. They all went for responsible, valuable, realistic careers. Lived in realistic places suitable for raising healthy kids on realistic incomes. It's embarrassing, really.'

'It should be the absolute opposite. You should be proud of them.'

'I am. I'm embarrassed about the contrast I present.'

'Don't be ridiculous,' said Emily, from the chopping board. 'Your choices have probably made you much happier than theirs made them.'

'Even if that were true, I can't see why that should make me any less embarrassed.'

'You really did grow up Catholic,' said Andrew.

'What time's Sophie due?' asked Emily.

'Soon,' said Andrew. 'And what was it like at your school, Paul?'

I told him.

'You need to be careful, Paul.'

'Careful?'

'Of relying too much on stories of hardship to explain your lack of direction.'

'I didn't say anything about hardship. It was fine – it just didn't have very high ambitions for us.'

'Some people aren't given advantages. I sympathise. But what can you do with my sympathy?'

'It was you who brought up my school. I was minding my own business.'

'I just think you need to think more positively. Act yourself into the right role. I grew up working class.'

'But don't you think the era made some practical difference to you? With grammar schools, plausible house prices . . .'

'You sound like my daughter.'

'You don't,' said Emily.

Then the doorbell rang and Andrew went to let Sophie in.

*

An hour had passed. The salad was delicious, there was a lentil stew with bright-green beans and basil, and a loaf of sourdough bread from the oven – though these culinary matters were mentioned very little at the table. Emily and I had been silent for a while, moving only to pour ourselves more wine. Andrew and Sophie had barely touched their glasses.

'But you weren't researching a novel. You were stealing a dress.'

'Which proves my point even further.'

'So why not admit that in the article?'

'Would you rather I had?'

'Do I want you to announce to the world you're a thief? I suppose actually I don't. You might need a job one day.'

'I have a career as a journalist already, thank you.'

'There are circles in which saying someone writes journalism is an insult, you know, Sophie.'

'Not ones I want to be part of, and that's rich, considering how much journalism you write. And I *was* researching an article, as it turned out. Why do you care?'

'Because this stuff matters.'

'Why?'

'Why does truth matter? Really?'

'The end justifies the means,' she said.

'What?'

'Do you not think it's abhorrent that I can get away with stealing that dress when someone else can't?'

'Yes, I do.'

'And I've drawn attention to that.'

'So what? What end have you reached by drawing attention to it? What solution to poverty have you proposed? And why did you call me? Why didn't you just use the lawyer they would have provided? Why didn't you leave me to eat my dinner that night?'

'Oh, I'm sorry I put you out, Dad.'

'You're better than this, Sophie. This bratty sarcasm.'

'I rang you because I was scared and I wanted to talk to you. I didn't expect a get-out-of-jail-free card.'

'Do you believe what you're saying?'

'Don't you see it's wrong that your friend could arrive and just get me out of there?'

'You better hope the Americans don't read your column.'

'What? Why?'

'They could stick your name on a list of UK citizens convicted of crimes of moral turpitude. And you would be turned away.'

'What? Then why did Sandra say I'd be OK with a caution?'

'She didn't know you were going to write a fucking column about it. For such an educated person you really can be quite stupid.'

'It's not stupid to speak out about injustice!'

Andrew's face twisted with derision. 'You're in serious danger of taking this useful, simplistic persona you've created for publishing your popular polemics and turning it into your actual personality. Which would be a shame, because you have a good mind beneath this bullshit. You wanted some material for a column, that's all. Of course it's wrong that you can get away with stealing a dress when someone else can't. That's your moral failure, not the system's. The system is like it is because people with your advantages don't tend to steal dresses, unless they're suffering a mental breakdown. So it was easy to convince them what you did was a result of a mental breakdown, and that you weren't on your way to steal another one. You've proven nothing of worth at all.'

This was an interesting lesson in how to argue. By now Amy and I would have got personal and started screaming at each other.

'People like me do steal dresses. Dad. And don't talk about my moral failings. I don't see why some of us are allowed to display outrageous morals and others aren't.'

And now it began to resemble the arguments I knew well.

Andrew slapped his hand down on the table. 'I am trying to stay calm here, Sophie. Which outrageous morals of mine are we talking about? Why don't you state it clearly rather than make these petty allusions?'

He pushed his chair back and strode from the room. We heard his sandals slapping on the floorboards as he walked the length of the corridors.

Emily topped up all of our glasses of wine, looking down at the table as she did, and opened her mouth in a yawn.

'Were we boring you, Emily?' asked Sophie, who was looking a bit shaken.

'Occasionally,' said Emily. 'Shall we try to change the subject before he's back?'

'What was it that was so boring to you?'

'I'm just not really into such muscular sports. It's like watching two thugs play tennis. Just *whack whack whack*.'

'We like to have debate over dinner in our family, Emily,' she said.

'We did not,' said Emily. 'And I'm willing to learn new things, but only up to a point.' She picked up her glass, took an infinitesimal sip, holding eye contact with Sophie, then lowered the glass back down.

Sophie turned to me. 'And were you bored too, Paul?'

I tried to think of something to change the subject. 'And how is your writing going?' had been a disastrous question.

Sophie carried on. 'Dad mentioned you two were going to go on holiday to the seaside together without him.'

We had made a plan to go there in a week's time. I was coming along for two nights, to let her in, and to check in with the estate agent. I could have spoken to the agent on the phone though Amy was taking care of that, and I didn't really need to check the house was all right, which Alan was still doing for us. But my reasons for being there sounded convincing. And after all, it was my home. I wanted to go there with her.

'It's not a holiday,' said Emily. 'Paul's just letting me in and doing some things he needs to do there, then he's leaving me to get some work done.'

'Yes, that's what Dad said too. But you can't go to the seaside and not have some fun. You'll want Paul to take you for a go on the Big One, surely?'

Sophie looked at me and raised her eyebrows. I made an awkward grin at her.

Emily noticed and scowled. 'I'll be doing nothing an old-age pensioner wouldn't do. Fifty-p cups of tea, blustery walks on the beach, and trying to write my book.'

'Do you miss Rochi?' Sophie asked me suddenly. 'You were spending a lot of time with her. And now you're not.'

'I didn't know you were keeping tabs on us,' I said.

'Who's Rochi?' said Emily.

'My friend. She was at the launch. Tall, Indian heritage. Attractive. She is attractive, isn't she, Paul?'

'I know who you mean,' said Emily. 'Of course she is. She's striking.'

I couldn't work out if the smile she was giving me was patronising or admiring.

'We had a nice time,' I said.

'Who had a nice time?' said Andrew, striding back into the room. 'Why's Paul gone red?'

'Rochi and Paul had a nice time,' said Emily.

'Rochi your friend?' asked Andrew.

'Rochi's great,' I said quickly. 'We went out a couple of times. We're buddies.'

'Buddies?' asked Sophie. 'English people don't say "buddies" unless they're silently pronouncing the word "fuck" before it.'

'Jesus, Sophie. Can we try to keep things civilised?' said Andrew.

'It's a vile phrase, I know, Dad,' said Sophie. 'But it's *la parlance du jour*. What else can you say? *Lovers?* You'd have to be at least your age to get away with that, and what's love got to do with it?'

'What's love but a second-hand emotion?' sang Emily.

Sophie glared at her.

'They do use the word "buddy" where I'm from,' I said.

'It's American,' said Sophie.

'"All right, buddy", "All right, bud". That's how men greet each other.'

'How strange,' said Sophie.

'You and Rochi, hey?' said Andrew.

'Jesus, you're not going to start some male perv club, are you?' said Sophie.

'*Sophie*,' said Andrew.

'No. Not me and Rochi,' I said.

Emily was looking at me and I still couldn't read her face. I saw Andrew notice she was studying me. 'Let's move on,' he said.

The speculation about my sex life had lightened the mood. Emily and Sophie began to chat about novels they'd read recently, while Andrew encouraged me to follow up on my conversation with Susannah. 'She likes you,' he said. 'She's keen to help you.'

'It's very good, your new novel,' Sophie was saying to Emily.

And perhaps Sophie's aggression towards her was tributary, a failed attempt to show respect, like a boy pulling the ponytail of a girl as a way of trying to tell her, and himself, that he liked her.

'Thank you,' said Emily.

'Very good indeed!'

'Thank you.'

'I've been telling everyone to read it. Apart from my mum. It's very intelligent! Funny, too!'

I could see Emily struggling to lower her eyebrows. It was hard to tell whether Sophie was being unwittingly condescending, or whether she was being as condescending as she could possibly be.

'And are *you* still planning to write fiction?' asked Emily.

'It's on the back burner while I finish my essay book. English fiction just seems so moribund? So defeated? There hasn't been a good political novelist since . . .'

She directed her speech to Emily first, then turned to her father. After a minute Emily stood up and walked from the room. Sophie turned to watch her leave. Andrew topped up our glasses again.

*

At about six I could tell it was time to leave, and I said I would be on my way.

'Where are you going?' asked Sophie.

'Just back east. Home.'

'Are you going out?'

'Not planning to.'

'Hmm. Walk me to the Tube, will you?'

'Of course.'

'Actually, Sophie, we did want to talk to you about something first,' said Andrew. He looked at me and round towards the door.

'Well, can Paul stay while you do?' she said.

'Um,' said Andrew. 'I suppose it doesn't matter.'

'And actually there're some books I wanted to borrow – can I take them?' Sophie said, leaving the room and pacing up and down the hallway.

'Yes, just show them to me first in case I need them for a course or a piece.'

Emily stood up. She ran a sink full of water and started putting pans into it.

'I'll do that later, darling,' said Andrew.

'Do you want me to wait in your living room?' I asked. 'While you talk about whatever you're talking about.'

'No, stay,' said Andrew. 'Right, Emily?'

'Yeah, why not?' she said, sitting down again, before getting back up and putting the kettle on.

We sat there waiting for Sophie, whose company I was beginning to look forward to having to myself. I was curious about the type of alliance we were going to form.

'So what was this thing you wanted to tell me?' she asked when she came back in with a pile of books, and her bag on her shoulder.

'Sit down, Sophie,' said Andrew.

'I'll hear you whether I'm standing up or sitting down,' she said, leaning against the kitchen counter.

'Fine. I've asked Emily to – '

'This is the best translation, isn't it?' said Sophie, holding up a book.

'I've asked Emily to – '

'We've decided together to,' said Emily.

'Yes, we've decided together to . . . that we'd like to get married.'

'Oh,' said Sophie.

No one had looked at me once during this exchange except Sophie, a quick glance of panic. I didn't say congratulations or anything at all.

Sophie coughed. 'Just to be clear: you are going to get married? When?'

'We won't wait long,' said Andrew. 'The end of the summer, perhaps early September.'

'Congratulations,' I said, to break the silence.

The engaged couple looked in my direction and smiled with their mouths shut. While they were looking away from her, Sophie pretended to vomit, composed herself and said, 'Yes, very well done. Now I presume it's my job to tell Mum about this. Have you thought about Mum at all in this?'

'I'll call her this evening,' said Andrew.

'Don't call her this evening. If you call her this evening I'll have to go home and pick up the pieces, and I might have other plans this evening.'

'There won't be any pieces to pick up, Sophie. We've been divorced for eight years.'

'Eight years is nothing. Eight years is eight weeks.'

'That's startlingly mature and nihilistic of you, Sophie, but in this case eight years is eight years. I do still speak to

Jean as you know, and she's fully aware of my relationship with Emily.'

'That's what you think. You don't live with her.'

'No. I live with Emily, and I will be marrying her this summer.'

'Well . . . congratulations. Congratulations, Dad. Congratulations, Emily.'

'Thank you,' said Emily, as flatly as Sophie.

'And you're getting married this summer?' I said, wishing I wasn't there.

Emily had carefully avoided looking at me until she couldn't any more. 'It won't be a big thing,' she said. 'The smallest room in the registry office. A handful of people.'

'So not as big a deal as your wedding to Carole, Dad?'

'Oh, Sophie . . .'

'Are you even inviting me?'

'Of course we're inviting you,' said Andrew. 'You will come?'

'Depends if I'm free,' said Sophie. 'I'm very busy this summer.'

'And you, Paul, I hope you'll come too,' he said, which Emily looked startled by before she said yes, and nodded her head at me.

'Perhaps we could both bring a witness,' said Andrew to Emily.

I was not even supposed to be witnessing this. I had the sense that he was trying not to smirk at me.

'I'm sorry there's no champagne,' he said. 'I should have said earlier when we hadn't drunk so much, but we weren't intending to tell you in front of Paul.'

Emily looked up at me then and made a little shrug of apology.

I excused myself and went to the bathroom, where I locked the door before opening the bathroom cabinet and looking around. There were some ominous-looking pills I liked the look of. Heart medicine, I hoped. Things to help dangerously high blood pressure. Or to stabilise suicidal moods. I shook a couple out and took a picture of the bottles. I couldn't see any Viagra, though he probably kept that in his bedroom, or in his office drawers. Hair dye? None that I could see. That was a shame. Valium! Xanax! Hello, old friends. Perhaps they were Emily's. Perhaps he was an anxious man behind the facade. About what? Where were his troubles? I borrowed a couple of each of the pills, anyway, before I unlocked the door and stepped out.

In the hall Andrew was hugging Sophie. She kept her arms loose by her side. When they parted Sophie's eyes were shut. She waited a few seconds before opening them.

After I'd hugged Emily, Andrew shook my hand while squeezing my shoulder with his other hand. Again, the smirk on his face that I had not worked out how to trouble. Not yet. 'Look after my daughter!' he said.

'Daddy,' she said. 'I'll look after him.'

THIRTEEN

Next time I come you ask me to list what it is that makes me angry.

'What it is?'

'Aren't there things that make you angry?'

'If people are things.'

'Well. Can you give me a list of people's actions that make you angry?'

'Oh, God, where to start?'

'Take your time.'

'It's like when people ask you what your favourite book is. There're too many shining examples to pick one. You always forget to say *Anna Karenina*.'

You look past me and I know it's at the other clock on the wall behind. I don't like thinking of the way we must exhaust you. I hope there's someone who listens to your problems.

'In general might we say it's when people refuse to see things the way you do?'

'You're asking if I'm just as bad as everyone else? One of those good guys who know that they're the good guys. God, I hate those fuckers. I hate the fucking good guys.'

You look at me for at least a minute and I keep quiet too, staring at the box of tissues on the coffee table between us. Is it wise to provoke the wankaholics like that? I think about saying. So I do. You ignore that and carry on.

'Do you think it's impossible to be a good guy?'

'No. Just extremely difficult.'

'By whose standards?'

'Jesus? J. K. Rowling?'

'I see. The very highest authorities. And you – you're not a good guy? You don't think you're a good guy?'

'Recently I've been behaving even worse than the good guys.'

It's not a big smile you make but it's something.

*

And so it came to the day of the EU vote, and the people voted. Except for me, for I was not on the electoral register, a consequence of my unusual address. But everyone I knew in London who could vote voted, and apart from the occasional lunatic exception we voted to stay. We were all calm, or pretending to be calm.

Mary and Jonathan were going out that night to a summer party in the Serpentine Pavilion. 'Pop stars and fashion designers, actors, that sort of thing,' said Jonathan.

'Save it for Mary,' I said, who had done herself up in a sequinned blue dress and bright silver sandals, her hair piled up in a way I'd never seen before.

'You look good,' I said.

'Yeah?'

'Your shoulders look very naked.'

'Get lost.'

She was back in my room two minutes later.

'Are you sure I look all right? This dress is just H&M. Is it a bit basic?'

'Your beauty is so bright it's blinding.' I reached over and put on my sunglasses. 'No, I still can't look at you.'

I put a pillow over my head and she went out.

Then Jonathan came in. 'How do I look, mate?'

'You've never once cared about my opinion of how you look.'

'Yeah, you're right. Why am I asking your opinion?'

He was wearing one of his skinny suits that had been so fashionable when he started at the magazine.

'Where's your hat?' I asked.

'I don't have a hat, you cunt.'

'Then where do you keep your razor in case you get into a bit of bother?'

'Let's go, Mary,' he said.

She checked herself in my mirror and pouted, tipped her face from side to side.

Lucky Jonathan. He moved into the mirror beside her and I watched them watching themselves framed together. They might have made a nice-looking couple for a few years; I might have been very jealous if I hadn't had my own assignation that evening.

*

In the morning, dazed and underslept, I waited for Emily on the terrace of Euston station. We were taking the train up to Preston where we'd get another train to the end of the line, and from there the tram further up the coast to the end of another line. The next day we had an excursion planned. Emily was writing a long essay for a literary magazine prompted by a new biography of Charlotte Brontë, and we were going to get the train east for an hour to visit the parsonage where she and her sisters had written their novels.

When she arrived we headed to Marks & Spencer's for supplies for the journey. Emily bought a bottle of water and some carrots. I bought some orange juice to mix into a breakfast cocktail with a bottle of fizzy French wine one or two letters away from champagne.

I needed the drink that day. I'd stayed up till five in the morning in a flat in Camden with Sophie and her friends, where we watched the results come in until it was clear there had been no mistake. I had invited Sophie back to mine when I got my Uber, but she couldn't stop watching. 'Stay a bit longer,' she said, lying back with her legs over the laps of me and a guy called Antonio, an actor from her college who claimed to be writing a sitcom about an entomologist, and I kept staying longer until I suspected she was trying to make me miss my train, and left on my own.

After two hours' sleep my alarm went off and I turned the telly on to watch the prime minister resign and Farage walk into what looked like a golf club full of cheering red-faced recruitment consultants wearing too much suit. Business journalists showed the pound crashing. On Facebook, acquaintances were taking it personally, talking about the racist pigs who lived outside of the city, who had ruined the country, from whom we needed to secede, form our own nation, which we would allow Scotland to be part of too.

Emily and I sat on the terrace in the sun with coffees and waited for our platform to be called while we discussed the new world we had woken into. Andrew had been up all night talking to friends on the phone, and now he was writing notes for articles, taking phone calls from radio producers. 'He lives for these moments,' she said.

'For catastrophe.'

'That's it. He's never happier than when he's appalled by something.'

'Like his daughter.' I didn't mention that Sophie had sent me a text an hour ago, telling me she had a commission for an article she was going to write that day and also an appearance on Radio 4 to talk about how the exit polls showed that the elder generation had betrayed the younger, and what the young needed to do about it now. She hadn't been to sleep at all, she wrote. She was furiously exhilarated. It was the worst and best thing that had ever happened to her.

The train was called and we walked through the concourse to our platform.

When we found seats at a table, Emily unzipped her suitcase to find the book she couldn't find in her handbag. I could smell the fabric softener of her clothes, and I looked with her at the neatly rolled tights, the folded dresses and jumpers packed in around paperbacks and her laptop, the side netting filled with creams and make-up. A woman's things. How I missed this stuff. I missed Monica and wanted her back. I missed Emily even as I sat beside her. I might have missed her for her generalness as much as her specificity, for the warmth of her body as much as her paraphernalia, for her shape as much as the outline of it. Sometimes, in front of toilet doors I would be unable to work out for a moment which were the men's and which were the women's; the stick man could be a stick woman until you added a black triangle, a skirt to make a woman a woman and a man her opposite.

'Would you like a glass of wine mixed with orange juice, Emily?' I asked.

'No, thanks. The same as when you asked if I'd help you drink it when you bought it, and whether I thought you should buy two bottles.'

'The offer remains open at any time. This is real French Charlemagne. You might not be able to get this stuff soon.'

'Let's read for a bit,' she said. 'I feel like I'll go mad if I don't.'

She read her novel and I tried to read mine. The sun beat through the warehouses and foliage and for whole minutes I would forget myself and trance out before I refreshed the news on my phone, typed an ill-advised reply to one of the London secessionists, who I hated at that moment even more than the Leave voters, who I hated considerably too. I was glad to be travelling away from London that day. The opinion pieces were multiplying already.

'Would you like a carrot?' asked Emily. A cool carrot on a summer's day. The flashing sun and fizzy citrus and rocking on the tracks, the fever of collapse – what I began to feel as the anger left me was euphoria, and I was careful to avoid looking directly at Emily, worried that my face would show her something that could only be read as love, chaotic love, enough to scare her into getting off the train and returning home.

When we stopped at Warrington fourteen men in nearly identical T-shirts boarded, all carrying an open tin of lager. They formed a line throughout the carriage, looking up and down and trying to work out where to sit. On the front of each of their bright-orange T-shirts it said 'Baz's Blackpool Stag Do 2016', and on the back each man had an individual nickname. From our vantage point we could only make out #dangleballs, #shewassixteenhonest!, #fishyfinger and #lukeskywanker.

'We seem to be surrounded by digital natives,' said Emily. 'I think I need an orange juice and Charlemagne.'

I happily poured her one and we kept our heads down while they mooed at each other. 'Who's the fitty sitting down?' said one of them, and Emily groaned.

'If I say I'm gay can I feel your tits?' came another disembodied voice.

'What does that even mean?' she whispered to me.

'Don't try to understand. We get off in five minutes,' I said.

We ran to change platforms in Preston and had the gratifying sight of seeing the first of their gang arrive at the doors just as they were shutting.

'Oh, this is wonderful!' she said as we pulled away. She blew a kiss to the man who had pounded on the door.

'Hashtag: victory to the fitty sitting down.'

'Hashtag: what kind of place have you fucking brought me to?'

'It's not like that where we are, don't worry,' I said. 'Their bodies would never be found if they drew attention to themselves like that where we're going.'

'I like the sound of this place,' she said.

'Steady on.'

Emily kept her book in her bag, and I finally felt I could ask her about her engagement. I noticed she wasn't wearing a ring.

She looked down at her left hand. 'No. God, no. He offered to buy me one but all that money wasted on a pretty "Keep Away" sign, with some gem mined by a modern-day slave in a country torn by civil war? Nah. Anyway, he didn't propose to me; we proposed to each other.'

'As it should be.'

'I don't know why I'm saying this. It was his idea. I was just very happy about it.'

'Were you?'

'I've never been happier in my life with someone. I don't want it to end. It's nice to know he feels the same way.'

'So did he get down on one knee?'

'No! Thank God!'

'Why thank God?'

'It would be embarrassing. Is that how you'd propose?'

'I can't propose to anyone. I have yet to make my fortune.'

'It's not the nineteenth century.'

'It's not not the nineteenth century either. Anyway, I probably wouldn't. Get down on one knee. It's a bit needy. If you do it in public it's outright manipulative. Especially if I'd asked your father too.'

'My father?'

'I thought we were talking about how I'd propose to you.'

'Not to me, to one.'

'To one.' I looked out of the window.

'If you asked my dad for permission first, that would be a definite refusal from me. Unless he refused. In which case a definite acceptance.'

'And where do I find your father? And how do I annoy him?'

'Oh, would you?' She rested her hand on my knee for a second and then took it off. 'Just stand next to him and breathe. Back at my gran's, in Partick. Just stand next to him and appear cheerful.'

'Perhaps he'd like me. I get on with most people.'

She looked me up and down. 'He'd detest you.'

'What about Andrew? Who would he hate the most?'

'Andrew.'

'Why?'

'He has more money than you. He's more concentratedly English. I don't mean English, I mean middle class. I don't mean middle class, I mean successful. He's more confident.'

'You're mistaking arrogance for confidence.'

'Hey!'

'But he does have more money than me. That's why I need to seek my fortune.'

'Let me know when you find it, though I'll certainly be married by then.'

'Oh, that's OK,' I said. 'You can't rush success.'

She smiled and shook her head. This wasn't serious. 'Any more questions before we move on?'

'Will you wear a white dress?'

'I will not.'

'You have that white dress you wore to your launch party.

Perhaps that's what gave him the idea. You looked very marriable that evening.'

She gave me a look and picked up her book again.

'We're just about to pull in,' I said.

She put her book down and took out her phone and we updated ourselves on the news in stunned silence.

Across the fields, the red tip of Blackpool Tower appeared in the cloudless blue. I pointed it out to Emily.

'Sorry if it was awkward for you, the other day,' she said, still looking out of the window. 'We didn't mean for you to be there then.'

'It's OK. I didn't mind.'

'Sophie took it better than I'd expected.'

'Really?'

'I imagined it being slightly worse.'

The tower disappeared behind a row of houses.

'What did you and Sophie do when you left together?' she asked.

'Oh, you know.'

'No?'

'We went to the pub.'

'Did you stay long?'

'No.'

'And – are you friends?'

'There are things I like about her.'

'Which things?'

'She's trying: she actually believes she can do something to change the world. When she's not insulting me or boasting about her achievements she's quite funny. She has this idea that everything is a battle – it's useful to her, it's how she writes her pieces – but she forgets it after a while. Or she does with me. She doesn't seem to feel the need to outshine me like she does you.'

'And you like that about her, do you?' Emily said, incredulously. Which stung a little.

*

Sophie's questions about my relationship with Emily had been more direct.

'What is it with you two anyway?' she said, as soon as we'd got into the Uber she'd ordered. 'Are you fucking?'

'Do you really think I'd come round for Sunday lunch with her and Andrew if we were having an affair?'

'You might find it erotic. You might get off on rubbing my dad's nose in it. In fact you look like just the sort who'd enjoy that.'

The driver glanced behind him.

'There's something between you,' she continued. 'Those little glances you give each other when you think we're not watching.'

'That's us being satirical when you say something objectionable.'

She didn't like this. 'So you feel superior to me, is that what you're saying?'

'Only when you say outrageous things.'

'And what have you two done to be able to judge whether I'm being outrageous or not? I can see it with her: she's got her books, her prizes – but you? What've you done, Paul? What have you achieved?'

'Not much. But nor have I ever tried to belittle someone because of their lack of achievements. You know, for someone who doesn't shut up about being a socialist, you sound just like a Tory.'

She breathed in quickly, then smiled. 'What else is wrong with me?'

'Oh, Jesus, you're perfect – there's nothing wrong with you.'

'*No*. What's wrong with me?'

'Really?'

'I want to know.'

'OK. You talk over people.'

'Yeah?'

'You don't listen. You have rehearsed opinions on things you haven't read. You're obsessed with privilege and unaware of how your own privilege makes you think. You're rude and aggressive. You're elitist. You're transparently on the make.'

'You are fucking her, aren't you?'

'All the time. It turns us on, slagging you off. We fuck in your dad's bed when he's out at work.'

'You're not really angry with me, are you?'

'I don't really understand why you want to be in here with me.'

'Tell me more about what's wrong with me.'

'I'm running out of things that are wrong with you. There's so much I like about you.'

'I can show you plenty more that's wrong about me if you want me to.'

The taxi driver turned round again to look at us.

'What shall we argue about?' I said.

'I don't know. How about education?'

'Great,' I said.

And we began.

*

Emily sat on a seat in front of mine when we caught the tram north, and we went quiet, shunting past the hundreds of B&Bs, looking west at the Irish Sea rippling around the coast until we were heading inland and past my old school. The tram dropped us off on the edge of the high street in town. Emily trundled her case beside me down the terraced streets, the wind in our faces. The gulls had taken exception to us; they wheeled in tight circles around us until one bird, cackling like a pervert entertainer, came down so slow and low that Emily had to duck and grab my arm.

'What's its fucking problem?' she asked.

'It can tell we've come from London. Or it's nesting. They've always been twats. Don't worry. We're just down here.'

The house was just as Mum had left it, as clean and free from dust as it always was. It wasn't a big place for the town, but big for London – a long, thin terrace with a living room and a dining room and a kitchen at the back with a small garden, three bedrooms above. All cleanly decorated, painted walls covered in prints, the floors wooden except for the thick carpet that was the touch of comfort over style in the room where she watched TV. Her boyfriend Alan came round once a week to dust surfaces and run a Hoover round. I had let him know Emily was staying and arranged to visit him for a coffee on Sunday.

I gave Emily the room I usually slept in, the only bedroom with a desk in it. I made her a cup of green tea with one of the bags – they may have been Amy's – that I found in the cupboard.

'It must be strange for you, being here,' said Emily, looking at me.

'It's, er, yeah,' I said. I had my hands on the wall of the kitchen, as though it might be about to fall in. I took them off and turned around.

'Shall we go for a walk?' Emily said. 'I'd like to see the sea.'

*

And on the beach, with the tide in, it was still possible to feel optimistic about the town. The skies were the bright blue dye of the school shirts we had worn on the first day back in September. The clean air filled our lungs and made us buoyant. We walked towards the site of our burned-down pier, listening to the waves arrive so diligently, so faithfully. I told her the story of the bawdy comedian who some people suspected had set it alight. On the bay's horizon I pointed out to Emily the mountains, the power station, the wide space where you could still see the cargo ships heading somewhere else to land. Though it was a clear, warm day we only met a handful of dog-walkers. We headed on and rounded the edge of the peninsula on the prom, past a statue of a woman and girl waving out towards Ireland. Bye-bye! Bye-bye! There was bunting strung up outside the amusement arcade, from the Queen's ninetieth, I presumed, unless it had been put up that morning in celebration of the Leave vote. I pointed through the fencing to show Emily where the ships had docked and we walked on into the town, where we passed three men in stationary mobility buggies, smoking and talking. A smoking man in a jogging suit pushed a little boy wearing Fonzie shades. Seagulls the size of microwave ovens swooped from the sky and scrapped for chips. There was life on the high street, people queuing for cash machines, at the Iceland checkout. Schoolgirls with white legs, smoking. Smaller boys buzzed round them in blazers. A giant Asda cast its shadow over the smaller shops.

'Pub?' I said.

'OK,' she said. 'I think today we can allow ourselves a few drinks.'

*

There was a party going on in the busiest pub in town. Beer mats objecting to Christine Lagarde winged through the air.

The bar was packed deep. An incongruous hipster with full Edwardian beard and an arm full of sailor's tattoos – a mermaid, an anchor, a leaping shark – dispensed pints as quickly as he could pour them. Plates full of the remains of fish and chips were being gathered by a waiter while another brought fresh ones out of the kitchen doors. Everyone smiled at us. 'All right, pal, all right, bud!'

A TV without the sound on replayed the arrival of Farage in another pub very like the one we were in.

'Do you want to get out of here?' I asked.

'No, no. Let's soak up the atmosphere,' she said.

'Paul,' said John from primary school, whom I hadn't spoken to for twenty years. He shook my hand. 'We did it,' he said. His head was shaved and there was a scar running from ear to ear.

'Yep,' I said.

'Are you back living here?' he asked.

'Nah, just visiting.'

'Where from?'

'London.'

His eyes went wide. 'Rather you than me, mate.'

We found a table on the outskirts of the room and I bought us drinks. I saw people I'd worked with as a street-sweeper at the council during my university summers. More people shook my hand, beaming.

'Is that your lass, Paul? She's a corker.'

'London! How much is a beer there?'

'You were a bright lad, Paul. I bet you're earning down there, yeah?'

I didn't like to disappoint them. I just nodded and fought my way back to Emily.

*

We stayed for a few hours in the end. Emily was at the bar talking to a group of men. One of them was Wozza, the man who had doubted the accidentalness of Carl's death on Facebook, the man who had made a contested but plausible claim to being 'cock of the town' in the mid-1990s. My phone rang.

'Jesus, where are you?' asked Sophie.

'I'm in a Wetherspoons,' I told her.

'Obvs.'

'Obvs. It's banging in here. Where are you?'

'I'm at home, working. God, are people happy there?'

'Absolutely. They're having a whale of a time.'

'Fuck.'

'It's the best atmosphere in here I've experienced for years.'

'Oh, God, let's not go there. How is she?'

'She's at the bar, making friends with the locals and buying me a drink.'

'So you weren't missing me, then?'

'No, not at all.'

'What!'

'I was distracted. I'm missing you now I can hear your voice.'

'Liar.'

'Look, she's on her way back now. Can I call you later?'

'I see. Choosing her over me.'

'She *is* bringing me a beer.'

Emily put the drinks down and grinned, looking back towards Wozza.

'Don't you even want to know what I'm wearing?' Sophie asked.

'Don't tell me. I couldn't cope. I'll call you back later.'

'I'll send you a photo.'

'Looking forward to talking later.'

'You do sound flustered.'

'Obvs. Talk to you later.'

I cut the call and smiled at Emily, raised my glass. 'Cheers.'

'Who was that?' she said.

'My sister.'

'You have quite a flirty tone with her.'

'Brotherly.'

My phone buzzed on the table. I snatched it up and put it in my jeans pocket.

Emily looked at me. 'I have some news,' she said. 'I was chatted up at the bar.'

'I saw you were popular. Which one was doing the chatting up?'

'The wide one. The rectangle in an orange tablecloth with a head on the top.'

'Human head or bulldog's head?'

'In the middle.'

'Yeah, that's Wozza.'

'Wotsit?'

'Wozza.'

I told her about a time he had held me upside down to remove and confiscate the money from the pockets of my school trousers.

'How long ago was this?'

'Oh, last Christmas. No: I would have been about fourteen or thereabouts. He once made me dance like Jarvis Cocker for him. After that he sort of liked me. As a mascot. I kept well away from him. What did he say to you?'

'Celebrating, are you?'

'What did you say?'

'I said, *No*. He asked me why not and I said I didn't think Brexit was a very good idea. *Why not?* he said, and I said I didn't think it would solve anything, just trash the economy, increase intolerance, stop me from living in France if I wanted to.'

'What would you want to live in France for?'

'He didn't actually ask that. He asked where I lived and nodded knowingly when I said London. Fair enough, love, he said, but it's different round here. Then he told me to let him know if anyone gives me any hassle and he'd have a word with them for me.'

'That's a useful offer.'

'Then I asked him why he was celebrating.'

'What did he say?'

'*Because we won! We won! There's more of us than there is of them.*'

'Who's them?'

'Us,' she said.

*

We went the long way back so Emily could see the sea again. It would be dark in London by now but the sun was only just setting here, pink sky and glints of flame in the puddles the tide had left behind. We walked down towards it, where the sand was wet and firm. Seagulls glided overhead and patrolled the tideline, mocking us in Liverpudlian accents, impersonating laser guns like kids with ADHD. In the distance the sea sloshed. A light shone on the horizon. Everything stank of sex.

Emily took a deep breath and said, 'This is peaceful. Thanks, Paul.'

She keeled over and lay on the ground.

'That was a stupid thing to do,' I said. 'You'll be all sandy now.'

I wondered if she wanted me to lie down next to her. I wondered too long.

She got back up and I laughed at her, brushed the sand off her back.

'You city types,' I said. 'You go silly at the sight of the seashore.'

I spent more time rubbing the sand from the small of her back than I suppose I really needed to.

When we got in we sat down on the sofa in the back room and started yawning.

'I'm tired,' she said. 'Which train are we getting tomorrow?'

'We'll get a taxi at nine for the half nine train.'

'I haven't got sand on your mum's sofa, have I?' She brushed at her knees and looked around her. When she looked back up at me she saw that I was looking at her knees and she pressed them closer together.

'You're fine,' I said, looking away. 'Would you like a cup of tea?'

'No, I should go to bed,' she said. She yawned again, and stood up.

'You have everything you need?' I asked.

'Everything,' she said.

You couldn't kiss someone goodbye who was staying in your house, but it felt cold just to let her leave, so I stood up and gave her a hug.

'Goodnight,' I said.

She went up and I followed up soon after. I left my bedroom door open and got into bed where I lay thinking about how the night had gone and imagining what might have happened if I had lain down next to her on the sand. They had installed a new street light just outside the window to illuminate the activities of youths hanging out in the alley. It was very bright, and I kept thinking that it was still daylight outside, long after it had gone dark. I lay awake for a while, listening out in case she made a noise, in case she called out for me.

FOURTEEN

The leaves on the tree outside your window have gone bright yellow. I tell you again about the wedding and what I did afterwards.

'I wonder if you can explain to me what it was that was so attractive to you about Emily,' you say. 'She doesn't sound like she was particularly nice to you.'

'No, no, that's a drab interpretation. She was wonderful to me.'

'In what way?'

'She spoke to me. She was interested in me.'

'But you should expect that, shouldn't you, from everyone?'

'In what utopia? We were on the same side. We had the same enemies. She was funny. She was perceptive. I think you and I might disagree about what friendship is. For me it has to be more than an exchange of kindnesses. That's just barter, just commerce. I liked her because she was scathing, because she was brilliant. And beautiful. God, she was beautiful, in such a . . . Hardly anyone is beautiful now.'

I take a tissue from the box and wipe my glasses clean. You watch me for a while and then ask, 'So you don't consider her to have betrayed you?'

'Not in the way you mean. Not like that.'

'So why were you so angry with her?'

'I don't know. Why don't you have any books in here?'

'Because I don't read in this room. Why were you so angry with her?'

*

The Lancashire countryside alternated with neat redbrick workers' terraces as we moved through the towns of nineteenth-century industry, Burnley, Accrington and Todmorden, the landscape getting wilder as we headed into the Moors and over into Yorkshire.

We were both still sleepy. There is always something wholesomely exhausting in the change of air; I had slept through the hysterical yearning of the seagulls better than Emily, who knocked on my door at eight and asked if I wanted a cup of tea.

It had been sunny for most of the trip but we disappeared into a cloud at Todmorden and got out in Hebden Bridge to a drizzle. Emily had dressed practically for the occasion, wearing jeans, jumper and a pair of athletic trainers I had not imagined her to possess. Now she pulled out a pac-a-mac, unfolded it and carefully put it on over her jumper. I zipped up my own cagoule and we set off like a married couple into town, crossing a bridge over the river, talking about how nice it would be to live here, where they had scenery, fresh air and an art-house cinema.

While we waited at the bus stop we looked in the window of an estate agent and cooed. Our dreams, really, were very conventional.

*

The bus reached the top of the moors and shook the hills out below us. The sun only shone through some of the clouds, lighting up bright-green planes tinged with orange and purple, casting great moving shadows upon the hillscape, squirming clots of darkness shifting shape like my worst envies. Small, crooked farmhouses passed in and out of the light, and we tried to guess which one was Wuthering Heights. A man turned round and asked if we were from round there. 'You're looking for Top Withens,' he said, 'a way over that peak.' He pointed out the Haworth old road branching left from the road we were on, going down into the valley while we climbed higher and higher.

'How long would it take to walk that way?' asked Emily. 'Maybe we should get off?'

'About three hours, love. If you're fit, that is, and you've got the right shoes on.'

I looked out at the paths and imagined us alone together there, on the grass that blazed green and darkened again.

'It'll be quicker from the parsonage, if you're going that way,' he said.

So we stayed on the bus and climbed up to Haworth.

It was raining again when the bus dropped us off. We trudged up the street, past souvenir shops, past galleries selling hobbyists' landscapes, until we reached the Black Bull, Branwell's local. A Chinese woman asked if I would take a picture of her and her husband under its sign, and I did so happily, asking her if she'd return the favour using my phone.

'This is so cheesy,' said Emily, as I put my hand on her shoulder and grinned.

'Shall we have one for Branwell?' I asked.

'We should have one for his sisters, stuck at home or earning money as governesses,' she said. 'Let's go to the museum before we have a drink. I might need to take notes.'

*

The first room we came to was the famous parlour where the sisters had written their novels, where Charlotte and Branwell had elaborated their childhood fantasies about their kingdom of Angria.

'Angrier,' I said. 'Do you think they knew about Brexit?'

We stood in front of the table where *Jane Eyre* and *Wuthering Heights* were written, behind a rope that kept us just inside the doorway. Three housedresses stood awkwardly on their own.

'Who sat where then?' asked Emily.

'We could do with those little place cards you get at weddings. I'm not getting much of an aura, are you?'

'No,' said Emily. 'Let's try. Imagine you're here a hundred and seventy years ago.'

'OK. I'm Emily, you're Charlotte. Which dress is yours and which is mine?'

'Don't you want to be Branwell?'

'Stop negging me. Let's split up. I'll see you upstairs. We're interfering with each other's receptors for ghostly vibes.'

I wandered round the kitchen and Patrick Brontë's study, then headed upstairs. There was some kind of art installation in one room – no, it was a recreation of Branwell's bedroom studio, excellent at the expense of accuracy, which some small print acknowledged: Branwell had shared a room with his father for a lot of his life; and this gloomy chamber was more like my bedroom in the château on a Sunday morning after I'd invited friends back, a disordered piling of books and newspapers and empties, scrawled poems and empty laudanum bottles – at least I assumed that's what they were, since you couldn't fit enough gin in them to get an alcoholic drunk, or certainly not this one. I wouldn't have been surprised to have found NOS canisters on the floor; or empty baggies with Bob Marley's face printed on them.

A tour guide in the hall outside was explaining about Branwell's ambitious affair with Mrs Robinson, mother of the children he and Anne were hired to teach. When her husband had died, Branwell had been convinced she would send for him.

I backed out and into Emily.

'This room is quite something,' I said. 'Look: he's been reading a copy of his own poem in the newspaper.'

'All these candles. I'm surprised he's never set his bed on fire.'

We peered around the room, like a forensics squad.

'Do you think people, er? Goths, er?' she said, indicating the rumpled sheets.

We looked down at them together and back at each other.

'Are you propositioning me?' I asked.

'I wonder what's through here,' she said, stepping through the door and out into a long room, full of letters and trinkets behind glass. I left her to it after a while, and wandered downstairs to the shop and then out onto the lawn where I sat on a bench and looked up at the front of the house. It was still drizzling. I put my hood up and felt damp creep into the seat of my jeans. There was more of an aura here, looking at the famous parlour from outside, where we would always be. I imagined the industry on the other side of the window, anger finding form, the money invested in the boy who was eclipsed by his sisters, whose achievements he never once mentioned in a letter, and which might have been kept from him. But of course he knew. I imagined being on the other side of the glass. Looking out at the bleached days of winter when the trees were stripped clean. The hope of the new bloom and the light. The feeling of being on the verge of some great unveiling, some beauty arriving to make sense of all the deaths and scarcity. Bitterness taking weight, itself and its cure, something to shape and send out.

*

I'm not very good at reading maps. Or playing chess. I have the ability to do both. But I'm impatient. I want to trust to instinct. So I move quickly. I lose. I get lost.

We were trying to find Wuthering Heights, surrounded by lambs and rams and broken walls. Emily was gingerly stepping around little balls of sheep shit. I wasn't sure I knew my way back so it was best to keep going onwards. The sun had come up glorious. We had stripped off our coats and jumpers.

Then we came to a gate in a large pool of water. I was wearing the waterproof walking trainers that I took to music festivals; Emily's mesh trainers would be soaked through in an instant.

'I'll carry you.'

'You will not.'

'Seriously, otherwise you'll have soaking feet and will want to go straight back. You're only a slip of a thing.'

'I am not.'

'You are. And I don't like to talk about it, but I possess enormous physical strength.'

'No way.'

'Come on. We've gone on holiday to the nineteenth century. Gentleman are always carrying women over obstacles. Think of *Persuasion*.'

'She slips and they become convinced she's dead.'

'But it all works out for the best.'

And with that I put a hand under one arm and one under a knee and picked her up.

'Put me down.'

I slopped into the water. 'Open the gate.'

She fumbled with the latch. I walked through and set her down in the dry.

'That was assault,' she said.

'It was our dignity or your feet's dryness.'

'We're turning back at the next big puddle, that's for sure.'

We headed up another hill and from the top saw the landscape spread out around us, the ground where it was raining and the ground where it wasn't.

'God, I just want to lie down here with you,' I said.

'Paul.'

'Sorry. I don't mean. Just all of this laid out for us. Don't you just want to surrender to it?'

'In the wet and the shit?'

We settled for standing up, watching the hillscape flicker between moods.

I realised we were on the right track when we began to see the signs: the Brontë bridge, the Brontë waterfall, and after a while we arrived at Top Withens, the ruins of Heathcliff's prison. There was no roof. A ram with pink earrings and droopy horns stared mellowly from the doorway.

'Do I get an NUS discount?' I asked him.

Walkers were sitting on the walls, pouring cups of coffee and eating sandwiches. The sun was still out but the wind was picking up and made us put our jumpers back on. We poked around inside, and smiled at the other tourists. When we came out we could see the rain coming in towards us.

On the way back, running out of energy, wishing we'd brought food and water with us, we stopped talking. I was anxious that I wasn't taking us the right way and she kept pulling her phone out and looking at it. But we reached the same gate in its pool of water. I picked her up once more, taking more notice this time of how her legs felt against my arms, exactly how her body filled the small space it had in this world, in my arms, right there. I walked her through the gate and set her down again.

*

The Black Bull is a big old place, with high windows looking out into the damp; full of friendly senior citizens eating pie and chips. We ordered drinks and I asked the young goth pouring them which was Branwell's chair.

'Oh, it's up on the staircase on its own, up there,' she pointed. 'I doubt that's where it was when he sat on it, unless he war a right miserable sod.'

'I've never liked men in pubs who lay claim to their own seats,' said Emily.

*

We stopped to pick up the papers from a newsagent on the way back to the station. 'I'm ready once more to read about the destruction of contemporary society,' said Emily. 'Andrew should have something in today.'

And Sophie too, I thought, and when we were on the train I googled her name to find out where she'd placed her piece about the old betraying the young. I found her radio interview, but higher on Google's ranking was another piece about intergenerational relationships that had also been published a couple of days ago.

THE ETHICS OF THE AGE GAP
Sophie Lancaster

I'm dating a man who is eight years older than me, and I'm wondering what I should think of that. My friends reassure me. We're both young (I'm 25, he's 33). He doesn't look old, just a bit crinkled, like a favourite jacket you wear too much to get round to dry-cleaning. You could not imagine him talking about cars, or investment portfolios, or saying something positive about Jeremy Clarkson.

But I can't stop wondering to what extent I have become complicit in my own oppression. Whether I'm just helping to normalise the idea that older men are still handsome and women in their thirties or older are there to be passed over for younger models, in our cheaply made clothes and vibrant colours, with our youthful idealism to condescend to. Are we Dracula's victims offering the neck too readily?

To think of my newish man as Dracula is a bit rough on him: I am still waiting for him to sink his teeth into me. But older men can be a real threat to our principles: with their picking up of the bill, their neo-liberalist certainties, apathies, their anti-Corbynism and misty eyes at the idea of the centre-left. Move in with us and forget the struggle to transform society into a place where you can afford to rent. Forget your friends. Leave them behind. Our mortgage repayments are very reasonable. (A mortgage! we cry.)

My current squeeze, like a romantic lead in an English romcom, works in a bookshop, and is as broke as I am. So I do not feel much at risk in his case that the patriarchy is purchasing me for its particular aims. (Chance would be a fine thing, I sometimes think, before I remember how lucky I am not to be compromised in this way.)

My older man's age does confer some benefits. He's not as anxious as boys my age about how to present himself. He's decided who he is, or at least what he looks like. He's been around long enough to know a lot of people. He writes for a silly magazine and gets invited to the kind of party where you can drink cocktails for free and get offered drugs by sexual degenerates.

Nevertheless, we always need to ask ourselves to what extent we're willing to sell our youth to the older generation. It's a constant temptation. We have what they want and they have some of what we want. Who can blame a woman for accommodating herself to the best options in a bad world? Let's not talk about blame, but we can do better than this. We have better options than we might think. We won't achieve equality if we sell ourselves cheap; or even if we sell ourselves dear.

While I was reading it, Emily's phone buzzed. 'Paul?' she said. 'Andrew's asked me to ask you something.'

'Yes?'

'Are you romantically involved with his daughter? His words, not mine. There's some article she's written or something that he thinks refers to you. He found it when he was trying to find a radio interview she did yesterday.'

'I've just finished reading that.' I handed her the phone.

'That girl,' she said when she'd finished reading. 'It makes it very clear what she thinks of me.'

'Is that what she's doing? I'm not sure it's about you. I'm not sure I come out particularly well there.'

'So that is you?'

'Unless she's using the outline of my life to disguise a relationship she's having with another man.'

'You and her?'

'It's, um. I didn't know that's how she thought of me. Or if she does.'

'Why didn't you tell me?'

'There wasn't anything to tell. It was just after that ridiculous lunch at yours. We got a taxi together when we were both pissed off with you and Andrew. I did wonder if she was using me to make some kind of statement to you. But, actually, we seem to like each other.'

'What were *you* pissed off about?'

'Being used to stop her from making a scene.'

'I invited you because you'd become a friend. You were supposed to be gone by the announcement. And in what way was that her making a statement to me?'

She looked away from me, out of the window on the other side of the carriage, at all the scenery spending itself.

'She asked me a lot of questions about the nature of our relationship,' I said.

'And what did you tell her?'

'We're friends. She thought she could detect conspiratorial glances between us.'

'Whenever she said something stupid!'

'I said that. And then she got cross.'

'But not so cross.'

'Yeah.' We looked away from each other. 'Well, why shouldn't I?'

'You're right. Why shouldn't you?' She shifted to the edge of the seat.

'It's probably not serious. She's just using me for a column, for some immediate gratification – to annoy her dad, to annoy you. It's not even her real personality in those things.'

'That's even worse, in that case, if she's just faking outrage.'

'It's just, I don't know, like Andrew said, polemics. She knows her audience.'

'If by polemical you mean unconsidered and cynical, then I agree with you. As long as you realise she's just using you to annoy her dad and me. Don't think I'm annoyed. It's got nothing to do with me. Though why would you let yourself be used like that?'

'I'll decide for myself whether I'm being used or not. I don't think it's that simple. I don't know why you are so annoyed.'

'I'm *not* annoyed. Except you lied to me about it. So I am

annoyed about that. It makes me realise you're not honest with me.'

'I thought you'd prefer not to know. I thought I was being tasteful.'

'There was a more tasteful option available to you,' she said, opening the newspaper again. After a minute of staring at the page she got up, told me she was going to make a call and walked down to the rear of the train.

I reread the article on my phone, thought about ringing Sophie, but I wasn't as annoyed with her as I was with Emily.

When Emily returned, she asked me, 'Is that really what people think of me? That I've sold what remains of my youth to Andrew for the privilege of living somewhere nice?'

'Not even Sophie said that. And I don't think his money is what you're most attracted to.'

'It's not.'

'It wouldn't even matter if it were. People are always falling in love with what is convenient to them. The age gap just makes it starker in your case.'

'I'm not with him because of fucking convenience.'

'I know.'

She looked at me, waiting for me to say something else.

'I like Andrew too,' I said.

'*Do* you, really?' she said.

'Yeah, he's been decent to me. He's decided he should put me on the right track. I could take offence at how easily he's concluded that I'm on the wrong track, but, well . . .'

'I can see how his manner might rub you up the wrong way,' said Emily. 'But he's trying to be helpful, and wouldn't you rather have a conversation with someone challenging than one of these bland idiots?' She threw the paper she'd been reading down on the seat beside her. 'He's by far the most intelligent man I know.'

I wasn't going to argue that point. We didn't talk for the rest of the journey.

*

We went to the same pub when we got back to town. I wasn't in the mood to cook. We didn't eat anyway. We drank.

'There's Wozza,' said Emily.

'You're going to know the whole pub after a couple of weeks here without me,' I said.

And there was Joanne too, waving at me from the other side of the bar. I waved back, and she looked at Emily and raised her eyebrows. Emily took a seat and I went to say hi to Joanne on the way to the bar.

'Is that your girlfriend?' she asked, and I told her we were just friends. 'She's beautiful,' she said, and I said, 'Oh, she's all right. You look great yourself.'

'Thanks,' she said. 'How's London? I thought you might call me, invite me down.'

'Would you have come? Would you have been able to? That would have been nice,' I said, after which there was an embarrassing pause. 'What's been happening with you?'

'It's the same old,' she said. 'Have you seen Carl's dad's here?'

I turned in the direction she pointed, where I saw Mike sitting on his own and looking at me. I waved and he nodded. The pub was a lot quieter than it had been yesterday – there were plenty of tables left. The lights were bright and there was a crowd of lads hanging around by the fruit machines. Wozza had walked over to the table Emily had chosen, and was leaning over to tell her something.

'I'll go and say hi to him,' I said. 'I'll come back here too for a proper catch-up.'

'Ah, don't worry. Look after your lass. We're off to the Euston after this – there's a band on.'

'Maybe we'll come over.'

'Maybe see you there. Kevin's back in town though. He gets jealous if he thinks men are trying to chat me up.'

'Surely men and women in this day and age are allowed to exchange pleasantries.'

'Oh, yeah,' she said. 'You just need to point that out to him.' On her way to the door she looked over her shoulder and waved at me.

Mike was looking down at his pint when I walked towards him. 'How are you, Mike?' I said.

He shrugged. 'What are you doing here again?'

'Stuff to do with the house. I brought a mate down to stay there for a few days. How's the family?'

'Oh, they're coping. Janine isn't so good. All this is a distraction, hey?' He picked up the 'Vote Leave' beer mat lying on the table and tossed it down again.

'Yeah.'

'I bet you're not into it, are you?'

'Nah.'

'Why not?'

'It's a load of bollocks.'

'That's what I thought too. They think we're going to get our fishing industry back? It's been dead forty year. Idiots.'

'Yeah.'

'You agree, then? That we're idiots?'

'Don't start this, Mike. I don't think you're an idiot. I don't think a lot of people here are idiots.'

'You're just being polite. Scared. Go on. Admit it. Admit that we're all idiots. Idiots like Carl was. Poor fucking idiots.'

'I better get back to my mate. Carl wasn't stupid.'

'His exam results said he was.'

'Yeah, well.'

'Poor fucker. He found it hard that you could walk away and he couldn't. To see life as stark as that. Everyone sorted into two categories.'

'I had to do some work for those results.'

'But you liked that work, eh?'

'Sometimes.'

'And he didn't. I'm not saying he couldn't have tried more. Of course he could.'

'I wish I'd kept in better touch.'

'He wanted to be someone else.'

'Most people do. He's not the only one to mess up his chances.'

'Yeah. Well.' He looked over where I was looking. 'I hope that's not true. Girlfriend?'

'I wish.'

Wozza had a hand on her shoulder and was bending over to tell her something.

'I think you'd better rescue her. Look after the pair of you.'

'Take care, Mike.'

He raised his fingerless hand and waved bye. 'Too late for that, pal.'

*

Wozza was still there when I got back with the drinks.

'I know you,' he said.

'Yeah,' I said. 'We used to see each other on the beach, back in the day.'

'You used to dance!' he said. 'You danced like Jarvis Cocker.'

'You liked to try to make me.'

'Go on, do it now.'

'No.'

'Go on!'

'Yeah, go on, Paul,' said Emily.

I sat down. Wozza glared at me. 'Only joking, buddy,' he said. 'Plenty of time for that later. Emily and I were just getting to know each other.'

'I'm pleased to hear it.'

I shoved Emily's gin and tonic towards her.

'You're Mr Wright's son, aren't you?' he said.

'Yeah,' I said.

'He taught me English. God, we used to have fun in that class. Worked him right over. What happened to him?'

'He had a breakdown, left us, moved to Liverpool, then died of a stress-related heart attack.'

'Er, right. Good one. Ha!'

'No, he did.'

'Right. Oh. I'm sorry to hear that. He were a laugh. Much better than the other cunts we had.' He stood up. 'I should probably –'

'Was that why you gave him such a hard time?' I said.

'Give over. We were just having a laugh.'

'I remember watching TV when a brick came through the window. "Sorry, Mr Shite," someone shouted. He said he recognised the voice. Was it you?'

'No,' he said.

'He was actually trying to do his best for you all.'

'So? It were his job. He were paid to do that.'

'Come on, Paul,' said Emily.

'I just want you to remember he was a good man; he was a good teacher; he did his best for you.'

'He were the one with a decent job, a decent salary, long summer holidays. If he weren't tough enough, it's not our fault.'

'Decent job? Teaching here? Fuck off.'

'All right, all right. Chill out, pal,' Wozza said. 'Don't start something you'll regret. I'll see you later, my lads are over there.' And he left, turning to give me the hard stare as he walked away, except he clipped a table as he did and stumbled. His mates started laughing and I turned away. If he caught my eye now he would have to fight me; that was the rule.

'Are you OK?' asked Emily.

'I'm fine. Just don't look at him.'

*

I knew Wozza and his friends were staring at me without having to look up.

'What's Andrew doing while you're away?' I asked, moving my chair so I had my back to them.

'Oh, he'll be enjoying himself. Going to all the dinners and drinks parties I don't want to accompany him to.'

'This must be the best time of the year for him. No teaching.'

'Yes, just his PhD students through the summer.'

'He's quite involved with them, isn't he?' I said.

'I suppose so. What do you mean, involved?'

'Friendly. Like the one who came to your launch and his talk. I've seen him with her a few times.'

'Chloe. She was at my launch? I don't remember seeing her. Yes, she's his biggest fan. And you've seen them together elsewhere?'

'Oh, in the shop. And then walking down the street later, going into a hotel.'

'A *hotel*?'

'A hotel bar, you know. It would have been the bar. The Hoxton – we go there sometimes after the pub shuts.'

'You watched them go into the bar.'

'Yeah, I was heading there myself. I even had a chat with him at the bar. This was before I'd met him, but I knew who he was.'

'You've never mentioned that.'

'What was to mention?'

'Right. And they were doing work?'

'I couldn't say. I wasn't spying on them.'

'OK. Really. A hotel?'

'A hotel bar.'

'And you saw them leave.'

'I saw them leave the bar area.'

'The bar area.'

'To go outside, I presume.'

'You presume.'

'Well, they must have done. They went somewhere.'

'Right. Do you want another drink? I certainly do.'

'Yes, please.'

*

I needed the toilet. I went upstairs and stood in front of a urinal. When I heard the door open I didn't look up.

But I could feel someone looking at me. I finished, zipped myself up and turned to face Wozza, who was standing between me and the door. I nodded at him, wandered to the sink, washed my hands and walked over to the dryer.

'You've been here ten minutes,' he said, 'and you start slagging me off straight away. Slagging me off for what I did twenty year ago.'

'Yeah,' I said and turned to face him.

'A lifetime ago. Do you want me to tell you about my life twenty year ago?'

'Yeah,' I said.

'You don't,' he said. 'Trust me about that.'

'You can if you want to.'

'Don't be soft. I came up here to leather you.'

'I wondered.'

He walked forwards and I fought the urge to cringe away. He took my shoulders in his hands and I waited for his head to descend and break my nose.

'I'm sorry,' he said. 'About your dad. He were all right, thinking about it.'

'It's OK,' I said.

He nodded. Then he turned and walked out. I turned the dryer on and rubbed my hands together. I could see my reflection in its chrome. This face that people didn't seem to mind at first: my friendly face, my mixture of Mum and Dad stamped over me. I had been told I looked young for my age.

My hands were dry now. I could believe in general that we were all formed by our past, fed by the soil in which we'd been planted, but I still hoped that if I remained alert I would find a way to be an exception to the rule. I looked at my face again and then I smashed my head against it.

*

My nose had stopped bleeding by the time I got home. I had held my bloody sweater to my face on the walk back, while Emily stroked my back and said reassuring things.

When we got in I washed my face again and opened a bottle of wine my mum might have been saving for Christmas. I poured a glass and took it into the front room and lay on the plush white carpet and imagined it blotting red through. Emily was in the bathroom and I shouted through for her to help herself to wine in the kitchen.

The woman next door was shouting at her children.

I closed my eyes and took careful sips of wine.

'You've got me wondering if it's safe to stay here,' she said.

I opened my eyes. She was standing in front of me in her jeans and walking jumper and socks, holding a glass of wine.

'I might have gone to Cornwall,' she said, taking a seat.

'Not for free, you wouldn't.'

I missed my mouth and a drop of red fell on the carpet. I leaped up and came back with kitchen roll to blot it.

'Are you sure your head's all right?' Emily said.

'I'm fine,' I said.

'Well, let's stay up for a while at least. In case you start behaving strangely.'

'Start?'

'Stop.'

She sat on the sofa and I stayed on the floor. There was a very small CD collection and I put on *Blonde on Blonde*. Gradually my head moved closer to her feet and I felt a strong urge to rest it on them. And then I did.

I couldn't see her face but she must have been wondering how she had got herself in this predicament. I felt wretched. I rolled over and moved my head away. I stood up and sat down on the sofa beside her.

'I'm not going to kiss you, Paul,' she said.

'I'm not going to kiss you either,' I said.

And then we kissed, which was a great relief from having to talk to each other, and after half a minute or so she pushed me away and said, 'No. Sorry.'

Then we did it again, with great surprising naturalness, which might have encouraged a sentimental person to believe that we were fated for each other, and after a bit longer she pushed me away and said, 'No. Sorry. I really mean it.'

I nodded and lay back.

'What a day,' she said.

'Thank you,' I said. 'It's improved considerably.'

'It was a nice kiss,' she said. 'But we can't do it again.'

It wasn't all I wanted. But it was a good enough start. It's like you keep telling me. We achieve our progress in increments.

FIFTEEN

When I get to your place early I have to sit in the bus stop across the road, keeping an eye out for the middle-aged woman who has the slot before me. She comes out at fifty-one minutes past, on the dot, every week. I study her face when she gets out, trying to see if she looks to have undergone significant emotional insight. But the face doesn't reveal such changes easily. She might just as well have come from a dentist's.

I wait a few minutes until she's gone and buzz the door. I'm glad to see you. And you are good at appearing glad to see me. But then we have to talk about my life.

'How do you feel now you've agreed the sale of your mother's house?'

'Bereft.'

There's a long silence between us. I have become familiar with this tactic of yours and have begun to wonder to what extent it is for therapeutic purposes and to what extent you are simply taking a paid break. I'm not saying you're negligent in your professional duties, but you must get weary of listening to all this moaning.

'Aren't you going to ask me something else?' I say.

'You've just admitted to feeling bereft. I'm waiting to see if you say something facetious, if you make a joke about it.'

'What did the salmon say when he swam into a wall?'

'I don't know.'

'Damn!'

You take another minute's paid break before you ask, 'Will you go back much?'

'Home? No. Well, there won't be a home to go to.'

'And how do you feel about that?'

'Oh, well . . . The whole place is poisoned now. Place without an *i*, that is. And not literally, I don't think. The famous fish and chips are in no danger at all. Especially as it's all imported from Iceland.'

'Bereft, you said earlier.'

'Yes . . . Do you think you might ask me about something else now?'

*

I could hear the tapping of a laptop from Emily's room; I brought her a cup of tea and glanced at her screen. She shut the lid and attempted to smile, and I knew it was time to go before she began to consider me a burden.

Before I left town I called for Alan, who was outside on his driveway, washing his car when I arrived. He invited me in and over a cup of tea we spoke awkwardly about Mum, how he was filling his time, the practicalities of selling the house in a depressed market. 'People are talking about reopening the train line here,' he said. 'That would help.'

'Do you think it will happen?'

'I doubt it's a priority, is it?' he said.

When we shook hands to say goodbye, he told me Amy and I would always be welcome to stay with him. 'Don't feel obliged,' he said quickly, when he saw my face.

'No,' I said. 'It's not that. I'd like to. It's only really dawning on me that when we sell the place we'll . . .'

'You both have a place to stay here whenever you want.'

It was something, and I was grateful.

I said goodbye to Alan and shook hands, then I caught a tram to Blackpool, two trains to London.

It was mid-afternoon when I unchained my bike from outside Euston, jumped on the canal at Camden Lock and rode home slowly by the water, dodging all the *flâneurs* on their Sunday stroll.

As I climbed the rickety stairs to the château I knew I was coming back to my real home, and the relief of this inspired the opposite feeling: where the hell was I going to end up in the autumn? I put a record on, opened a window and let the rush of traffic in before I lay on the bed.

When neither Mary nor Jonathan had appeared after an hour, I went looking for signs of their presence. For once the living room was more like a living room than a bedroom; Jonathan's bedding was folded up neatly and the air was what passes for fresh round here. I wondered where he had been sleeping and went upstairs to stick my head around Mary's door. It was the usual mess. I was glad to see no evidence of Jonathan's belongings in the room.

It was my interview for the job at the publisher's in the morning. I thought about what to say, and went to bed early while the house was still empty.

*

'How would you feel about being slightly older than a lot of the entry-level staff?' asked the marketing director, a woman about my own age.

'It's very kind of you to say *slightly*,' I said.

She smiled but I got the sense I might be overdoing the self-deprecation.

'I live in Dalston. Everyone is younger than me every time I leave the front door.'

She kept smiling, politely.

'I'd work hard,' I said, 'and be ambitious, and I'd hope my experience in the world and in the book trade would enable me to distinguish myself and progress quickly.'

This was another of Susannah's set answers. I surprised myself by almost believing it.

She was seeing some other people that week, she said, but she'd let me know.

*

And everyone in London talked about nothing but Brexit. You asked a friend or a customer how they were, and they moaned the word 'Brexit'. Politicians resigned from their jobs and went on holiday to avoid having to think about Brexit. I stopped talking to people whenever possible. For the first three weeks I read everything there was to read about Brexit and then I couldn't digest any more. We joined or left the Labour Party, depending on whether we had been members in the first place. I tried to give up newspapers and retreat to novels. But if you didn't bring up Brexit in the first ten words of a conversation then you knew that the person you were talking to thought you lacked moral seriousness. I wished I was Irish. I had grown up Catholic on the coast of the Irish Sea! I was not Irish in any way at all. And we were probably about to make another mess of Ireland too.

Sophie was about to go on holiday with some of her friends, to a villa that one of their parents owned in Italy. I hadn't been invited, and didn't expect to be, but the idea of lying with her by a pool winded me whenever I thought about it. Helen caught me on the staircase holding my stomach.

'Brexit?' she asked.

Outside the shop the sun was shining all the time. The courtyard filled up with men in shirts and elongated leather shoes. Orange women drank pink wine. Our customers, pushed up against the wall, lit cigarettes and sucked vape machines and made disparaging comments about the fair-weather crowd who had once again stolen their tables and chairs.

When I wasn't at work I rode out to canal-side bars, met friends for beer and pizza, took photos of women with exceptional haircuts. Filed it to Stev'n. Did it again. *White Jesus* had decided against the legal highs column in the face of new legislation; they had replaced it with a cycle-rage page in which Macaulay Culkin drove around with a GoPro camera strapped to his head, trying to provoke tradesmen to abandon their vans and punch him. He had become a viral sensation ('Where's my helmet? At the end of my big dick!') and received a promotion.

Meanwhile, Emily had stayed on at the house longer than the two weeks she'd first suggested. She didn't reply to the first emails I sent to her, and I didn't know if she was going somewhere to check them. Then she sent me a quick one to ask if she could spend two more weeks there, to tell me she was making progress on the novel and wanted to continue working there. *Fine*, I wrote. *Are you all right?*

I'm fine, she said, but little more.

It was during the first of these weeks, while Sophie was still on holiday, that Andrew wrote me an email to ask if I'd meet him for a drink after work one day.

*

The courtyard was still fluorescing, squarely. Men juggled suit jackets, pints of beer and cigarettes. Women in strappy dresses carried jugs of Pimm's. An idea of English leisure summoned with the right props. Red squash and cricket whites, freshly mown lawns. Grass rhymes with arse. Dennis plays tennis.

From the shop counter I watched out for Andrew and when I saw him arrive, overcoat slung over a shoulder, I said goodbye to Helen and finished up for the day.

We shook hands. 'Hi, Paul,' he said, nodding towards the bar, and we walked there together.

'I've been meaning to tell you,' I said. 'I got the job Susannah recommended I apply for. I'm so grateful to you for introducing us.'

'Great,' he said. 'Well done.'

He didn't smile, which confirmed my suspicion that he was here to tell me off. I pretended not to pick up on that. 'Let me buy you a drink,' I said. 'What do you want?'

'I'll come with you.'

There was a tight crowd squashed around the bar. We were wedged together tightly as different sections of the pack expanded to let people out with the drinks they'd bought.

'There are a lot of jugs of Pimm's being ordered,' he observed.

'Yes.'

'Do you like Pimm's?'

'No.'

'Me neither.'

The silence that followed was uncomfortable so I broke it with some inane small talk.

'You won't be handing out glasses of it at your wedding, then?'

'To all six guests?'

'Is that all you'll have?'

'Emily's not had much of luck with her family.'

'How is she?'

'Don't you know? I thought you were in regular contact?'

'Not really.'

'It's hard to get through to her sometimes. Phone signals are dodgy in these places, aren't they?'

'My phone works well there. Must be a network thing.'

'Must be a network thing,' he said.

'Must be,' I said.

'Things have been a little fraught, actually,' he said.

'Right.'

'For reasons I'm going to ask you about.'

'OK. Ask away.'

'Let's get a drink and sit down.'

'OK. But she's all right?'

'Yes, yes. When I get hold of her she says she's working well. She's enjoying the town.'

'The town?'

'Or am I putting words into her mouth? The quiet. She's getting work done. It's kind of you to lend her the house.'

I pretended again that I didn't catch his tone. 'It's nice to have her in there. We've finally had a bit of interest in it, actually. We might be able to sell it soon.'

'Well. That will be a handy bit of cash.'

'My sister thinks that if we club together it will be enough for a deposit on an ex-council flat in very far south-south-east London where I can live and pay the mortgage while we wait for the value to shoot up when it becomes the last place anyone can afford to live. The place she has in mind is called Downhill, which sounds like somewhere in a Dickens novel. I've been sent a list of places she wants me to go and check out.'

'How is your sister? I liked her.'

'She's OK. I hope.'

'Does she always take charge of your life?'

'Let me give her a ring and ask her.'

Either Andrew hadn't noticed I was being witty, or he hadn't considered that I was being witty. He had attracted the barman's attention and was ordering two pints.

'I was going to get those,' I said.

'It's fine.' He handed me my pint. 'Come on, let's get out of here,' he said, leading his way out of the scrum with his right shoulder. We went outside and found a couple of wicker chairs to sit down in next to the shop front of an architect's office.

'Well,' he said.

'OK?'

'Emily asked me whether I'd been sleeping with one of my PhD students. Chloe. Whom we spoke about at the launch.'

'Yes.'

'And with whom you saw me going into a *hotel*, apparently?'

'Yes?'

'And you told Emily you'd seen us going into a hotel?'

'Yes. The Hoxton round the corner from where I work. You and I even spoke at the bar.'

'What?'

'You were in the bar with her. I recognised you. You came over to ask me what I was looking at and bought me a pint. I was reading a biography of George Eliot, which you commented on.'

'Wait, that does ring a bell. That was you? Why've you never mentioned that?'

'You didn't recognise me when Emily introduced us. I wasn't offended. I didn't want to make you feel embarrassed about it.'

'I wouldn't have felt embarrassed. I think I – I remember that! Was that you?'

'Yes.'

'Well, that's *weird*. What were you doing there?'

'Reading.'

The crease in the middle of his forehead deepened. 'Whether you were there or not, it doesn't change what you did. I want to know why you've implied to Emily that I'm having an affair.'

'I didn't do that.'

'It sounds to me like that is exactly what you did.'

'I didn't think you were having an affair. Are you having an affair?'

'No, I'm not, and that's none of your business.'

'Great, then why don't you apologise to me, and stop being so paranoid?'

He spluttered. 'Apologise to you? You've arrived in my life from nowhere, Paul, looking on at me in bars, coming round for lunch – '

'You *invited* me for lunch . . .'

' – and taking my fiancée away for a weekend and installing her in a house after suggesting to her that I'm having an affair! A house she has not returned from. And not only that but you're pursuing my daughter!'

During this speech I had been watching a woman approach us, a journalist who was often in the shop.

'We're about to be interrupted,' I said.

'What?'

'Jenny. That one, there.'

'Oh, yes. She seems familiar. Can you get rid of her?'

'I can try.'

'Paul!' she said, and I stood to kiss her hello.

'This is – '

'I know exactly who this is, that's why I ran over. Andrew Lancaster, so nice to see you again! How do you two know each other?'

'Oh, hello. Yes, you're familiar. How do I know Paul? Paul here is sleeping with my daughter,' said Andrew.

Jenny laughed and patted me on the arm. Andrew stayed sitting down. 'He's such a joker. Are you, Paul?'

'He hasn't said as much,' continued Andrew, 'but my daughter has written a column about it, so we can all enjoy the details. You've probably read it. Perhaps you've even slept with Paul too, Jenny?'

'No! What a question. We haven't, have we, Paul?'

'It probably wouldn't be very memorable,' said Andrew.

'Andrew's a terrific lover,' I said. 'He first made love in the 1960s and has been practising ever since.'

'Oh, fuck off, Paul.'

'This is where I work. You fuck off.'

'Well, I — nice seeing you both,' said Jenny, backing away.

'Sorry, Jenny. I'm afraid this is a bad time,' he said. 'We were just about to have an argument.'

'That's quite OK,' she said, and left, looking over her shoulder to see if we'd come to blows yet. I sat back down and we were quiet until she had disappeared around the corner.

'It was the 1970s,' he said. 'What is happening with you and Sophie?'

'I don't know. I like her. She seems to like me. Ask her.'

'I will. Are you sure about that?'

I stood up. 'Why shouldn't she like me?'

'Oh, of course she likes you: she likes everyone who annoys me. Calm down. Drink your fucking beer.'

I sat back down again.

'Sorry to ask you this, Paul,' he said, 'but I'm going to. Is it Sophie or Emily you want?'

'I didn't know I was being offered the choice.'

'You are not being offered the fucking choice,' he said, standing up himself now.

'Calm down. Drink your fucking beer.'

He sat down and laughed without humour.

'You should be more gracious,' I said.

'I should be more gracious?'

'Why are you so convinced I'm out to steal something from you? For a lucky generation you're not very gracious. Look: they've got nothing, they must be desperate for what we have, let's protect ourselves from them. Let's sneer at their achievements.'

'Your achievements.' He laughed. 'Well, I certainly know how you feel now. I suppose you'd have it that everything *I've* achieved is just down to luck.'

'Sophie wouldn't say it was luck. She'd say it was the deliberate perpetuation of advantage. Exploitation.'

'Sophie is twenty-five years old.'

'Don't you think that might give her more insight than you into what it's like to be young?'

'Oh, it must be so boring to see the world in your terms. Everything a matter of power and justice and unfairness. Privileged vision. No agency. I know it's circumstances that have done this to you, but it doesn't make you any more attractive. At least Emily resists this carping on.'

'Do you mind if I don't state the obvious riposte to that?' My drink was nearly finished now. I was glad about that.

'You and Sophie are adults,' he said. 'Even if you don't act like it. I wouldn't mind what you got up to if I didn't suspect you were gunning for me and Emily.'

'Oh, come on. That's Sophie, not me.'

'I understand how Sophie feels about Emily. It's your position I'm unsure of. What did you say? We've got everything and you've got nothing. Sophie's not a thing, you know? She's not my possession. You don't win something back by having her.'

'Seriously, fuck off.'

He sighed loudly and swept his hair back. 'If I've misjudged things I apologise, Paul, but I can't be a good father and not try to satisfy myself of your motives with Sophie.'

'I like Sophie a lot more than other people seem to. I've really missed her while she's been away.'

He put his empty pint glass down and sighed. 'Perhaps I'm going mad. OK. Let's stop. Let's say no more.'

'Do you want another?' I asked.

'I'm all right.'

'I hope Emily comes back soon,' I said.

'Actually, she's back tomorrow.'

'Tomorrow? Oh, great. She hadn't let me know.'

'Good. I mean, it's good she's coming back. Coming home. I hope you enjoy your reunion with Sophie too. I think. And Paul – the warning goes both ways with her. You might not want to get too attached to her for your own sake.'

I wanted to ask what he meant, but I suspected I knew. Certain relationships take place over borders too bothersome to keep climbing over. He hadn't considered that the age difference might be such a border for him and Emily, or perhaps that's exactly what he was considering and why he was talking this way to me.

'Thanks for your concern,' I said.

When we said goodbye we shook hands, and I held on, feeling how warm and strong his grip was, for now.

SIXTEEN

Towards the end of the session you ask me if I realise I only ever talk about Andrew with a tone of moral disapproval.

'Do I?'

Even though the rest of the time I pride myself on not adopting 'conventional morality'.

'I don't mind conventional morals at all, if they've been given thought. I don't see what that's got to do with it.'

But monogamy isn't important to me, is it?

'It should be for him. I don't know how he has the energy at his age. He'll give himself a heart attack.'

Which is a neat way of avoiding making explicit your judgement.

'What judgement?'

What judgement could I make of him? Of this type of behaviour?

'. . . That he treats Emily badly. That he treats Chloe badly. That conducting non-monogamous relationships is harmful, is that what you're driving at? That there's something compulsive and cruel about it?'

That's what I seem to think.

'Fine. If you insist. Monogamy is the best system we have to avoid hurting people, to avoid chaos. We should all get married as soon as possible.'

*

Sophie and I were texting. She was still on holiday.

You're not bothered about monogamy, are you? she wrote.

Not really. I don't need to own the person I'm with.

I didn't think so.

Why?

I've just been thinking about polyamory. I think I'm a polyamorist.

Right.

And you are too?

I wouldn't put it on my CV. It's a sexual perversion to commit secretly, not a philosophy we should proudly brag about.

You are so old. It is not a perversion!

I don't mean that's a bad thing. Nothing wrong with perversion, not in private. Or in clubs for those with niche interests.

I think it's something we should be honest about. State it proudly. Desire can be an emancipatory force.

So who else do you want to fuck?

The texts had been arriving quickly but the reply to this one took longer to come through.

Er, the thing is, I slept with an old friend last night.

I took some time to think about this and her texts carried on.

Antonio. Please don't mind. It didn't mean anything. We were all quite high.

I thought for a while, about Antonio, and the sitcom he was writing, and his pleasant good manners, his fastidiously clean white trainers, his baby-smooth cheeks, and his earnest penis which he probably popped in a glass of disinfectant when he went to bed at night, and I wrote back, *That's OK. Don't worry.*

You're so enlightened.

You're so slutty.

I don't use that word even ironically.

I haven't ever used it negatively.

That's irlvnt.

I'm sorry.

That's OK.

I'm not sorry.

That's OK too. Given the circumstances. Would you mind if I did it again?

She was good at talking dirty.

I had no idea what she was doing with me.

I suspected I had some idea of what she was doing with me.

But even relationships sparked by malice and anger develop a tenderness to them.

Just please tell me it was only once when you get back.

*

Amy hadn't sounded so approving of me for a long time when I told her I had been offered the job at the publishing house. She came over one Sunday after running her stall on Brick Lane.

'That must have been tiring,' I said.

She was visibly pregnant now, with a neat little bump showing though her jumper above her denim skirt.

'Nah, I just sit down when I need to,' she said. 'And people seem to buy more from me. It's like I've achieved charitable status.'

We were sitting in the kitchen, drinking tea. She looked around her and I saw the wonky cupboard doors and old cooker through her eyes.

'It's a good cooker, that,' I said. 'Much more useful than the modern style. See the grill pan at the top, separate from the oven? That's incredibly useful.'

'I believe you.'

'Because if you're grilling something in the oven, the fat goes everywhere and you have to clean your oven every – '

'I believe you! Though I don't believe that oven has ever been cleaned.'

I did not confirm or deny this.

'I can't believe you're actually going to leave this place,' she said.

'Nor me.'

'It will be good for you.'

'In what way? I will lose all my freedom and have to spend every hour working to pay the rent or the mortgage.'

'*Mortgage*. We can do this.'

There had been movements with Mum's house. Since the price had dropped more people had come to see it and one couple seemed keen. 'They liked Mum's sense of style,' Amy told me. 'Emily's been helpful. She kept the place tidy and let people in.'

'Emily's great,' I said.

'Are you . . .?'

'What?'

'You have a look in your eye.'

'Emily is lovely. Emily is getting married to a man who owns a flat worth close to two million pounds.'

'How do you know how much it costs?'

'I've looked it up.'

'I thought you hated property websites.'

'I despise them.'

'Yeah, well. You can soon have your own two-bedroom bachelor pad to woo her with, if you pay attention to them for a little bit.'

'It's not exactly going to be a babe magnet. This place you're on about is in the middle of nowhere.'

'It has great transport links.'

'It does not.'

'You can be in the centre in half an hour.'

'Thirty-four minutes. One distant corner of the centre. After a quarter of an hour's walk to the train station. It would take forever to get here.'

'What's so good about here?'

'Oh, nothing, I suppose. It's just home, that's all.'

'You need to stop being so sentimental. You need to be realistic.'

'I know.'

'How was your trip home?' she asked, in a softer tone.

'Chaos. It won't even be *home* after we've sold the place, you realise? The house or the town. We'll lose them both at the same time.'

She slapped her hand on the table. Of course she had realised. She'd been trying to get me to realise that ever since Mum died. 'We need to make our own homes now. This' – she looked around her, at the torn lino, the chipped paint and yellowing walls – 'is not it.'

My phone began to ring before I could disagree. Sophie. She was walking past. She was going to pop in.

'Sophie's going to nip over,' I said.

'Sophie? You're still knocking around with her, that one who wrote the column about you?'

'About slumming it with a decrepit hipster, yeah.'

'She's not *home*, either.'

'No, she's round the corner.'

'You know what I mean.'

'Give her a chance. I like her. What about you? Your man in Bristol? The yoga guy.'

'Acupuncturist.'

'That's what I meant. What are you going to do about him?'

'They're not nearly the same thing. But that's my news. I've told him. Ben, his name is. I've told Ben.'

'Wow. What did Ben say?'

'He said, like I suppose was reasonable, "Are you sure it's mine?" though I flew off the handle a bit at the time.'

'Well. He might have responded more sensitively.'

'He might have. Anyway, the violence of my reaction seemed to convince him that it probably was his.'

'Right. And what did the rage therapist say when you told her that?'

'She said, "*Men.*"'

'And the man? What does he think?'

'He says he wants to be involved.'

'Great.'

'He seemed almost pleased after he got over the shock. He's going to come to the next scan, the twenty-week one.'

'Right.'

'Which is weird, right?'

'It doesn't have to be. Perhaps he likes you.'

'I barely know him at all.'

'And now you're, er . . .'

'Stuck with him, yeah. Well, I'm not, as much as my baby is.'

'But you liked him when you met him, presumably.'

'I did. Anyway. He's coming over in a couple of weeks to help get the new flat ready for the baby. Do you want to come and meet him, and make sure he doesn't murder us both?'

'Yes, of course,' I said, and then there was a knock on the door. I went to let Sophie in.

'Sophie, my sister Amy. You met each other briefly at Emily's launch.'

They smiled at each other and Sophie looked down at Amy's bump. 'Wow,' she said. 'Wow.'

Amy smiled again. 'I was just about to leave.'

'Congratulations.'

'Thanks.'

But on the way out Amy took some time running over the plan again for buying a place, to make sure I understood, and was convinced, and knew what I would need to do – and Sophie, who had sat down on the kitchen counter, grew restless while she did.

'Property, property, property,' she muttered.

'I'm sorry,' said Amy.

'Oh, don't mind me.'

'OK.'

'Just remember that it's property investors who are killing this city.'

'If you were listening,' said Amy, 'we were talking about a plan to use the small amount of money we'll get from our mother's house as a deposit to buy somewhere for Paul to live. This money from a house which she paid for by working as a teacher for her entire adult life.'

'Then why do you keep going on about what a great investment it is?'

'Am I right that you live . . . with your mother, I think Paul mentioned?'

'Yes. Because I can't afford to buy somewhere because of all the speculators and buy-to-letters.'

'I sympathise. London townhouses are so expensive these days. You might as well live at your mother's until you can inherit it. But, you know? I'm currently seeing a therapist so I don't stress my unborn baby out, so I definitely will go now and catch up with Paul later on the phone.'

Sophie looked down and carried on reading, as if she hadn't heard her. Perhaps she was embarrassed.

When I had seen Amy down the fire escape and come back, Sophie said, 'She doesn't like me.'

'Well. She'll come round.'

'I don't care. All that property talk is so boring. And immoral. You'd agree with me if she weren't your sister.'

'And she'd probably like you more if you didn't act like such a superior cunt to her.'

*

After that argument finished we went out for dinner and when we came back we continued to avoid talking about what had happened with Antonio by having a debate in bed about gender, inspired by a Facebook thread I was reading over her shoulder which discussed an article about 'Books No Woman Should Read'. It was nothing to get annoyed about, dashed off in response to a dull compilation of 'great novels' by men published in *Esquire* magazine that didn't include the words 'by men', and the tone of the article that everyone was discussing seemed intentionally glib, in keeping with the hack work it was attacking and parodying, though the people commenting on it took it as literal, the law. Eager men who were keen to demonstrate they did not hate all women joined in the conversation to announce that they would never read a book by Saul Bellow or John Updike, not never again, but never at all.

I made the mistake of wondering out loud to Sophie whether one of the great damages men might have done to women was to make it natural for them to believe anything bad that is said about men. All the arrogant explaining which many of us have been guilty of, the complacent interruptions, the forceful articulation of our perspective on things – the existence of this recognised to the extent that it is impossible to disagree about an overstatement of the case without seeming to prove the overstated case itself.

'And this aspect of gender inequality is most pressing, is it?' asked Sophie.

'I knew you were going to say that!' I said. 'It's rhetorical brilliance. Now I feel like I'm deeply sexist for mentioning it. So all I can do is shut up.'

'Why don't you? Or you could read the whole book by her instead of getting annoyed by what some idiots say on Facebook about one article? Practise what you preach?'

'Fine!' I said. I took the book off her shelf, made a show of finding a pencil, lay down next to her and started reading.

*

Wandering around a gallery on a day off I mooched along behind a woman pushing a buggy, thinking of how similar she looked to Monica from behind. I felt so thirsty looking at her, not only for Monica and the woman who resembled her but also for the melancholic feelings she flooded me with, for those memories that were delicious in their painfulness, memories that became harder and harder to reach and which I didn't want to drift away from more than I had already. I don't know what I expected to gain from this doomed internal record-keeping. Numbness and forgetting should be coveted. But I still tried to remember as vividly as I could what her skin had felt like next to mine. I wished we had made porno-graphic videos together; we had not been early adopters of smartphones, or digital cameras. How foolish and smug we had been about avoiding the fads of technology and now I could not summon a picture of her naked in bed. Nothing about the sheets we slept in, the underwear she put on in the morning. I remembered her voice very well, the way it veered from a drawl to the singing brightness of a good student in a good school explaining something she'd learned. We used to speak a lot on the phone. I knew what her voice sounded like in bed, in separate beds, across a line. I could make it speak to me even now.

The woman stopped to lean over the buggy and I side-stepped, and —

'Monica?'

A miracle. My saviour.

No. It wasn't her. It never would be.

SEVENTEEN

'Let's try this again,' you say. 'Can you give me some examples of when you don't feel in control of your anger? You don't need to say why, just when. Take all the time you need.'

Arguing with Amy, of course. I go from disagreeing with her about something trivial and specific – the exact definition of homeopathy, for instance – to letting her know about everything she does that I think is stupid, pointing out every detail I can think of that might confirm her anxieties about herself. She does this to me too, by the way. And it's she who starts it.

Then there're cars. Fucking drivers. Having to chase cars down who've driven too close or beeped at me, and bang on their windows at traffic lights and demand an apology. It's dangerous. Shouting at them on the Kingsland Road, holding up the traffic, reaching into my pockets for my keys to threaten to gouge a chunk out of their paintwork. Not just cars, bikes too. Cyclists who say something, try to hurry me on. Punching one of them once, twice, punching two cyclists once, the last more of a push, a shoulder shove, it was meant to be. Inventing a dead friend. They take your anger more seriously if they think it comes from grief. It jump-starts their deadened imagination.

But I am grieving? Well, maybe.

It was impossible to argue with my dad after he left. He'd just sigh and put the phone down. Impossible not to argue with my mum. About anything. She was always asking questions about him. I didn't want to even think about him. She'd keep asking. She didn't have to ask for my loyalty, she knew we were loyal, never asked us to take sides. But because we couldn't argue with him we argued with her. We all tore into each other. About anything. Literally anything. The reasonable volume of the music I was playing. The corruption of one's finer being through the endless perusal and discussion of online property listings. The treatment of women. The treatment of people.

The empty skies. The money gone. The going home. The blank account, the bruised fist. The swept glass. The sudden bangs and shouts in the night. The pain of others. The power-lessness to stop their pain. The stopping the starting the stopping. The man beeping his horn behind her. The fucker beeping his horn and thinking you wouldn't do anything about it. I really feel sometimes like I could hit someone. I really feel sometimes like I could kill someone.

There should be some kind of justice. Don't you think there should be?

'Take all the time you need,' you say.

*

It had been a couple of years since I had helped Amy decorate a place. She had to be pretty desperate to ask me to lend a hand; her days as an art student had made her far more skilled in painting and decorating, in knocking stuff together out of MDF. Every time she asked me to help I remembered how badly we had fought on the last occasion, and determined that this time would be different. It was a generous thing for a brother to do, a brother who often felt in need of ennobling himself, and on those mornings I would skip off to meet her. But when I arrived, my envy that she had found a way to buy and live in these places would provoke me into saying something about the need for legislation to prevent people making all this money out of buying and selling and renting property, on the pressing need to redistribute wealth.

'Well, thank God we have people like you, willing to redistribute your wealth to landlords and the Albanian mafia,' Amy would say. 'When there are such scumbags out there, saving their money and trying to pull themselves up.'

Then I might point out that she was just lucky to get her timing right, and she'd say I was born two years before her, and I might say I was busy thinking of things more important than money, and she'd say nightclubs? haircuts? ecstasy? and ask me where that had got me, and I'd say – well, and where has all the money you saved and earned got you?

Calmer and better decorating would be done if I absented myself. We would eventually agree this, but not calmly.

*

But I felt optimistic as I biked across the park to her new flat, a couple of miles from the one she'd just sold for nearly three times the price she'd paid for it ten years ago. I was becoming more and more aware how ordinary my aspirations were, how I admired wealth in those depths of the heart that are immune to convictions. I believed, like Sophie, that no one should own their own house, except for all the beautiful young parents chasing their children round the playground on the top of the hill, those mothers caught in the golden light of a catalogue's autumn range, these bearded fathers with slight tummies over Japanese jeans, a bright advert for the urban dream, a Brooklyn here on earth. I wanted to be one of them, to circumscribe my life with bricks and money and the proximity of green space.

Amy's new place was the bottom floor of a big detached house facing the park. I saw the man who must have been Ben the acupuncturist through the window, on a stepladder, painting the ceiling with a roller.

*

He was a small guy, shaven-headed, with a calm demeanour that would be reassuring for people who were going to let him put pins in them. You wouldn't want me to put pins in you, I'm sure you've already come to that conclusion. When Ben shook my hand his black T-shirt and baggy trousers made me think of martial arts pyjamas.

'It's nice to meet you,' I said.

'You too.'

'Thank you for helping Amy decorate.'

He watched me warily as I held his hand.

'Is there another roller?' I said. 'Do you want a hand?'

Amy had only got into the place yesterday and it was a mess, with peeling wallpaper in the process of being ripped down, and stained carpets being ripped up. Amy was not interested in buying places which she could not immediately improve the value of through sudden intervention. An old woman had been living in it with her dog for years. The garden was full of vicious brambles and burst bin bags. The ceilings were the colour of the inside of a teapot. All easy to solve with a bit of hard work, so she said. There was a skip outside and I set about pulling up the carpets in the bedrooms.

As we worked Amy explained to me about testing the market, about making low offers for houses you weren't sure you wanted to move into.

'I don't like the sound of that,' I said.

Amy stared at me.

'We'll discuss things after I've seen the places,' I said. I was going to jump on my bike and look round some flats that afternoon.

Her bump had really grown in the last few weeks.

'I'm not sure you should be doing this,' I said, after we had got the last of the carpet up. 'Can't you get some help?'

'You and Ben are helping.'

'Paid help.'

'I don't have the money.'

I bet she had the money. It was her thinking that she didn't have the money that meant she did have the money and it was me thinking I had the money that meant I didn't have the money. It was unlikely we'd ever reconcile our different valuations of the rewards of being prudent.

'We'll get through it in no time,' she said.

She was lying. It was going to take some time. Still, I had time, for now. After we'd finished painting the living room and stripped some more wallpaper from the hallway I got on my bike and set off to Downhill for the first of the viewings.

*

I rode through rows of Victorian terraces, then over the South Circular where things got shabbier and more modern. I traced the length of two long cemeteries, and then I was riding uphill to Downhill, wondering what that said about the optimism of the people who had named the place. Though of course, downhill is an easier journey than uphill. It's not all negative connotations. Off a road of chicken shops and nail bars I climbed my way through an estate of small pebble-dashed houses much like the estates my school friends had lived in, one hundred and fifty shades of brown. It was as quiet as those estates too, the middle of the day. Concrete driveways and cars, tradesmen's vans parked up, the occasional senior citizen pulling a two-wheel shopping trolley.

I liked the last flat the estate agent showed me. It was on the ground floor of a council block, with a large living room, two bedrooms and a kitchen with a door leading out to a strip of grass. I walked to the end and turned around and a man smoking on the balcony above raised his hand in a greeting I returned. 'Good afternoon!' I shouted. 'Good afternoon!' he shouted back, in an Eastern European accent.

'Is this is a nice place to live?' I said.

'Ah,' he said. 'I don't know. Are you nice? I am nice.'

'Great neighbours, see,' said the estate agent. 'Very friendly.'

'I'm nice,' I shouted back at him.

'Are you sure?' he shouted. 'You don't look nice.' Then he grinned.

A patch of grass to lie on, on a summer's day. A neighbour to wave at. A lawnmower. That paint you put on fences. Raking up the leaves in autumn. Barbecues with friends. A woman to come home to. A child to take to the park on a Saturday morning. It was not entirely implausible. Or undesirable. Not entirely.

*

On my way back to Amy's, I went by a park at the peak of the hill and stopped to look down at the city, at my life for the last fifteen years as a distant sparkle on the horizon beyond Canary Wharf. I typed the château's postcode into Google Maps – twelve miles away as the crow flies. An hour and ten minutes' cycle, an hour and twenty by public transport. If I moved here I would hardly ever go back again, and I wouldn't meet the same sort of people when I went out, the earnestly cool people, the anxiously fashionable young who were as optimistic and decent and vain and self-obsessed as any other people and who I condescended to only out of my worst instincts. The people I talked to when I smoked outside bars, those who I liked much more than I disliked. How much older would I become without them around me? Amy's theory was that exactly these people would move here, and open cafés and bars and bike shops, and we'd sell the flat to them for a decent profit, doing our little bit to make the city expensive for them and survivable for us. But when I looked at these interwar terraces squatting sullenly, I saw what a long-term project this might be, longer than my lifetime. The most sensible young people would abandon London for the west and the north, this country for Berlin and Lisbon and Athens, if they still could, long before they colonised this far. Start again. Declare the place finished. Even London could not be entirely gentrified. People in my position should have taken heart from this but we were conflicted. The wall had been low enough for us to look over at the enemy; a part of us wanted to climb over and forgive them if they promised not to set the dogs on us.

*

Amy was on her own when I got back.

'Where's he gone?' I said.

'He's gone to meet a friend for a couple of hours.'

'You haven't fallen out already, have you?'

'No. He was always going to do that. There's nothing romantic happening,' she warned me.

'Do you want there to be?'

'In this state?'

'Well, it is his baby. Doesn't mean there can't be romance.'

'I'm not thinking any further than this.' She put her hands on her stomach. 'Now tell me about the flats.'

I told her about them. We looked again at the one I liked online, and then I rang the estate agent to make an offer, at a price dictated by Amy, who would go round and see the place for herself the next day. The estate agent said she'd get back to me.

'So this is great,' I said, looking around at her furniture covered in plastic sheeting, at paint and tools and unpacked boxes. 'What do you do when you want to relax? Paint sitting down? Lie down to varnish the floorboards?'

She put her head in her hands. 'I know,' she said. 'What have I done?'

Just what she always did. Inflicted something exhausting on herself. Deferred immediate comfort for future comfort. Tried to correct the balance, to even the score. Behaved responsibly.

'I'm so tired,' she said.

'Go to sleep,' I said.

'I can't. There's so much to do.'

'Let me do it.'

'You don't know what you're doing.'

'Just tell me what to do. I can do it.'

With reluctance and some gratitude she went to bed and I carried on painting. The windows were open and the street was quiet outside, except for the rattle of a magpie. My painting arm grew heavy. After an hour the acupuncturist knocked on the glass.

I let him in. 'How was your friend?' I asked.

'Fine,' he said.

'Where does he live?' I said.

'She,' he said. 'Lauren. Streatham.'

'An old friend.'

'An old friend, exactly.'

I looked at him.

'This is a bit weird,' he said. 'I feel like you're a disapproving father I need to make like me.'

'Sorry. I don't disapprove. I'm just interested in you, in a suspicious way.'

'Suspicious.'

'Just in a brotherly way. Let's put the radio on. Maybe I should get us a couple of beers to have while we work?'

I got us a four-pack from the local corner shop and we listened to Gilles Peterson's show while stripping wallpaper and painting.

'Amy says you work in a bookshop,' he said.

'For a few more days.'

'Oh, yeah?'

'I've got a new job starting soon.' I heard the words 'digital marketing' come up my throat with thick inverted commas round them.

'That's good?' he said.

'I don't know,' I said. 'It could be an awful mistake. But you probably have to make some mistakes to stop yourself from making other mistakes.'

'Yeah,' he said. 'That's what I've been thinking recently too.'

By the time we'd finished the beers we'd transformed the long hallway and living room into a clean white space, and revealed wooden floorboards that would look good when sanded and polished. We took a break and he came outside into the garden to talk to me while I smoked.

Later, as the light began to fade and we carried on working, Amy opened the door of the bedroom she had gone to sleep in and pulled her head back in shock at the work we'd managed to get done.

'Wow,' she said. 'Thank you.'

EIGHTEEN

We have gone through tactics of how to avoid interrupting people and, in doing this, accelerating arguments beyond the point of recovery. So I am sorry that I continue to interrupt you sometimes.

' – Do you really believe in that term?' I ask. 'Self-medication?'

Because surely, I say, the desire to go out, lose one's inhibitions, make new friends, dance around, kiss strangers – surely that's mostly a desire to enjoy our finite and beautiful lives, rather than the need to replace some sort of absent prescribed pharmaceuticals and therapy that are the correct way of compensating for our mortality?

You shrug. I press my advantage. 'Don't you want to do that sometimes?'

'Of course I do,' you say.

'Do you?'

'Yes.'

'What are you doing on Friday?'

You shake your head. 'Certainly not the kind of thing you mean. I'm far too old for that kind of thing now.'

'You're no older than me.'

'You know – if you were seeing a Lacanian analyst, that might be the moment she would stop the session.'

Which I thought was a bit below the belt of you.

*

Our second offer for the flat in Downhill was accepted. And so was somebody else's for the château. We had to be out of there by the start of October. Jonathan's stuff was still in the house but he had not been home ever since one night when he had gone out to meet Julia, so it appeared his campaign to win her back was progressing. It was quiet in the evenings without him, even when Mary was around. She had quit her job in the bar and was seeing less of Nathan. 'I've no idea where he is,' she snapped, when I asked if she'd seen Jonathan. She had been reacting strangely to the mention of his name ever since the night they went out together to the summer party. I had offered her the spare room in Downhill for a cheap price, but not so cheap, she said, that it would encourage a woman in her mid-twenties to move from the twenty-first century to the 1930s. She had started going for interviews in small living rooms, with twenty-somethings who asked her what she liked watching on Netflix and what she thought she would bring to their household.

'Er, rent?' she said, pouring the last of a bottle of wine we'd been sharing. 'Seven hundred and fifty pounds a month for that little box room you've just shown me. Isn't that enough? I know, I know: they're all paying the same. They're not the ones I should be angry with: they're just trying to check if I'm tidy and sane; trying to claim some power for themselves and act like the middle managers they aspire to become one day. They're the same as me, the same as all of us, we're all fucked. And you and Jonathan have ruined me for normal company. I think there's something sinister going on if someone isn't questioning my decisions, or talking in the world-weary voice of a man who's lived for a thousand years.'

'Thirty-four thousand next week,' I reminded her.

*

To celebrate my birthday and commiserate the end of our time living together we blagged our way onto the guest list of a dance music festival in Victoria Park. Sophie was going with her friends, also on freebies. For us fringe members of the media class, this was the closest we could come to feeling like the tax exiles or expense-fiddling MPs we despised and envied, and we took on a certain hauteur as we approached the gates en masse and headed to the guest entrance, looking on with horror at the longer queues for those who had paid to get in.

I did not feel superior for very long. My friends put their heads down and scattered into the festival when a sniffer dog lunged for my trousers.

*

'Do you have any drugs in your possession, sir?' asked the owner of the drug dog, and when I denied I did he explained that because the dog could smell what she thought were drugs on me I was going to have to be arrested and strip-searched. The dog was delighted with herself, the little snitch. 'Have you taken any drugs recently, sir? Could that be it?'

Oh, yes, I said. 'I spilled a line of coke on these trousers last night, just there where your dog was sniffing. That must be it.'

'That would explain things,' he said, reasonably, and he led me away to a curtained-off cubicle inside a tent. Here I consented happily to taking all my clothes off, all the while apologising for putting him out. It is no doubt because I am a white man, university educated, with the polite and helpful manner of a bookseller, that my experiences with the police have been positive, even when the situation has been negative. I admire their sense of purpose and the camaraderie they have with each other, and whenever they are processing me for whatever misdemeanour I have committed I always think how much I might like to join their ranks, if only I hadn't just been caught doing something that precluded me from ever joining their ranks. 'It can't be very pleasant for you, this,' I said, as he shone his torch up my bum.

'Oh, you get used to it,' he said. 'If the person's cooperative, it's a quick process.'

The last thing my man did, now that I was fully dressed again, was to check the contents of my pockets, pulling up a couple of tubes of filter tips from my box, and glancing down inside.

'Are you working late?' I asked, as though he was an Uber driver taking me home.

'Just till teatime,' he said, and whether he spotted those small bags stuffed at the bottom of the packet or not he behaved just as if he hadn't.

'I'll have to walk you through the gate,' he said. 'Or the dogs will go for you again. I'd stick your jeans in the wash when you get home if I were you.'

*

By the time he had escorted me through the dogs, I had long lost Mary and Sophie and the rest of the gang. The next twelve hours went by in what seemed like an hour or two. I began to worry the police officer had seen my drugs after all and had me followed, so that I would lead him to my friends and he could arrest us all, and me for supply rather than possession. He had extracted a code from my phone upon arresting me, so I turned my phone off, locked myself in a Portaloo and destroyed a substantial part of the incriminating evidence, then I went to work to find some subjects for the *London Review of Haircuts.* The friendly city is at its friendliest in such places. Becky was blonde and slightly taller than me. Annie was smaller but equally dramatic, with big mahogany eyes rimmed with kohl like smudged flames. They helped me destroy some more of the evidence and we became a three-person production team. I had to turn my phone on again to take photos, which they assured me would be fine in flight mode; they had seen a documentary about moped gangs that snatched phones and so long as they had flight mode on they couldn't be tracked, at least not by normal police. Before I switched to flight mode I checked for messages or missed calls from Sophie or Mary, but there were none; phones were never reliable in such congested places. Then we took more photos, shakier photos, as we continued to dutifully destroy the evidence of my crime, until all traces of guilt had vanished completely, and my new friends and I could knock off for the day and enjoy ourselves.

*

I began to experience time in jump cuts. Sophie appeared, with one hand in the back pocket of a taller man than me, so tall that her arm must have been getting tired. 'We thought you were in prison!' she said. 'This is Jack; Jack, this is the man I was telling you about.'

'You *do* have an open relationship,' said Becky, who earlier had said to me, 'That's what all men with girlfriends say when they get you alone in a Portaloo.'

While the tallest members of the group introduced themselves, Sophie went to kiss me and I turned my head. 'I don't know where you've been,' I said.

'If you're good, I'll tell you later. Where have *you* been?'

'Cubicles. Police cubicles, Portaloo cubicles. A man made me take my clothes off and looked up my bum.'

'A policeman or a new boyfriend?'

'A policeman. I didn't ask him out; he was very professional. Becky and her friend have been helping me get rid of what nearly became police evidence.'

'How on earth did you get away with it?'

'I have an influential daddy. I'm going to write a column about the injustice of it as soon as I get home.'

'Plagiarist.'

Sophie's new friend was lighting my new friend's cigarette.

'He's handsome.'

'He is.'

'Aren't you going to say, "So are you"?'

'You're very handsome. I adore you.'

'Really?'

'Come on. Your eyes are like saucers. Let's get a beer.'

*

I was hugging Rochi. I hadn't seen her since she'd curtailed my expectations. She was beautiful. She was – where was she? I'd lost her.

*

And whoosh. Mary was on the phone. I was still on my own. 'Meet me in –' 'You're cutting out!' 'Nathan's not –' 'I can't hear you!' ' – you a text!' 'I'm not getting texts! Hello! Hello!'

*

Text received 7.04 p.m.: *Meet me by the mixing desk opposite main stage at 7.30. I'll wait for you there. Nathan off with new gf. Jonathan doesn't reply. I'm on my own, having shit time. Please come!*

*

I was dancing on my own by the mixing desk of the main stage, hoping Mary would come along, though I'd arrived twenty-five minutes late. A woman in a vest with I Have No Tits written across it put her finger in a baggie and offered it to me. I sucked it. Disgusting. Thank you very much. Have some of my beer. Let's get more beer. I like your T-shirt. I like your glasses.

Into the VIP area, where there was no one important, just Stev'n, Macaulay Culkin and Jerry the Deviant. The toilets were magnificent. Kissing. More kissing. Mouths too dry. We needed beer to kiss. Back to the bar for beer. Hello! said Stev'n! Hello! said Becky! Hello! said Sophie! Into the toilets again with her. I Have No Tits disappeared, never to be seen again. Hello! said Sophie's tall irregular man. He was wearing a hat he was not wearing before. All together now.

*

The music stopped and we were on the streets again, clanking down the road with some of our new friends and enemies, carrier bags full of beer and Prosecco, ice and Irish whiskey. Stev'n's flat was at the top of an old warehouse on Dalston Lane.

Where are you? said my phone, which had 3 per cent battery left.

Stev'n's. Want to come? Just round the corner from ours. Flat 8, 2 Dalston Lane.

No answer before the phone died.

No Mary either.

Smoking with the taller man on the long balcony all the length of the big open living room. The rasp of a nitrous oxide machine from the other end of the balcony where a boy and a girl giggled under a blanket.

'So I just go in buildings and value them up. By space, mostly, times area value. Age. Here, Sophie, she says you two, you're not, er . . .?'

'Something in-between.'

'What, like . . .?'

'I really don't know what like.'

*

Stev'n and Culkin had set out various plates of drugs in the bedroom and this had taken most of the people out of the living room to ingest them. Becky and Annie were queuing to do lines off a chest of drawers. The walls were covered with blow-ups of *White Jesus* shoots. A girl in cut-off dungarees and chunky men's shoes, lying on her front across the seats of a Tube carriage. A woman in a white dress and bright blue eye make-up covered in cockroaches. A woman in a 1950s housedress kneeling in front of an open oven. A sexy female soldier carrying a gun. A photographic tribute to John William Waterhouse, except the woman is carrying a large rock into the water with her. The white legs and broken body of a woman taken from the balcony from which she has jumped. The en-suite bathroom with its door open which Stev'n said women can use only if they don't close the door. 'Just joking!' he said, when Becky and Annie said in which case they were leaving.

'You better had be. Jesus, what is that? That's not coke,' said Annie.

'You wanted coke?'

'You *told* me that was coke,' she said.

Macaulay Culkin laughed and fell back on the bed. 'That's ketamine, baby.'

The walls were painted pale pink. A wardrobe covered one side of the wall, full to the brim with shirts decorated with small skulls, and jewellery made from the small skulls of animals, tortured and killed by Stev'n, and a collection of ankle socks worn by the models on his covers. Annie said she couldn't stand up any more.

'Here, this is coke,' offered Stev'n.

But we didn't let Annie have any. Becky and I propped her up and walked her back to the sofa in the living room.

'I can see myself from a camera in the corner of the room,' she said. 'I can see I'm the village drunk but can't do anything about it.'

And then she started to be sick into a carrier bag that I grabbed quickly and Becky held for her while I rubbed her back.

Sophie came in to check on us. 'Was that an accident?'

'We don't know,' said Becky.

'I doubt it,' I said. 'Let's leave. This is a horrible party. I can't believe I work for this prick.'

'He's totally vile,' said Sophie. 'But it's quite interesting to study him. Perhaps I'll write about him.'

The surveyor came in and said he had in his possession what he knew one hundred per cent to be coke.

'Can I have some?' said Sophie.

'Sure. I'll put some out in the other bedroom.'

Sophie left to have a 'quick line with him'.

I carried on talking to Becky. Stroking Annie's head. Becky called an Uber for them.

We took an arm each and walked down the stairs together to the taxi.

'Thanks for all your help.'

'I'm sorry you met me. You wouldn't have ended up here otherwise.'

'It's not your fault. We often end up in places like this.'

I kissed them both goodbye and made my way back upstairs.

I opened the door of Stev'n's room and looked in. Everyone horizontal. Plates being passed round. No Sophie.

I tried the other bedroom door. The lights were off. Two shapes were wrapping around each other on the bed.

'Paul?' said Sophie.

*

There was one thing I needed to do before I left.

One, two, three plates into the bowl of Stev'n's en-suite toilet.

'What the fuck did you do that for?' asked Culkin, and started to laugh.

'You fucking mummy's boy,' said Stev'n.

Someone else was fishing them out of the toilet. 'I think some of it's salvageable,' he was saying.

'We'll just ring some more in, you twat,' said Stev'n. 'Fucking mummy's boy. You're finished at the magazine.'

'I'm finished,' I agreed, and turned to take down the framed image next to me of the woman's body broken stylishly. Stev'n stood up and sat back down as I made as if to swing it into his face. I thought about stepping out on to the balcony and hurling it off, but I would probably kill someone, or it would end up on Instagram as an artistic gesture in the magazine's name, so I tucked it under my arm instead and left the flat.

*

When I got home Mary was lying on the sofa that had until recently been Jonathan's bed. She was wearing a dress and I found a blanket to put over her legs. There was a mouthful of white wine left in a glass resting on the carpet. She had not taken her trainers off, and they were lightly scuffed with grass stains. I rested the photo I had stolen against a wall.

'Are you asleep?' I said.

'Yes,' she said, not opening her eyes.

'Are you playing it cool and pretending you're not delighted to see me?'

'I can't see you. I would have liked to see you a lot earlier.' She opened her eyes. 'What the fuck is that thing?'

'I stole it from Stev'n. It's a photo of a model posing as a woman committing suicide.'

'Is that what you want?'

'To die?'

'No, do you want beautiful women to die? Is that what men secretly long for?'

'I don't know: I'm not men, I'm me. I don't want anyone to die.'

'Not anyone?'

'Well, one or two men, but no women who I can think of. Don't worry, I stole it to destroy it, not to hang it on our wall. What's up with you, anyway? What happened to Nathan?'

'We met up. Then he introduced me to his new girlfriend.'

'New girlfriend? But he's in love with you.'

She sat up and put her hand on my arm. 'Do you think he is?'

'It seemed obvious to me and Jonathan.'

'Jonathan.'

'I thought so too.'

'Well, I did too. I think we were wrong.'

I made us both a cup of tea and added one sugar to each, an emergency measure. Nathan had never made a move, she told me. They would share a bed sometimes and she could feel how he wanted her, and how much she liked knowing that, and how she would have responded if he'd touched her, but she wasn't in a hurry for him to touch her. 'I wasn't totally sure I wanted him until I realised I couldn't have him. I thought we could take things easy until something happened. I wanted to be free for a bit longer.'

We had forgotten that freedom was more important as a means than an end. Sophie didn't call but during the three hours I stayed up talking to Mary I tried not to think about her, only suffering the occasional juddering vision of what might be happening. I was too embarrassed to tell Mary about the invitation I had turned down.

'I saw Jonathan with his wife earlier,' she said, and then she told me what I had suspected; that she had slept with Jonathan on the night he was thrown out of the Serpentine party for forcibly kissing his wife's new boyfriend, and that Mary had spent some time before and after imagining what it might be like to be his girlfriend.

'So they're definitely back on?' she asked me.

'Looks like it. He's not been back here for days now.'

I made us some more tea and she played me some of the new music she was promoting for her record label. We lay side by side on the sofa, her facing away from me. I had my head in her hair and my arms round her.

'Are you sad about selling your mum's house?' she asked me at one point.

'Desperately,' I said.

'That's what you have to do though, isn't it?'

'Yes.'

'What was she like, your mum?'

'She was nice. What about yours?'

'Stop deflecting me. You never talk about her. What was she like?'

'I don't know how to start. She was decent and self-sacrificing. That's not interesting, is it? If she was uptight it was only about the unimportant things. The little worries. She was open-minded. Thought for herself. Didn't perform the expected emotions. Forgiving. Anti-establishment. When I was fifteen and on study leave for my GCSEs we all went round to a mate's house for a party while his parents were at work, and I put on one of his dad's suits to go to the off-licence and buy booze for us all. You know, seventeen cans of Stella, five cans of cider, three bottles of Mad Dog Twenty-Twenty kiwi flavour – a standard office party. The police picked me up on the way back and I got suspended. The policeman came over that night to see Mum. I don't know where my dad was. The policeman started to lecture me. "You know what you've done," he said. "You've destroyed the trust between you and your mother." "No, he hasn't," Mum said. "Let's keep things in perspective." She was loyal to me and Amy. He'd brought the carrier bags of booze over with him. "Would you like me to destroy these?" he asked. " No," she said. "We'll do that for you." The look on his face. You don't realise what it's like to have someone who's always on your side until you don't any more . . .'

I spoke about her for a while and then Mary told me about her friend who had died in the cycle accident. She showed me Instagram photos of them riding mopeds around a Greek island, and I pretended I hadn't already looked at them. I was touched by the way they publicly adored each other. Mary's last post on Facebook was the funeral arrangements for her friend, in a church in a village in Norfolk.

'I lied about my friend dying,' I said to her. 'When we first met. I didn't have a friend who died.'

Her head was on my shoulder and I was stroking her hair. She looked up at me, confused. 'What are you talking about?'

'Oh, nothing. It doesn't matter.'

We must have fallen asleep then. I woke up in the night with my arms around Mary and didn't know who she was at first. Then I woke up in the morning and she was gone.

NINETEEN

We talk about my mother. We talk about my father. The tissue box stays unused. I know I'm being a poor sport here.

'How would people describe *you*, do you think?' you ask.

'It depends which people,' I say.

'Colleagues, friends, family.'

'They'd . . . I'd hope they'd say I was kind, sympathetic, honest.'

'Honest?'

'Yes.'

'Because you seem to relish telling me about your slippery behaviour with Emily and Andrew.'

'I don't relish it at all. Do I? Maybe I've read too many old novels.'

'What do you mean?'

'The duplicitous hero, rising from the bottom to the top. It's a consoling fantasy.'

'But you don't really aspire to that, do you? To being a liar who tricks people to get on?'

'No. *No*.'

'In an earlier session you said you hate good people, good guys.'

'See: progress! You're curing me. I'll be sending out tweets about important issues soon.'

'It's good to joke but do you believe in anything enough to do that?'

'To tweet? Do I believe in anything enough to *tweet* about it?'

'Do you believe in anything enough to make a statement about it?'

'I believe . . . people should be kind – Jesus, I sound like a tweet.'

'You don't believe people should be kind?'

'Of course! Of fucking course! What is the likelihood of it? We'd have to give up too much. The people tweeting about kindness would have to give up more than anyone. It's utterly meaningless. It should be hard to state what you believe in, shouldn't it? That's what we're here for, isn't it? To try to do it truthfully?'

'So let's try!' you say, slapping your hands on the desk. 'Let's keep on trying.'

*

On my penultimate shift I waited for Emily on a park bench. The sun had gone in as I sat down and the afternoon was turning gloomy. I saw her enter the square on the north side and come towards me wearing a trench coat. I thought of a spy handling her source and stood up to meet her as the rain began to come down. She put up an umbrella.

'It's been ages,' I said.

We didn't hug.

'I know. Come on. Come under here. Let's get inside.'

We went to the pub opposite the museum where the tourists were consuming their all-season meat-and-gravy dinners. I got her a lime soda and myself a pint.

'I was glad you texted,' I said. 'I wasn't sure whether we might have decided to drift away. I had quite a fractious conversation with Andrew.'

'I know. I thought about ringing you when he told me.'

'What did he tell you?'

'He worried he was a bit heavy-handed and pissed you off. He said he was surprised by how much you seemed to hate him.'

'That's a bit melodramatic. I don't hate him. I just objected to being lectured to like I was one of his fucking servants.'

'He doesn't actually have any servants, you know. Unless you count me.'

'You're not his servant.'

'I am not his fucking servant. I'm glad we agree.'

I looked up and across the pub but when I found nothing to distract me I turned back to her. 'He accused me of − I don't know what he accused me of. Using his daughter as part of some baroque plan to steal his fiancée.'

She smiled. 'Really? How funny.'

'Something like that.'

'It's understandable that he's protective of Sophie. She has a habit of doing stupid things.'

'Which I'm one of. Though isn't he just keen to keep the riff-raff away from her?'

'You're imagining that. You're quite good enough for her.'

'For her?'

'Well.' She looked out of the window. 'She seems to have developed into a Marxist *sex columnist*. What's going on there? That recent piece was quite something.'

'I haven't seen it. I've tried to keep away from the internet recently.'

I had deleted all my social media accounts to avoid accidentally seeing what Sophie had been up to, and to make me feel less antagonistic with the culture, less at risk of turning right-wing out of contrariness. I could change my mind within thirty days, but I was very close to this now, and in a day or two I might lose forever the ability to broadcast pictures of haircuts with witty captions to my seven thousand followers, which would be a problem if I hadn't vowed to never talk to Stev'n again.

'Her life is quite an adventure if any of it's true,' she said.

'Really? Am I in there?'

'I don't know, Paul. Are you in there?'

'What does it say?'

'Oh, I can't say. I'm too shy.'

'I bet you're not.'

She raised her eyebrows. 'Well, read the column for yourself.'

She had me worried now and I reached for my phone.

'Oh, no. Look when I'm gone. Please. I don't want to know if it's true.'

I looked back down at my phone and put it away. 'Is Andrew actually pissed off about me and Sophie? Or was it that I provided you with a place to hide away from him for so long?'

'After you'd accused him of going to a hotel with his student.'

'A hotel bar.'

'You didn't say "hotel bar" at first. You said "hotel".'

'Did I? So you think I was stirring things up too?'

'I don't know. Maybe.'

'Maybe I was, unintentionally on purpose.'

'Or on purpose, pretending to be unintentionally on purpose.'

'Does he know you're meeting with me now?'

'He does. He's fine with it.'

'Is he?'

She shrugged.

'And so why *did* you stay there so long?' I asked.

She looked down and spoke to the table. 'I was working. I got a lot done.' Then she met my eyes. 'And I did wonder what it would be like to be away from him. I wanted to remember what it was like to be on my own.'

'What was it like?'

'Strange. Though that might have been the particular circumstances. But thank you for letting me stay there. Here, I've got the keys for you.'

'You're welcome. I wish you could go back there again.'

She grinned. 'Well. I'm not sure I'm in *such* a big hurry to go back.'

'Did you see our friends from the pub again?'

'No. I stayed right away.'

'Did you go to the discount retail park?'

'Eventually, actually, I did,' she said.

'Sorry to hear that. I'll miss the place though. The town, not the retail park. Some nice things happened there as well as the awful ones.'

'Um, yeah.' She folded her arms across her chest.

'Amy and I'll have to go back soon to start to pack the place up.'

'Have you got a new place sorted?'

'Yes. But it's too boring to talk about. Something in the pipeline. Literally in the pipeline. A pied-à-terre in the sewers.'

'Underground is the new above ground,' she said.

'Exactly. Perpetual darkness is the new sunlight.'

She unfolded her arms and spread her fingers across the table and looked at them.

'Do you still want me as a witness at the wedding?' I asked. 'The man who wants to split you up?'

'You don't want to, do you?'

I looked at her and didn't say anything.

'Not as a witness,' she said. 'That was Andrew being silly. But you're still welcome. Do you want to come?'

'Andrew wants me to come?'

'Yes. If we're going to be friends.'

'If? I'd like to be.'

'I didn't know if you'd . . . Oh, let's not be too dull.'

'No.'

'You could come with Sophie. She's decided her diary permits her attendance.'

'Maybe.'

'Aren't you . . .?'

'We were never really . . .'

'Really what?'

'Serious.' This sounded untrue, suddenly.

'Are you ever serious?'

I reached over and put my hands over hers. 'Of course I'm serious.' The couple eating pie and chips at the next table looked up at us. I let go of her hands and focused on her face, though I wanted to turn away from what she was seeing about me.

'It would be easier sometimes to take you seriously if you said what you mean and stopped joking about everything. You're difficult to work out.'

'Well, how about this? I don't like your fiancé. Don't marry him.'

Emily put her hands under the table. 'I'm going to marry him.'

'I know you are.'

'Oh, Paul . . .'

'So let's not be serious.'

She nodded, squinting at me as if what she was seeing wasn't in focus.

'Let's be frivolous. I have not taken my decision to be frivolous without some serious fucking thought involved.'

'OK.' She breathed out. 'We need another drink. I need a proper one.'

'Yes. Me too.'

just sent from Emily's sent items, followed by the screenshots from her gallery, and I got the phone into her bag just as she came back up the stairs.

My phone buzzed as she sat down.

'You look guilty,' she said. 'Is that Sophie? You haven't read her column, have you?'

'I haven't. Cross my heart and hope to die.'

'I don't believe you.'

When we got up to leave the barmaid watched me all the way to the door.

THREE IS AN ODD NUMBER
Sophie Lancaster

How many of you out there have had a threesome? No, I don't really want to know. OK: I'm not uninterested. What I really want to know (and forgive me that I'm talking in this case to women who have sex with men) is with whom you have had your threesomes. No, not their names! I mean: was it with a man and a woman, or with two men?

I was out with the current squeeze at a music festival the other weekend. Let's call him Peter. The rock of cocaine on which Jesus built his church. He was not rock-like at all that day. We lost each other on the way in after Peter attracted the attention of Shelley, an English springer spaniel currently employed by the London Met. It is perilous to work for a style magazine if you don't believe in washing denim. As a result of the ensuing strip search, we spent much of the festival apart, and when we found each other we were both with new friends, who happened to be very tall members of the opposite sex.

Released without charge, somehow, Peter didn't seem angry when he found me in the arms of his temporary replacement. Our tall people took something of a shine to each other, so everything felt serendipitous and Midsummer Night's Dreamy. Peter and I are generous enough to allow each other the right to be a bit selfish, to enjoy a little freedom. But are we equally generous, equally selfish, equally free?

At an afterparty at Peter's boss's house, my beau found himself helping the tall woman's friend be sick into a bin bag for a long time. Very compassionate of him, but I wasn't needed, or wanted, and nor was he, really, as the tall woman was also helping out.

Which left the tall man unattended again, and we got talking, sitting on the bed of the spare room, and etc., with the bedroom door shut, until we were interrupted by Peter looking for me. He left in a hurry, knowing I'd chase him, and of course I did.

'Why don't you come back?' I asked him. The party was fun and I couldn't see why we'd want to leave so early. And I know too that he would have been very much up for it if I had proposed we lie around together on a bed with a woman he'd been kissing all day. He admitted as much when I challenged him on this.

Peter certainly puts on the appearance of being an open-minded boy, but in principle is not the same as in practice. Women friends of mine who have had threesomes – all of them with two women and one man – have had similar scruples, but they've pushed past them. I don't blame Peter for having scruples. I don't want him to do anything he doesn't want to. No one has the right to do that to anyone, and the fact that it is us women being pressured most of the time doesn't give us permission to act like the men who pressure women to do things we don't want to. But isn't it telling how much more willing we are to go along with men's fantasies, and how less willing they are to go along with ours? How much of this is the way we have been conditioned by the patriarchy to be obedient and compliant? Are we just much sexier than men, less vanilla, is it just easier to find each other attractive, to want to cooperate? Or have men tricked us into believing this for their own selfish interest?

I think this last question was running through my mind when I told him I didn't mind if he left but I was going to stay. 'OK,' he said, 'I'm going.' He took a long time to go, standing at the door of the flat and looking at me. Then he changed his mind and came back. For a little bit. A very small amount of time. Then he left, and we haven't spoken since.

I strode up Gower Street towards the campus where Andrew worked, light on my feet and joyful in the way my disappointment was unhinging me. I was very late back to work and did not care. Term might not have been fully under way but there were a lot of young people with backpacks looking up at the buildings around us in the way that newcomers to the city do. You could have such a fine time in these streets when the other people were in their offices.

I had only ever walked past the courtyard of the campus at a clip, seen it out of the corner of my eye, but it made a different impression when you turned into it and looked up at the grand roof on its white stone pillars. It was a long way from the college on the Elephant and Castle roundabout. I sat on a bench and took it in.

But enough of that. When I stood up I asked a woman if she knew where the History department was, and she directed me out onto Gordon Square. It was only a few doors down from Virginia's house, from John Maynard's. I walked past the reception and smiled and headed up some stairs. No one I passed in the corridor looked at me like I didn't belong.

Eventually I found Andrew Lancaster's office. Nothing stuck to his door but his name and one piece of paper which listed one office hour. I knocked. Nothing. I turned the door handle and it opened. I looked up and down the corridor then stepped in, closing the door behind me. It was a big room, with tables pushed together with enough chairs around them to accommodate a seminar group. Two walls were completely covered with books, and outside his window was a big oak tree, and beyond that was Gordon Square. The light of his computer tower was flickering at his desk by the window. I strummed his keyboard and his screen turned on. Password required. I typed 'EmilyNardini1981' and other variations, before it told me I needed to wait half an hour to try again. His desk was stacked with books and scribbled notes. I read the notes. They were not salacious. And leaning against his monitor was a photo of Emily, looking up from an outdoor café table somewhere – Paris? – a mock-suspicious look, coquettish and sceptical, the why-do-I-love-you? look.

I took the photo and put it inside my jacket pocket. Then I opened the door, checked the corridor and left without anyone seeing me. Rather than go back the way I had come, I carried on up the corridor, reading about lecturers' niche interests on the posters on their doors. One room, with a glass window, was labelled as the PhD study room. I looked through the window and saw two men and a woman working at computers. The woman was Andrew's student, the one with whom he definitely wasn't having an affair. I opened the door and everyone looked up.

'Hi,' I said to her. 'Chloe, isn't it?'

'Er. Hi?'

'I'm Paul. Andrew's friend. We had dinner that time.'

'Oh, yes. You left abruptly with Emily.'

'Yes.'

She was looking at me warily, but there was curiosity mixed in with her distrust.

'You haven't seen him, have you? I've just tried his office but he's not there.'

'No. I haven't seen him yet today.' Her mouth was beginning to smile.

'Yet. OK. Well, if you do see him, let him know I was looking for him, won't you?'

'Sure. Shall I tell him what you want with him?'

'No. Unless you have time for a coffee? I could explain better then.'

She started by shaking her head. 'Oh, no, no. Oh, I'm − OK,' she said. 'Sure. OK. Yes.'

TWENTY

'When are you happiest?' you ask.

'I don't know. A good day in the shop, talking to customers. Staying at home with a book. Flirting with someone at the bar. Heading out with a wallet full of twenties and a fully charged phone.'

'You almost sounded wholesome for a second there.'

'I'm still unconvinced that any of those activities are any more wholesome than the others.'

'Really?'

'What's wrong with getting inebriated and going to bed with strangers? Surely it's wonderful, a reason to be alive.'

'There are consequences though, aren't there?'

'I know. But I'm not cut out to be *wholesome*.'

'Everyone can be as wholesome as they want to be.'

'You sound very American there.'

'And you sound very British.'

'Yeah?'

'Glib, superior, dodging away from analysis, unwilling to focus on self-improvement.'

'Happiest in the past.'

'Unable to be happy in the future.'

'You think?'

'It looks that way. But you specifically – I think you might be able to be happy.'

'Great! How do I do it?'

'Change the way you live your life.'

'Oh, right. Well. What a con. It's like the last noble truth of Buddhism – one defeats sorrow by . . . following the twelvefold path of Enlightenment. You think you've finished and you've got a list of loads more to do.'

'I didn't know you'd studied Buddhism, Paul.'

'That was when I stopped. Now you're doing that straight face again you do when you're secretly laughing at me. Stop it.'

*

On my last day Helen had ordered me a leaving cake decorated with a pair of scissors, and the cake-makers seemed to have assumed that I was a hairdresser; we all gathered around the box as Helen opened it to reveal something the shape of a record deck smothered in glittery icing, topped not only with a pair of scissors, but a to-scale sculpture in marzipan of a pair of hair straighteners, and a comb made from black icing.

'Can you eat glitter?' asked Helen.

'You never told me you were so gay, Paul,' said Leo.

'I'm just not into men who look like you.'

'Have you read Sophie Lancaster's last column?' asked Helen.

'That's not me she's referring to,' I said, but Leo was already on his phone looking for it.

Helen had congratulated me cautiously when I told her I was leaving, as if I was playing some kind of prank. She repeated 'digital marketing' in the same tone she might have 'the Catholic priesthood'. Leo quoted Bill Hicks and advised me to think again, or to kill myself. There was no rationalising what I would do: I would be one of Satan's little helpers.

'Trying to persuade people to buy books? Literary fiction? Critiques of neo-liberalism?'

'I'm joking. And wow. It's weird hearing the word *neoliberalism* come out of your mouth.'

'I've never really got used to it coming out of anyone's mouth.'

'It has a specific meaning, you know?'

'Yeah, and . . . seven syllables.'

'You won't be doing that stuff, anyway. You'll be making book trailers for Jeffrey Archer.'

'What's a book trailer?'

'How did you get this job again?'

'I needed it.'

Which wasn't strictly true. Helen had offered to find me more shifts when I'd told her that the reason I was leaving was so I could get a mortgage. After a few months my bank statements together with our deposit might have looked plausible to moneylenders. But I didn't want to wait. I was scared they would change their mind, that there had been a mistake. The new job clarified things neatly for the lenders, and now I was this far stepped in shit, it was easiest to buy a new pair of shoes.

*

Towards the end of the day I began to say hello to a suspicious number of my friends who were converging on the shop.

'What's going on?' I asked Helen.

'Everyone has come to enjoy their last glimpse of one of the strangest characters this shop has seen.'

'I see what's happening here,' I said.

'Good. In that case it won't ruin the surprise if you help Leo carry up the Prosecco and the ice bucket. We bought quite a lot, as it's for you.'

*

A lot of my friends and favourite customers were there. No Jonathan, who had disappeared from my life again. But Mary was there with Nathan, and I hadn't ever seen Nathan looking so happy. She'd told me the night before that she'd found a place in Clapton to move into; Nathan was going to help her move.

Helen was hassling me to give a speech when I felt hands on my waist, and I turned to see Sophie, smiling ruefully up at me.

'You,' I said.

'Me,' she said.

'Are you Sophie Lancaster?' asked Leo. 'I'm a big fan of your column.'

'Are you? I thought it was mostly women who read it.'

'Oh, no, of course not. Not all men are uninterested in the perspectives of women.'

I thought I might be sick.

Sophie was coughing on her prosecco. 'That's a . . . refreshing attitude,' she said, when she had recovered.

'Do you mind if I give you a proof copy of my novel? Penguin are publishing it in January?' said Leo.

I thought I might be violently sick.

'Thank you,' she said, glancing at me. 'I'd love one.'

Leo looked at me too, then back to her. 'Let me go and fetch you one. They've really pushed the boat out. Limited-edition hardbacks.'

'Poor guy. I expect it's going to be a huge flop,' I said, when he had gone away.

'Don't be bitter, Paul.'

'If you read the thing and like it and express that opinion in public, you will never hear from me again.'

'I'll keep that in mind in case it comes in handy.'

'It's nice to speak to you, though,' I said, 'in spite of that job you did on me in your article.'

'It was you not doing a job on him, as I remember.'

'There is a difference between being selfish and not wanting to give a man I'd just met a blow job.'

'Not according to most of you men.'

'You meet too many of the wrong sort. Like that phoney who'll be back in a minute. I might write a book for women about how to spot awful men, seeing as a lot of you don't seem very good at it. *Paul has been a dickhead all his life. Join him as he reveals all the tricks that dickheads use to pretend they're not dickheads.* I have the shoutline already: *It takes a wanker to know a wanker.*'

'You're not so bad,' she said. 'I still think you stormed out earlier than you needed to from that party, but I'm sorry. It was an awful scene. I should have left with you. I was just – I had it in my head that I was doing the right thing, that the right thing is difficult sometimes, antithetical, that the right thing involves hurting people. It would be easier just to be nice, but there's something larger at stake.'

'That, and you were high and horny and fancied him.'

'Well, that too. But if I had the choice again, I would leave with you.'

'Really?'

'Really. Though think of the fun we could have – '

'Oh, look – it's your dad.'

Andrew and Emily were walking in the door at the front of the shop. Andrew made himself smile at me and walked over to us with his hand on the small of his faithless fiancée's back. He nodded at me then turned to his daughter.

'Hello, Sophie! You've been very busy in print.'

'So've you, Dad.'

He moved forwards and kissed her, then he held out his hand to me. I took it, and leaned over to kiss Emily too.

'Are you well, Paul?' he said, squinting a little.

'I'm well,' I said.

Helen came over, tapped Emily on the shoulder and asked her to sign some stock. That left Sophie and me alone with her father.

'How are you, darling?' he said.

'I told you, I'm fine,' I said.

Both of them looked at me and shook their heads. Leo strode towards us, brandishing his book and beaming.

'I just need to use the toilet,' I said, and walked off.

*

I had never been so pleased to see Amy as when I returned to the shop floor. She was frowning, looking in the direction of Sophie and Leo.

'Thank God I've found you,' we said simultaneously. 'Thanks for coming,' I said.

'I'm not sure I would have, if I'd known that she would be here. I thought that was over.'

'She's all right.'

'You seem committed to deceiving yourself about that.'

'Honestly, she can be quite lovely. It's just not her official brand. And don't worry. It's over between us. Almost certainly.'

'What happened? And why would you want to be with someone whose best quality is being less obnoxious than she seems? Watch out: she's spotted us.'

She had. She was looking over Leo's book while he talked to her. I watched her put her hand on his arm.

'She's flirting with him because I'm watching,' I said. 'The man is unfanciable. It's sad, really.'

'Is he unfanciable?' said Amy.

'Don't say things like that. I can't afford to fall out with you for good too.'

'Let's change the subject then. Have you thought any more about what we might do to mark Mum's first anniversary?'

'I haven't. I mean, I have, but I haven't thought of anything good.'

'Plant a tree?'

'Where? We haven't got anywhere to plant a tree.'

'OK, not a fucking tree then. I know I'm not the only one who cares about this, so why are you pretending not to?'

'I'm not. I care. I'm sorry. I'll think harder about it.'

'You have to.' She looked around her at the crowded room. 'Are you OK? About leaving here? You've been here forever.'

'I have no idea how I am. Are you OK? How are you feeling?'

'I have no idea how I am. I'm scared.'

'Me too,' I said.

'At least you can have a drink.'

'I'm going to have twenty.'

'Mine and yours?'

'You can always rely on me to pick up the slack, Amy.'

'What a lucky sister I am.'

'I'm a lucky brother. I mean that, seriously. Thanks for coming.'

'It's OK,' she said. 'Don't be soppy.'

'Are you still in touch with Ben?'

'Yeah. I was going to tell you. He came to the last scan and now I've asked him to be the birth partner. He's going to come up for some NCT stuff I've signed up for.'

'Great.'

'You're not put out? I took your offer seriously, you know?'

'I'm not the dad. Of course I'm not put out. I'm relieved.'

'It would be weird having you in there.'

'You're telling me. Thank God for Ben. But I'll come over, stay over, whenever you want me. You can rely on me.'

'Thanks,' she said. 'We'll see.'

*

I approached Andrew later, after I'd had a few drinks and said goodbye to Amy.

'Would you like a piece of hairdresser cake?' I asked.

'No, thank you. I hear you came looking for me in my office.'

'Oh, yeah. I wanted to clear the air.'

'OK.'

'Don't you?'

'The air was clear, as far as I'm concerned. I explained to you what I had noticed and you reacted to it angrily. Perhaps reasonably. I'm sorry if I got you wrong.'

'Don't worry about it.'

'I wasn't worrying about it.' He looked over to his daughter who was laughing at something Leo had just told her. 'Sophie says you're not together now.'

'We were never really together.'

'That's what she said. When you came looking for me, did you go into my room, by any chance?'

'No, I just knocked on the door.'

'Because I've noticed something's missing.'

'Do you not lock your door?'

'I do now. How was your coffee with Chloe?'

'Nice,' I said.

'OK,' he said.

'What did she say to you about it?'

'Nothing,' he said. 'She said she thought you were just being friendly.'

'I am friendly.'

'Some might say over-friendly.'

'Are you looking forward to your wedding?' I asked.

'Yes,' he said. 'I am.'

'Me too,' I said.

I thought I might be about to tell him something. Then Leo came over to demand I made a speech.

*

The cake was eaten, even the marzipan hair straighteners. Twenty-four bottles of Prosecco had been poured. Two hundred and eighty-eight units of alcohol, I told people, proud of my long multiplication. Sophie was going to let her dad buy her dinner and Emily had opted out. The gang were dragging me towards a bar with a dance floor on Hanway Street.

'Coming?' I asked Emily.

'Tempting, but I should get back. I've drunk enough already.'

'Come on. You're getting married next weekend. Call this your hen do.'

'I've been to Blackpool already.'

'You can't have a hen do on your own. Except, I suppose . . .'

'What?'

'Nothing.'

'I haven't danced in about five years.'

'Well, that's far too long, obviously. You have to come. I insist.'

She relented and ten of us staggered down the road, passing round the few bottles of Prosecco we had discovered scattered around the bookshop which still had some wine left in them. We binned them at Tottenham Court Road and made our way up into the little bar we always went to if a party in the shop had taken life. It has a dance floor the size of a living room which encourages physical intimacy and conversational shouting. The DJ was playing Motown. We all just bopped along. I shook my invisible maracas. Emily danced around her handbag, like an old woman trying to edge her way into a bad-mannered bus queue. Tequilas were passed around, bottles of lager. We practised our Spanish on tourists who practised their English on us. It was great. The time went by in what seemed like ten minutes, and then the place was closing.

*

'Please don't walk me home,' Emily said, as I walked her along Oxford Street.

'Get a taxi then, or the bus.'

'I need to walk to sober myself up a bit.'

'I'll leave you alone, but only if you insist. I like hanging out with you.'

'I'm putting you out.'

'You're not.'

'Why's my bag so heavy? There was hardly anything in it before.' She pulled out a copy of Leo's limited-edition hardback proof. 'Oh,' she said, and posted it into a litter bin.

'You could never put me out,' I said.

'It's totally safe, you know.'

'Yes, the edge of a dark park. Totally safe. What could possibly go wrong there?'

'Please don't make me scared of the way I walk home.'

'It's not normally so late and you're not normally so drunk. Let me put you in a taxi.'

'Maybe in a bit. Let's just walk for a bit. I want to do karaoke. Do you know where there's a karaoke bar?'

'I don't.'

'Let's see,' she said, getting out her phone.

'You don't like karaoke.'

'I love karaoke. Don't you?'

'I like singing.'

'In which case you like karaoke.'

*

We found a place in Soho. The smallest booths were for four people so we had to pay for two ghosts as well as both of us. Emily paid for the room hire on her card: 'That's the advance gone.' I ordered her a Coke and me a beer. She demanded vodka in her Coke. She was quite unsteady on her feet now. 'What song are you going to open with?' I asked and she forgot about the vodka.

Our heads were still filled with old soul tunes.

This old heart of mine . . .

A thousand times . . .

Let me go.

She had a clear, high voice that didn't sound drunk at all when she was singing. I thought of the Diana Ross I could not separate from northern indie discos, lasses in heels queuing in the wind and drizzle, dance floors blue with fag smoke.

I joined in on the chorus, leaning into the same mic. I love you! I love you! We sang as loud as we could, bashing our hips together in time to the piano riff and collapsing into each other's arms as we reached the song's crescendo. I kissed her on the lips and she let me for a while before the song finished and she twisted away.

'This is my favourite thing. I'm having so much fun.' She leaned over the console and began to type into it.

'Is this what you and Andrew do together?'

'Absolutely not. Can you imagine?'

'I didn't really imagine this. Who do you do this with?'

'Oh, my friend Richard, when I was back in Leeds.'

'Oh,' I said, and as the song started I turned away.

'Paul?' she said, touching me on my neck and I turned around and saw her notice something in my face before I hid it from her.

*

We stayed until the place shut. We were too busy singing and dancing to drink much more, and as we sobered up with each song I realised that there had been a chance of something happening which had now nearly slipped away, again. We were back in Soho, in central London, three miles away from the flat she shared with the man she was marrying.

'Time to go, then,' she said. The disco lights turned her face blue yellow red. I moved my head closer to hers and we assessed each other.

'You are the best karaoke partner,' I said. 'I didn't know this could be fun.'

'Like I said: I'm a veteran.'

'With that lad from the launch.'

'With that lad. You sound annoyed about it.'

I shrugged.

'You look annoyed too. Wait, did you say something earlier about my time at your mum's? You didn't, did you?'

'Didn't what?'

'Did you have . . . cameras? Spying on me?'

'How drunk are you? Cameras?'

'OK. You didn't have cameras.'

'What would I have seen in these fucking cameras?'

'Nothing.'

'Doesn't sound like nothing. Cameras?'

'Right. Sorry.'

'About what?'

'Oh, everything.'

The strobe above us spun petals of light across her face and body.

'I'll have my own flat soon. You could come and live with me.'

'Oh, Paul. Shut up.'

'Seriously. You could.'

'Shut up. I mean it. You're not serious. We've established that.'

'I'm being serious.'

'I like you because you're not serious.'

I put my hand on her shoulder. I put my hands in her hair and she took them in hers and brought them down to where I could have held her hips if she decided to let them go.

I waited to see what she'd decide.

TWENTY-ONE

'Do you think she might ever write about you? Would you read it if she did?'

'Yes.'

'How would you feel?'

'Naked. Humiliated.'

'You wouldn't feel proud that you made an impact on her life?'

'I think her portrayal would do enough to remove any sense of pride. She'd destroy me.'

'Perhaps you shouldn't read it if she does.'

'Oh, I know I shouldn't. I would, though, if she does, and the awful thing is I'll be more offended if she doesn't. It's not every day two people crash into each other's lives like that. I think I've got at least a year or two until she eviscerates me, if she's going to. I want to put some distance between her portrait of me and whoever I've become by then. If I can see what she writes as a historical document that applies to a historical person? That would be the best thing, if I can do that.'

'You sound like you might actually want her to punish you.'

'Wouldn't you rather be punished than forgotten?'

*

When Sophie arrived at the pub before the ceremony, she confessed to me that she would have made it out of the house in a denim skirt, vest top and Adidas trainers, all ready to make the point that this was not a significant occasion for *her*, except that her mother had looked at her and inclined her head slightly, and so Sophie had gone back upstairs to change into a dress and heels. Now she sought reassurance from me. 'I don't look like I've made *much* of an effort, do I?'

It was a cool autumn morning, one of those I had begun to enjoy more than its equivalent in spring. The soft sun, and brushed percussion of the leaves like the music playing in the morning at the end of the party. Time to let go of summer's hunger.

We were on the corner of the King's Road close to the registry office, under another of those grand porticos that my new friends kept bringing me to. We drank our beers and discussed where we were going to go together afterwards, at what point we would escape. I was still willing to take my happiness one night at a time; if willing is the right word for it.

*

Susannah was smoking outside the registry office with a man I recognised from somewhere.

'My new colleague!' she said, as we approached. 'I knew you'd impress us.'

I had neither impressed nor unimpressed anyone yet. I hadn't seen Susannah once, who worked on a completely different floor to me, but it was good of her to communicate the impression to Sophie that I was not useless. Sophie was not listening in any case, as she was being squeezed by Andrew's

284

best man, whom I had recognised by now: a journalist and essayist whose books I liked.

'I've barely started yet,' I said to Susannah.

'I bet you haven't!'

'No: I mean I –'

'We know what you mean, darling. You've scrubbed up well today.'

*

And it was true that I was wearing more expensive clothes than usual. I owned a couple of suits, but after scrutinising the impression we presented together to the mirror I decided the occasion demanded something more elegant, and so I detoured to borrow something from Jonathan. He was back living at Julia's, the place I used to think of as their place, but now we all knew whose place it was. Julia kissed me on both cheeks, but made no attempt to apologise or look even faintly rueful about her part in the marital pause that had forced me to live with her husband for the last few months. I had wondered if I might get a thank you, but understood her tactic: pretend it had never happened; reverse to the fork where they went wrong and take the other way. Jonathan was in a kitchen with a high glass wall and roof that had not been there the last time I had been round a few years ago; it looked like the foyer of a brand-new contemporary art gallery. He was wearing an apron and slicing shallots while people on Radio 4 were arguing about a theatre production.

He took me up to the bedroom where he rifled through a rack of twenty-odd suits; after some negotiation I picked out a tight black number I could probably get a thousand pounds for on eBay.

'Who did you steal this off?' I asked.

'We photoed some crack-fiend musician in it. He was angling to steal it himself so I ran off with it when he was tooting up in the toilets and blamed him.'

I could just get the trousers to fasten.

'That's snug,' I said.

'And I had them loosened last year too,' he admitted. 'I hope she's impressed. You look all right. For you, you look all right. Go on: you can keep it if you like.'

I looked at him in his apron. 'How did you fix things with Julia, then?'

'Oh, you know. We've decided to try for a baby.'

'That's good?'

'*Yeah.* I hope so. I can't do a worse job than my parents, anyway. How's Mary?'

'She's all right. She's moving out. She thinks you're an arsehole.'

'Good for her. I am an arsehole. First rule of Arseholes Anonymous, isn't it? Declare yourself. Admit you can't help it. Avoid situations where you might be an arsehole.'

'Which are?'

'Almost any in which one talks to members of the opposite sex.'

I looked at myself in the mirror again and straightened my tie. 'That's too far for me. I'll have to try to be a functioning arsehole.'

*

'And how are you?' said Susannah to Sophie. 'You're becoming such a star these days. Paul – do you know Gary?'

I felt like I already knew Gary a bit from his articles and books, and from a friend's account of going to bed with him a few years ago, when she had invited him to speak at a festival.

He was Andrew's best friend from Oxford, and though they were both energetic men nearing sixty it would never have occurred to me they were contemporaries. Not for Gary the gradual smartening and professionalism of the distinguished late male. His hair had silvered but it had not gone, and it was cut short, clipped cheaply like a raver's, a five-quid job, maybe even a DIY-clippers number; he wore the minimum requirements of a suit like a slouching schoolboy, a black blazer and white shirt with a floppy collar, tie hanging low beneath an open top button, and below this a pair of black jeans in the loose fit he would have worn in his late twenties, early thirties, the period in a man's life when he must make his choices and stick with them, or risk looking vain and foolish. It had been the 1980s such a very short time ago to Gary, who unlike Andrew had stayed interested in new cultural movements, in club culture, and never had kids or worked a nine-to-five. I did not mention to him that I knew someone he knew; I wouldn't have even if his partner hadn't shown up while we were talking. I liked him and didn't want to make him uncomfortable. He was irritable and droll and quick to laugh. He was a hero of mine, really, I wanted to live his life or have him as a friend.

In spite of this, there will come a point when we will be persuaded that we should kill all men like him, as much as we might like them on an individual basis. We will be encouraged not to respond to their charm. They have what the young want and they won't let go of it.

I don't think I could go along with that, though perhaps I could. You never know what kind of thrust you can support when you only see the handle of the knife and not the tip.

It's obvious why the next generation are hardening their morality, their stringency of expression, why they are turning away from irony, the grey area, why we are all black-and-whitening the world. Why wouldn't they look for reasons to fail you, or me, to find us wanting? Why shouldn't they judge and convict the enemies? There is no kindness due to those in the way of justice, to those who won't surrender. They are readying for war.

*

I tried not to notice when Susannah and Sophie looked across at me at the same time – a problem they may have been discussing a solution to.

*

Andrew and Emily walked together down the aisle, past all three rows of seats, on the thick blue carpet dotted with yellow flowers, to the sound of a string quartet on a portable CD player operated by Gary.

In the twenty or so seconds between Gary turning the CD on and off again I managed to open my phone and shazam the track: 'Beethoven, No. 12 in E-Flat Major – ' 'Be quiet,' said Sophie, when I whispered this to her, showing her my phone screen. She slapped my wrist. Put it away. She was, instinctually, a good girl, a model student, who achieved her rebelliousness with the same diligent work with which she had achieved her double first. She was protective of her father as well as critical; it was not OK for me to point out what remained of the gauche young man, the Leonard Bast who had risen from the provinces, the mistakes of style his daughter would not inherit. The secular wedding was a great temptation towards such mistakes, with its invocation to pick your significant songs and poems, as long as they didn't mention God. It was too close to the projection of a carefully created social media profile. For those of us who once believed in God, the problem with atheism, that reasonable position, is exactly its reasonableness, its marriage officials, its humanist funeral people. This special occasion. This very special day that means a great deal. They are so breezy, so chirpy, so comfortable with sentiment; they smile too much, they seem to like their job, and people, and saying the word 'human'; do they think humans are a good thing? Have they not learned how to suffer? That there is a style to it?

'You're all very quiet in here,' she boomed. She had the flat South London accent of the recently resigned England football manager.

I raised my eyebrows at Sophie, who looked away from me.

'Are you all all right?' she bellowed.

We nodded back at her.

'Well,' she said, and then pointed out the fire exits and told us to turn off our mobile phones. 'What a happy day for Andrew and Emily,' she said, and explained what a civil ceremony was and the role we had to play in it. Minimal, in theory, except I had in my pocket two sealed envelopes containing cards I had bought on the Kings Road, elegant cards in thick cream envelopes, addressed individually to Emily and Andrew.

In each of the three rows, there were two chairs on either side of the aisle, twelve chairs in all. The marriage official was facing Emily and Andrew from across a vase of flowers in the centre of a desk at the front of the room. A row ahead of us to our right was Gary and his partner, Angela, who was a documentary film-maker, and who looked a bit younger than him, perhaps by a whole decade, but certainly not by two decades and five years.

Susannah was sitting in front of us with her son Felix, an affable young man about to start university. He had been inside reading when I met his mother and Gary smoking outside.

Apart from the minister, Emily and Andrew, there were just us six guests. Emily hadn't invited anyone but me, not, she told me, because she had no friends, but because she didn't think it would be particularly fun for them. There were no people she had to worry about offending by not inviting. Her mother was three years dead. Her father: he would make a scene. Her sister – well, maybe, but she lived in Canada now; she couldn't bring her all the way over the Atlantic for this. So her sister didn't even know that Emily was getting married.

The small number of people in the room was only obvious at the points when we were invited to offer applause. There were just enough of us to make clapping plausible but not enough of us to make the spread of noise that one needed to feel like applause was occurring. This was through no fault of mine or Felix's; we both slapped our hands together as hard as we could while the official at the front fluttered hers together without her palms ever touching. Sophie glared at me. Susannah put her hand on her son's shoulder. The documentary film-maker had a camera and took a couple of shots, without using a flash, as requested earlier by the minster.

Emily had insisted on no poetry, allowing Andrew the music as compromise. Poetry should never be made trite, she explained to me, by forcing it to express profound statements of love. She had kept her face straight and I didn't know whether she was teasing me.

Did anyone know of any lawful impediment why Emily and Andrew could not be joined in martyr money?

I had hoped Richard or Chloe might burst in at this point. 'I'm sorry,' they would say, 'but there is something that the bride and groom should admit to each other first.'

The minister left a polite pause. I wondered how many times in such a minister's life they hear the question answered in the negative.

It was down to me alone. I could call out and read aloud the contents of each card in my pocket.

We all listened to the drone of a motor: the air conditioning or heating somewhere, a PC with a broken fan; the ambient clatter that rattles through all bureaucratic buildings.

And then they were asked to face each other, confirm their names and repeat after me.

Andrew was in a navy-blue suit and open-neck shirt, a white flower in his lapel. Emily in a red dress that cinched at her waist and made me remember what it had felt like to hold her there while she sang to me. She was shaking. She was scared. The stiletto of the heel trembled as she repeated those old adverbial phrases, as he repeated his in turn, as they smiled with great concentration at each other while the other said their lines. Was Sophie touched by this? Was her mind changed? Did she think that I was surrendering to soppiness as I used my hand to tell her that I was there, close to her, available if she wanted me?

She shivered slightly to push my hand away and I put my hand down by my side again. She looked at me with her mouth shut and back again at Andrew and Emily. A breeze through the window stirred the leaves of the plants that decorated the ledges of the room.

Emily would not meet my eyes, but Andrew made sure to turn to me and grin.

It didn't look like a very passionate kiss when they kissed.

*

I had no intention of giving Andrew the card into which I had folded the printouts of Emily's texts with the married man she met up with in Blackpool, the man she took back, I can only presume, to my mother's house, to have sex with in my bedroom, or on the living-room carpet I had never walked on while wearing shoes. Most of the time the gun on the wall is just for show, just the owner's substitute for personality. I didn't want to be a destroyer, just to know that I could be a destroyer, for my fantasies to carry a credible weight. I wanted to know that what was in my pocket was sitting there, so that when Andrew grinned at me like that, like I knew he would, and made it clear to me how powerless he thought I was, I could put my hand inside my jacket and feel the grain of the paper, imagine the blade of an old-fashioned letter-knife slicing through it.

I had something in the other envelope too. Chloe and I had spent much longer together than the time it takes to drink a coffee. And though our dignity demanded that we spoke like we were only pretending, she had sent me just the evidence I had asked her for.

*

We made our way on foot to a pub where a section had been reserved and food ordered for 'a little afternoon party', as Andrew described it. He put his arm around me twice while he told me the arrangements. He was so jubilant I thought he might be about to put me in a neck hold and give me a head scrub.

'How are you?' I asked Emily, as we made our way there and walked slightly ahead together. They were the first words I'd said to her that day.

'I'm good, thanks. Glad that's over.'

'What did you think of her who did it?'

'She was fine. Functional. I wish we'd just done it on our own though.'

'There were only six guests.'

'I know. A bit much to walk in to taped violins, wasn't it?'

'No, no.'

'Well, I'm not regretting things!' she said.

'Of course you're not.' I put my hand on her arm. 'It was fine.'

'Stop making off with my bride,' called Andrew from behind us, and we waited up for the rest of the party.

'I haven't told you how beautiful you look in that dress,' I said, just as Andrew arrived.

'Now you have,' she said. 'You look very sharp yourself.'

'Thank you,' I said. I hugged her so I didn't have to look at her face.

'Cool down, Cassio,' said Gary.

'Those trousers aren't constricting you, are they, Paul?' said Andrew. 'They're very tight.'

Sophie caught my arm when I disengaged from Emily and I hung back to talk to her.

'You two are very friendly,' she said. 'I was also tempted to tell you to get your hands off my father's wife.'

'That's the spirit,' I said. 'Protective of their union.'

She screwed up her face, and I laughed.

'It's done,' she said. 'What can I do?'

'Devise a dastardly plot to split them up?'

'Yes, I suppose I could. How would I go about it?'

I pretended I was thinking about this for the first time. 'I suppose you could find or manufacture evidence to suggest one or the other was cheating on the other.'

'Oh, God, no. Old people and their ancient morality. I couldn't take it seriously.'

'That's principled of you. So if you knew Emily was cheating on your father you wouldn't think it any of his business?'

'The important thing is honesty, not monogamy. Yes, I wouldn't want to know.'

I didn't say anything and faced straight forwards as we walked.

'Is she?' she blurted. 'She'd tell you, wouldn't she?'

'I have no idea why you'd think that.'

She grabbed my arm. 'What's that tone about?'

'There's no tone.'

'You sound angry.'

'No.'

'*Have* you?'

'Have I what?'

She spun her head to gesture with her chin at Emily.

'No.'

She squeezed my arm harder.

'Seriously, have you?'

'No.'

'I don't know if I believe you. If you haven't, it's probably not through lack of trying.'

'Why would I want to try? It's you I like.'

'I don't believe that either. Don't you feel entitled to a certain amount of revenge?'

'On who?'

'Me.'

We followed the party down a path through the grounds of a large Gothic-looking church.

'You haven't answered,' she said.

'I know,' I said. 'I'm still thinking about it.'

*

Five bottles of champagne waited for us in an ice bucket. Little pastries and sandwiches, hot, spiced things made from chickpeas. And our party got along quite merrily, to begin with, on our raised platform in the back of the pub. There were seats to sit on but we remained standing. Felix eyed my cigarette packet wistfully as I nipped out, before emerging to steal one from me, looking over his shoulder every few seconds for any sign of his mother. I liked Felix. He thought I had a 'cool life' when I told him, through force of habit, that I was a bookseller, with a magazine column, and that I lived in a shared flat on the Kingsland Road. 'You sound like you have it sorted, mate,' he said, and I realised that, yes, I had lived a teenager's idea of a perfect life for the last thirteen years.

Back inside we talked and drank and ate and when I went to pour everyone another glass of champagne from the last bottle it ran out before I could pour myself one. Andrew called over to me to get a couple more, stick them on his tab.

So off I went to the bar, where a TV presenter in front of me was wearing a leather jacket. He looked around at me and nodded. I pretended I didn't recognise him. 'Congratulations,' he said, looking at Emily.

'Oh, yeah. Thanks.'

'Want a drink?'

'No, thanks. I'm getting a couple of bottles.'

'You have a beautiful wife.'

'I really don't.'

'It's a bit early to be disenchanted already, isn't it?'

'I mean, she's not my wife. She married the older gentleman over there.'

'Oh! God. Right, well, *he* really does have a beautiful wife.'

'Yes, he does.'

He turned back to the bar but I tapped him on the shoulder. 'Why did you think we were married?'

'I don't know. You both look like you're getting married. And you know, you're the same sort of age.'

'I'm with her,' I said, pointing out Sophie, keen to impress him for reasons I would wince about when I had time to examine them. 'I think.'

'She looks very pretty too. I'd thought she was your sister. My girlfriend and I have been watching you from our table. Funny the way we think we can read a situation from the surface, but get it totally wrong.'

While this was going on Emily had walked over.

'Hello,' I said.

'We need fizzy water too.'

'Congratulations,' said the TV presenter.

Emily did a double take. 'Thank you.'

'He thought *we'd* just got married.'

'Oh!' she said.

'Sorry,' he said. 'Anyway, have a great day.'

'Thank you,' she said, and we watched him take two glasses of wine over to a table in the corner where a woman was waiting.

'*Great*,' she said.

'It's going OK, though, isn't it?'

'Yeah. It's nice.'

'Were you worried about Sophie acting up?'

'Of course.'

'She seems less against you than before.'

'That's probably the pre-nup.'

'Ha ha.'

She looked back towards our platform and back to me.

'Of course. There probably was something like that.'

'Mm hm,' she said. 'I thought it would ease the tension.'

'Is that what the tension was about? I thought it was her mum.'

She took a mirror from her bag and looked at herself in it.

'These things don't really occur to me,' I lied. 'I suppose it's pretty complicated. Inheritance.'

The barman popped the cork of a bottle of champagne and set it down.

She put the mirror back in her bag. 'It's just to reassure the family that I won't run off with all his money if he happens to die suddenly, or if I catch him fucking his students and divorce him.'

'Would you mind?'

She shrugged and looked away. 'Yes.'

'Sophie would think that unenlightened of you.'

'Yes, she's full of theoretical positions. I suspect she's capable of jealousy too.'

'Certainly where you're concerned.'

She pulled a face, though I thought she looked slightly pleased.

'And you're not feeling upset, that you were pressurised into something less than you deserved?'

'Jesus, fuck, Paul.' She didn't look pleased any more. 'Did you just say that? On my wedding day?'

'About the *money*. Not about Andrew.'

'That's not much better,' she sighed. 'I'm sorry. I just wanted to get on with life the way it was, and this seemed a good way to do that. I met a man who I'm happy with, much to my surprise. I fell in love with him, not his money. He's kind, intelligent, handsome. Don't roll your eyes.'

'Convince yourself when I'm not around, please.'

'What?'

'You came back with me the other night and you're talking like nothing at all happened.'

'Paul. Please.'

'I mean: I'm not actually sensitive about it. It's the principle of the thing. That you might at least consider that you might want to be sensitive about it.'

'Come on,' she said, putting her hand on my waist. 'You can't have wounded feelings while sleeping with my boyf— my *husband*'s daughter.'

'Jesus, listen to this sordid fucking . . . Yuck.'

'I know. What are you doing here, Paul? What are you hoping for?'

'Right now, just a dignified end to it. Then a new start.'

'Well, amen to that.' She fiddled with her ring. 'I suppose I am convincing myself a bit. What a funny thing this is. I have a husband. I have this ring on my finger. This marker.'

'It's easy enough to take it off.'

'It really isn't,' she said. 'I mean actually. I think it's stuck on.'

'You twist,' I said.

'Still stuck.'

'Twist and pull. Here,' I said, taking her hand, twisting and pulling, meeting resistance until I didn't and the ring skidded across the pub floor to land under the table of the TV presenter and his companion.

'For heaven's sake,' called Andrew, who had probably been watching our conversation for a while, they all probably had. 'What *is* going on?'

'It's OK,' I said, rushing to the other side of the pub with Emily. 'I saw where it landed.'

'Jesus *Christ.*'

The TV presenter and his girlfriend were peering under their table. Emily got on her hands and knees and crawled under it, and her dress rode up. I looked away, in the direction of Andrew who was striding towards me. Then I got on my hands and knees too. 'Let me, Emily,' I said. 'I'm not wearing a dress.'

She straightened up and banged her head, backed out while rubbing it.

'What does it look like?' asked the TV presenter.

'A wedding ring,' said Emily.

'How did that happen?' said Andrew.

The ring had disappeared.

'Congratulations,' said the TV presenter and his girlfriend. 'I'm sure he'll find it.'

I had found it. I was tempted to slip it into my pocket and pawn it later.

'Here it is,' I said, coming out from the table on my knees.

Emily held out her hand. Instead of dropping it into her palm I slid it over the end of her finger, all the way to the base.

'Why, Paul, were you removing Emily's wedding ring?' Andrew asked, after we'd moved away from the table.

'Calm down,' said Emily. 'I was just saying it was stuck already, and he was explaining, demonstrating, how to take it off.'

He looked at me, his forehead as knotty as old tree bark. I was pleased I'd annoyed him. I put my hand in my jacket to make sure I still had my cards. My reflex was to apologise but I bit down hard on it and said I was going for a cigarette.

*

While I was smoking, Sophie came out and we had a conversation I don't like to think about. No, I said, I did not throw Emily's ring across the pub on purpose, as a comment on the marriage, and it was not even a Freudian slip of the hand.

Whatever you might think.

But I suggested to Sophie that it was now a good opportunity to proceed with our plan and go off somewhere on our own, wasn't it?

'Ah,' she said.

She had been thinking actually, she said, that she should go back and check on her mum, and we could hang out another time, was that all right?

'Right?' I said. 'Right?'

'Stop saying right. Is it all right?'

'How it could it not be all right? How could any reasonable man insist you leave your miserable mum on her own, if that's what she is, miserable and at home and on her own.'

The sun was fading out, and we were nearly finished. I only had to turn around and go. But I didn't.

'So it's not OK,' she said. 'I understand you're disappointed but I don't think you have the right to be annoyed, given the circumstances.'

'We'd made an arrangement. I was looking forward to it.'

'So was I!'

'Come on.'

'You really are needy. I don't make excuses.'

'You certainly believe the press releases you write for yourself.'

'Oh, fuck you.'

'It's just inconsiderate and insensitive. To puff yourself up with virtuousness by evoking your sad mother to me.'

'Oh, Paul, I'm sorry about your mum, but I just won't do emotional blackmail.'

We might have come back from the brink if I'd walked away then. It would probably have been the end but we might have remained friends.

'I'm sorry,' I said. 'I just thought we were going to take care of each other today.'

Her expression softened and she'd stepped up close to me before something occurred to her. 'Why would you need taking care of? What's your disappointment here?'

'There's no disappointment. I just mean – '

'What do you mean?'

'Nothing.'

'What was I to you? Just a way of making her jealous? Pissing off my dad?'

'If you want? Would that let you off the hook? Yes, then, if that's what you want: you were nothing to me. I used you to annoy Emily, to get at your dad. I was laughing at you all the way. That's the kind of man I am. Just a clever schemer.'

'Clever?' she said. 'What have you got away with?'

*

I thought I would try to leave with one last display of grace.

Back inside, Sophie was making her own farewells to everyone. I hung back so I'd be the last person she'd walk past, and I leaned against the wall, watching the others watch me. Sophie hugged Emily awkwardly, then Andrew swept her up in his arms and spoke into her ear.

She nodded. She shook her head. They both turned to look at me.

'I'm sorry,' I said, as she walked past me.

'Yeah, me too,' she said, and she patted me on the arm and left.

Andrew walked over to me.

'I'm really sorry about before with the ring,' I said.

'Sophie said you've been arguing.'

'Yes.'

'She didn't want to tell me what about but I can guess.'

'It was a misunderstanding.'

'Well. Let's make sure you and me understand each other. Are you planning on staying here or are you going to go now?'

'I'll, er. I'll say goodbye.'

'Correct answer.'

I nearly said something then, but I turned away to make my other farewells. When I came back to Andrew and held out my hand for him to shake, saying 'Congratulations' in a way I meant to mean 'You win', he looked at it and turned away.

Emily walked me to the door. 'Did you see that?' I asked her.

'Yes. He thinks you've been horrible to his daughter.'

'We've been horrible to each other.'

She sighed.

'Look,' I said. 'Before I go, just let me say – '

'No,' she said. 'Please don't. There's nothing to say.'

'OK.'

'I asked you to go home that night but you insisted on following me. I was trying to avoid this.'

'You make me sound like such a creep. Following you around.'

'I just mean that it's best you don't any more.'

'Right.'

'So I'm going to go back in now and enjoy the rest of my wedding day.'

'But – '

'No,' she said, 'that's the end,' and she turned away from me to go back to him.

'Emily?' I said, when she was at the door.

She turned around. 'What?'

'How do you do it?'

'Do what?'

'How do you fuck him, Emily?'

She held up her hand between us and went inside.

*

But it was only the end if I agreed it was the end, and it wasn't much more than half an hour's walk back to their street in Holland Park. Enough time for me to cool down, and enough time for me to heat up. It would have been so easy for them if I walked away, so easy for me to stop existing. Even though

I had imagined them so thoroughly, even though I could close my eyes and see them in front of me, show them the places where they were transparent. They would never get to know how wrong they were about me, how refined my perceptions really were. I would think of them and they would not think of me.

I came up through an underpass into a council estate that turned quickly into the townhouses of Holland Park. I slowed my pace now as I walked past those house fronts iced like wedding cakes in thick white stucco. The traffic noise was receding into the distance; but even on a Saturday builders were converting attics and calling to each other from scaffolding.

When I arrived at the corner of their street, I went slower still, but eventually I had to arrive at their building. I looked up at it for a long moment, up at the top windows where the tall trees from the private garden square reflected, and I looked along the road at the pillars and railings lined up in perfect order. Above the windows and the edges of the roof there were moulded little flourishes of decoration, careful strokes of beauty, the whole road sculpted to calm and reassure, to convince us of our civilisation. I didn't want it to civilise me so I climbed the steps to their door and stood there looking at the mouth of their letter box.

You know what I did next. I took the cards out of my jacket and I opened the letter box and I pushed them through. Then I turned my back and sat down on their steps. I sneezed. I could smell cut grass from the gardens. The sun was shining on the other side of the street, on the curved walls and pillars, the cream plaster like the bonded writing paper you might ink with a last will and testament. Each morning, for the foreseeable, Emily and Andrew would come down these steps and start their new day.

I hated them for that, but I didn't hate them enough.

When I got up again I jabbed several of the doorbells belonging to the other flats in the building until a Slavic-sounding voice answered.

'I posted the wrong letter,' I said. 'Could you let me in to pick it up?'

'I'm sorry. Who are you?'

'I'm a friend of Emily and Andrew's.'

'Sorry. Don't know you. Can't let you in.'

I rang the doorbell again. And again. Someone else answered.

'I'm sorry,' he said. 'But I don't know you.'

'Please.'

'I am calling the police if you don't go.'

'Please,' I said. 'This is life or death.'

'Stop ringing, please. You need to go away.'

I walked back down the steps and looked up at the building. 'Hello! Hello!' I shouted. An open sash window dropped like a guillotine.

'Please!' I shouted. 'I posted some letters I need to get back.'

No one came. The street was empty. The windows were blank. I went back to the doors and pressed the buzzers for all the flats. Nothing. I looked into the lens of the camera and held my hands out.

'I just need my letters back!' I shouted. 'I just need you to let me in. You don't need to be scared of me! You don't need to shut yourselves away!'

When I went back down the steps and looked back up again, I saw a man's figure retreat from the window that had shut on me.

'You!' I shouted. 'Sir! You, sir, who shut the window! Please, just buzz me in. I've made a mistake! I need to correct it.'

I looked around for something light I could throw against his window to get his attention again. There was a skip a few doors down, and I rummaged around in it until I found a little chunk of masonry that didn't feel too heavy.

I tried the buzzers one more time.

All they had to do was let me in, and I would have left them alone forever. I called again. 'Hello! Hello!' Then I threw the little piece of rubble up at the window. The window didn't break; no one was in any danger. It just cracked a bit.

The window opened. A white-haired man looked down at me. 'What the hell are you doing? The police were called five minutes ago, you know, and all of this is on camera.'

'Please,' I said. 'Just let me in. I posted the wrong letter!'

He retreated from the window again, and I sat back down on the steps and put my head in my hands. Then I stood back up.

'Fine!' I shouted. 'I tried! Let them know I tried!'

The building loomed over me, serene, the windows filled with reflected greenery.

I set off walking, dawdling past the doorways, stopping to look back in the direction from where I was coming. I still believed then that I could reverse things, that I could come back in an hour and explain – that the man whose window I'd broken would see the funny side and perhaps even let me off the repair bill when I offered to pay him.

I still believed that they would let me in, that this was all a mistake.

When a police car came past on a corner, the officer in the passenger seat looking hard at me, I smiled at him as though I belonged and kept moving. And as soon as I was round the corner and out of their sight I ran as fast as I could to the Tube. I didn't dare to wait for the elevator down. Instead I skipped down the stairs, all ninety-three of them, and when I got to the platform I threw myself through some closing doors and I sat down and started to laugh as the train took us east. People were looking at me and shuffling away but I didn't care. They didn't let me in. They would never let me in. I was not coming back here.

TWENTY-TWO

I don't regret what I did, not when I'm angry. It was the only thing I could do to get their attention. It was in bad taste and led to the end of my short new career. But it was that moment. You have to understand the context. I thought I had more to lose by being decent than by being awful. I was wrong, but it felt good then.

And of course I wish I hadn't done it. Of course! I'm not stupid.

'I know that,' you say. 'See you next week?'

'Yes, thanks. Unless you fancy a drink later?'

You look up at me, startled for a second then weary. 'See you next week,' you say. 'We still have work to do.'

*

On the last weekend before Mum's house was sold, Amy and I walked down to the beach together at sunset. The wind was up high, rustling the scrub grass and blowing new shapes out of the sand that had escaped onto the promenade. Grit scoured our cheeks, and it was about to rain; pink burned over the top of some thinner clouds and opened a gap; sunlight skimmed across the water and set alight the windows of the grand terraces that faced the sea. It was here a year ago that we had scattered her ashes, after a stupid argument about whether or not Catholics had to have their ashes buried or not. Mum had never specified what she wanted, in her will or to us; she hadn't come close to dying until she did. Amy and I had to make educated guesses about how we were supposed to honour her. We would never know if we were doing it right, and it would never matter if we weren't.

We'd picked that evening after looking online to see when high tide would come in, and we hadn't been the only ones: men were positioned at intervals along the edge of the sea, sitting on camping chairs with their rods bending into the lines they'd cast.

It had been hard to decide on something ceremonial to perform for her and us in the wide open space. We couldn't lay down flowers without littering, without the sea swallowing them. Instead we had taken carrier bags with us and now we set about picking up the litter from the bay where we had scattered her ashes, keeping that part of the coast clean for her, putting tins of strong lager and bottles of cider and jumbo bags of crisps into a carrier bag, a pair of knickers and a tray of curry and chips, and many boxes now empty of super-sized cigarettes. I pulled up a carrier bag tangled in a line of seaweed and a troop of sandhoppers scattered. There was a seagull carcass there I would come back for later.

'Paul? Amy?'

One of the fishers pulled down his hood and waved.

'Hi, Mike,' we called, and walked over to him.

'What the hell are you doing?' he asked.

'It's been a year,' said Amy, 'since we scattered Mum's ashes here. We're just sort of keeping it clean for her. Something to do.'

'Right. That's something,' he agreed.

'How's the catch tonight?' I asked.

'I've had nothing yet, but might still. Lad down there picked up a decent codling.'

We looked to the lad down there. He was sitting on his stool with his head in his hands.

'Doesn't seem to have made him very happy,' I said.

'None of us lads out here are bursting with joy,' said Mike. 'At least not on the outside. Did I see there's a *Sold* sign outside your mum's?'

'That's why we're here,' said Amy. 'Our last weekend. They're moving in on Thursday.'

'Right. I suppose that's the last I'll see of you, is it?'

'I hope not,' I said.

'Me too,' said Amy. 'We'll come back.'

'Will you really? You say that, but.'

'We will do. To remember Mum. And keep this bit clean for her. Once a year, anyway.'

The sun came out for a few seconds and lit his face before the cloud cast him in shadow again. 'I can do that sometimes,' he said. 'When you're away.'

'That's good of you,' I said. 'We'll be here every year, on the anniversary, at least.'

'I wonder if we should have cremated our Carl and scattered him out here. I'd have liked that. But Janine wouldn't; it's her who matters most. She likes being able to take flowers down, in the mornings, to the cemetery.'

Behind him his rod started to twitch. 'I think you might have something,' said Amy.

*

We watched him bring it in. He held the rod in a tight grip with his right thumb and reeled it in with his good left hand. Even in the grey light of the cloud cover, the fish, a little longer than my hand, flashed from yellow to silver.

'What is it?' asked Amy.

'Whiting,' said Mike, holding it against his chest while he reached down into its mouth to take the hook out.

'Are you going to eat it?'

'I could do. This one's not much of a meal though. Do you want it?'

We didn't.

'Yeah,' he said. 'More hassle than it's worth. Do you want to have a look at it before I let it go? Hold it tight, don't let it thrash around or it'll be too weak to go back in.'

Amy took the fish in her hands.

'Have you hurt it?'

'Nah.'

'How do you know?'

'I don't. But I can take the hook out without damaging it, you see. You just thread it through. Here, why don't you two let it go?'

I looked down at the creature in Amy's hands. 'OK. Do we just throw it?'

'Try and put it in gently, or it'll get stunned and a seagull will swoop on it.'

I looked up and there were already two circling above us.

'Give me a hand, Paul.'

I came over and we held the fish together.

'Do it when the tide's going back,' Mike said.

A wave came in and we came too close to it; the water went into my shoes and socks.

'Fuck it,' we said, and stepped out further into the freezing water.

'Now,' said Amy, and we let the fish slip out of our hands. We looked up at the seagulls and waved our hands. Wah! Wah! Fuck off, you beasts! And then we looked back to the water, looking for the flash of silver, imagining we could see it, and that we knew what it was like to be out there, untethered, without the pull of the line; the freedom we would never be sure we wanted.

Amy put her hands on her stomach. 'Let's go home and get warm.'

We said goodbye to Mike. 'It was nice knowing you,' he said.

'We'll still come home,' I said. 'We'll see you again.'

'Well,' he said. 'I'm not going anywhere. I'll be here when the tide's up, seeing what gets washed in.'

He faced back to the water, and checked his rod. We turned and headed up over the shingle back to the prom. On the way I picked up the dead seagull by the feet and bagged it, left it by a bin, and Amy and I walked back to the house together listening to the waves, and looking out to the lights on the water, the homing points the small boats used to find the channel into harbour.

We could call it home for now. It would be home until we left it behind.

ACKNOWLEDGEMENTS

Thank you to my agent Peter Straus, and to his colleagues at Rogers, Coleridge & White. To my editor Stefan Tobler and to Javerya Iqbal, Eleanor Kent, Nichola Smalley and Tara Tobler at And Other Stories. To my friends who read and offered advice on early drafts of the book: Keiran Goddard, Joe Thomas, Francis Bickmore, Lee Brackstone, Mark Richards, Clare Conville, Sophie Mackintosh, Catherine O'Flynn, Ed Lake, Natasha Stallard and Steven McGregor, and in particular to Alan Mahar and Anna Kelly. To Jacques Testard, Ben Eastham and Francesca Wade for publishing and editing part of an early version of the novel in the *White Review* in 2015. To Joe Stretch, Martin Catterall and Yvonne Dodoo-Catterall, my generous hosts in Manchester. To Stuart Hammond, for welcoming me into the palace above Greggs. To Arts Council England, for financial support throughout my writing career and during the writing of this book. To my colleagues at the Centre for New Writing, Manchester. To my family and friends from Fleetwood and the Fylde coast. And to Anna Kelly again, for much more than editorial advice.

Dear readers,

As well as relying on bookshop sales, And Other Stories relies on subscriptions from people like you for many of our books, whose stories other publishers often consider too risky to take on.

Our subscribers don't just make the books physically happen. They also help us approach booksellers, because we can demonstrate that our books already have readers and fans. And they give us the security to publish in line with our values, which are collaborative, imaginative and 'shamelessly literary'.

All of our subscribers:

- receive a first-edition copy of each of the books they subscribe to
- are thanked by name at the end of our subscriber-supported books
- receive little extras from us by way of thank you, for example: postcards created by our authors

BECOME A SUBSCRIBER,
OR GIVE A SUBSCRIPTION TO A FRIEND

Visit andotherstories.org/subscriptions to help make our books happen. You can subscribe to books we're in the process of making. To purchase books we have already published, we urge you to support your local or favourite bookshop and order directly from them – the often unsung heroes of publishing.

OTHER WAYS TO GET INVOLVED

If you'd like to know about upcoming events and reading groups (our foreign-language reading groups help us choose books to publish, for example) you can:

- join our mailing list at: andotherstories.org
- follow us on Twitter: @andothertweets
- join us on Facebook: facebook.com/AndOtherStoriesBooks
- admire our books on Instagram: @andotherpics
- follow our blog: andotherstories.org/ampersand

This book was made possible thanks to the support of:

Aaron McEnery
Aaron Schneider
Adam Lenson
Adriana Diaz Enciso
Ailsa Peate
Aine Andrews
Aisha McLean
Aisling Reina
Ajay Sharma
Alan Donnelly
Alan Simpson
Alana Rupnarain
Alastair Gillespie
Alex Hoffman
Alex Pearce
Alex Ramsey
Alex Robertson
Alexander Barbour
Alexandra Stewart
Alexandra Stewart
Ali Riley
Ali Smith
Alice Toulmin
Alicia Bishop
Alison Winston
Aliya Rashid
Alyse Ceirante
Alyssa Rinaldi
Alyssa Tauber
Amado Floresca
Amalia Gladhart
Amanda Astley
Amanda Dalton
Amanda Silvester
Amanda
Amanda Greenstein
Amanda Read
Amber Da
Amelia Dowe
Amy Bojang
Amy Rushton
Andra Dusu
Andrea Reece
Andrew Jarred
Andrew Kerr-Jarrett
Andrew Lees
Andrew Marston
Andrew McCallum
Andrew Rego
Andriy Dovbenko
Andy Marshall

Angus Walker
Anna Corbett
Anna Gibson
Anna Glendenning
Anna Milsom
Anna Pigott
Anna Zaranko
Anne Carus
Anne Craven
Anne Kangley
Anne Sticksel
Anne-Marie
    Renshaw
Anneliese O'Malley
Anonymous
Anonymous
Anonymous
Anthony Brown
Anthony Cotton
Anthony Quinn
Anthony Thomas
Antonia Lloyd-Jones
Antonia Saske
Antony Pearce
Aoife Boyd
Archie Davies
Asako Serizawa
Asher Louise
    Sydenham
Ashleigh Sutton
Ashley Cairns
Asif Jehangir
Audrey Mash
Aviv Teller
Avril Marren
Barbara Mellor
Barbara Wheatley
Barbara Spicer
Barry John Fletcher
Ben Schofield
Ben Thornton
Ben Walter
Benjamin Judge
Beryl Wesley and Kev
    Carmody
Bethlehem Attfield
Beverly Jackson
Bianca Duec
Bianca Jackson
Bianca Winter
Bill Fletcher

Bjørnar Djupevik
    Hagen
Briallen Hopper
Brian Anderson
Brian Byrne
Brian Smith
Brigita Ptackova
Briony Hey
Bruna Rotzsch –
    Thomas
Burkhard Fehsenfeld
Caitlin Erskine Smith
Caitlin Halpern
Caitlin Liebenberg
Caitriona Lally
Callum Mackay
Cam Scott
Campbell McEwan
Carol Mavor
Carolina Pineiro
Caroline Picard
Caroline West
Cassidy Hughes
Catharine
    Braithwaite
Catherine Barton
Catherine Blanchard
Catherine Lambert
Catie Kosinski
Catriona Gibbs
Cecilia Rossi
Cecilia Uribe
Ceri Webb
Chantal Wright
Charles Fernyhough
Charles Raby
Charles Dee Mitchell
Charlotte Briggs
Charlotte Holtam
Charlotte Middleton
Charlotte Whittle
China Miéville
Chris Gostick
Chris Gribble
Chris Lintott
Chris Maguire
Chris McCann
Chris & Kathleen
    Repper-Day
Chris Stevenson
Chris Tomlinson

Christian Kopf
Christian
  Schuhmann
Christina Moutsou
Christine Bartels
Christine Lewis
Christopher Allen
Christopher Mitchell
Christopher Stout
Christopher Young
Ciara Ní Riain
Ciara Nugent
Claire Adams
Claire Adams
Claire Brooksby
Claire Tristram
Claire Williams
Clare Young
Clarice Borges
Claudia Nannini
Clive Bellingham
Clotilde Beaumont
Cody Copeland
Colin Denyer
Colin Matthews
Colin Hewlett
Collin Brooke
Coral Johnson
Courtney Lilly
Csilla Toldy
Cyrus Massoudi
Daisy Savage
Dale Wisely
Dana Behrman
Daniel Coxon
Daniel Gillespie
Daniel Hahn
Daniel Ng
Daniel Oudshoorn
Daniel Pope
Daniel Wood
Daniela Steierberg
Danny Turze
Darina Brejtrova
Darren Davies
Dave Lander
Davi Rocha
David Anderson
David Bevan
David Gould
David Hebblethwaite
David Higgins
David Johnson-Davies
David F Long

David McIntyre
David Miller
David Musgrave
David Shriver
David Smith
David Steege
David Thornton
David Travis
David Willey
Davis MacMillan
Dawn Bass
Dean Taucher
Debbie Pinfold
Declan Gardner
Declan O'Driscoll
Deirdre Nic
  Mhathuna
Denis Larose
Denis Stillewagt &
  Anca Fronescu
Denton Djurasevich
Dermot McAleese
Diana Adell
Diana Cragg
Diana Digges
Diana Hutchison
Diana Romer
Dinesh Prasad
Dominic Nolan
Dominick Santa
  Cattarina
Dominique Brocard
Duncan Clubb
Duncan Marks
Dyanne Prinsen
Eamonn Foster
Earl James
Ed Burness
Ed Errington
Ed Tronick
Edward Rathke
Ekaterina Beliakova
Elaine Kennedy
Eleanor Dawson
Eleanor Maier
Eleanor Updegraff
Elie Howe
Elif Aganoglu
Elina Zicmane
Elisabeth Cook
Elisabeth Pike
Elizabeth Dillon
Elizabeth Draper
Elizabeth Franz

Elizabeth Leach
Emily Armitage
Emily McCarthy
Emily Taylor
Emily Webber
Emily Yaewon Lee &
  Gregory Limpens
Emma Barraclough
Emma Bielecki
Emma Knock
Emma Louise Grove
Emma Page
Emma Patel
Emma Perry
Emma Post
Emma Selby
Emma Timpany
Eric Anderson
Eric Tucker
Erin Cameron Allen
Erin Williamson
Esmée de Heer
Eve Anderson
Ewan Tant
F Gary Knapp
Felix Valdivieso
Filiz Emre-Cooke
Finbarr Farragher
Fiona Galloway
Fiona Liddle
Fiona Mozley
Florence Reynolds
Florian Duijsens
Forrest Pelsue
Fran Sanderson
Francesca Brooks
Francis Mathias
Freddie Radford
Frederick Lockett
Friederike Knabe
Gabriel Vogt
Gabriela Lucia Garza
  de Linde
Gabrielle Crockatt
Garan Holcombe
Garry Craig Powell
Gary Gorton
Gavin Smith
Gawain Espley
Genaro Palomo Jr
Genia Ogrenchuk
Geoff Thrower
Geoffrey Cohen
Geoffrey Urland

George Christie
George Stanbury
George Wilkinson
Georgia Dennison
German Cortez-
  Hernandez
Gerry Craddock
Gill Boag-Munroe
Gillian Ackroyd
Gillian Grant
Gillian Spencer
Gillian Stern
Gordon Cameron
Gosia Pennar
Grady Wray
Graham Blenkinsop
Graham R Foster
Greg Bowman
Hadil Balzan
Hamish Russell
Hannah Dougherty
Hannah Freeman
Hannah Procter
Hannah Vidmark
Hannah Jane
  Lownsbrough
Hans Lazda
Harriet Stiles
Haydon Spenceley
Hayley Newman
Heather Mason
Heather & Andrew
  Ordover
Heather Roche
Hebe George
Heidi Cheung
Helen Brady
Helen Brooker
Helen Coombes
Helen Peacock
Helen Wormald
Henrike Laehnemann
Henry Patino
Holly Down
Howard Robinson
Hugh Gilmore
Hyoung-Won Park
Iain Forsyth
Ian Barnett
Ian C. Fraser
Ian McMillan
Ian Mond
Ian Hagues
Iciar Murphy

Ifer Moore
Ilona Abb
Ingrid Olsen
Irene Croal
Irene Mansfield
Irina Tzanova
Isabel Adey
Isabella Garment
Isabella Weibrecht
Isobel Foxford
J Collins
Jacinta Perez Gavilan
  Torres
Jack Brown
Jack Hargreaves
Jacob Blizard
Jacob Swan Hyam
Jacqueline Lademann
Jacqueline Ting Lin
Jacqui Jackson
Jake Nicholls
James Beck
James Crossley
James Cubbon
James Dahm
James Kinsley
James Lehmann
James Lesniak
James Leveque
James Mewis
James Plummer
James Portlock
James Russell
James Scudamore
Jamie Cox
Jamie Mollart
Jamie Walsh
Jane Bryce
Jane Fairweather
Jane Leuchter
Jane Roberts
Jane Roberts
Jane Woollard
Jannik Lyhne
Jasmine Gideon
Jasmine Haniff
Jayne Watson
JC Sutcliffe
Jeff Collins
Jeff Questad
Jeff Van Campen
Jeffrey Danielson
Jenifer Logie
Jennifer Arnold

Jennifer Bernstein
Jennifer Fatzinger
Jennifer Higgins
Jennifer Watts
Jennifer Wiegele
Jenny Huth
Jenny Messenger
Jenny Newton
Jeremy Morton
Jerry Simcock
Jess Howard-
  Armitage
Jesse Coleman
Jesse Thayre
Jessica Laine
Jessica Martin
Jessica Queree
Jethro Soutar
Jill Westby
Jillian Jones
Jo Goodall
Jo Harding
Jo Woolf
Joanna Luloff
Joanne Smith
Joao Pedro Bragatti
  Winckler
JoDee Brandon
Jodie Adams
Joe Gill
Joel Swerdlow
Johannes Holmqvist
John Bennett
John Berube
John Bogg
John Carnahan
John Conway
John Coyne
John Down
John Gent
John Hodgson
John Kelly
John Royley
John Shaw
John Steigerwald
John Winkelman
Jon Riches
Jon Talbot
Jonathan Blaney
Jonathan Fiedler
Jonathan Huston
Jonathan Paterson
Jonathan Ruppin
Jonathan Watkiss

Jonny Kiehlmann
Joseph Camilleri
Joseph Cooney
Joseph Darlington
Joseph Hiller
Joseph Schreiber
Josh Sumner
Joshua Davis
Joy Paul
Judyth Emanuel
Julia Peters
Julia Ellis Burnet
Julie Greenwalt
Julie Hutchinson
Julie Miller
Juliet Swann
Justin Ahlbach
Justine Goodchild
K Elkes
Kaarina Hollo
Karen Waloschek
Karl Kleinknecht &
   Monika Motylinska
Kasim Husain
Kasper Haakansson
Kasper Hartmann
Kat Burdon
Kate Attwooll
Kate Beswick
Kate Morgan
Kate Shires
Katharina Herzberger
Katharine Freeman
Katharine Robbins
Katherine El-Salahi
Katherine Gray
Katherine Mackinnon
Kathryn Edwards
Kathryn Oliver
Kathryn Williams
Katie Brown
Katie Grant
Katie Lewin
Katie Smart
Katrina Thomas
Keila Vall
Keith Walker
Kenneth Blythe
Kenneth Michaels
Kerry Parke
Kieran McGrath
Kieran Rollin
Kieron James
Kimberley Khan

Kirsten Hey
Kirsty Doole
KL Ee
Klara Rešetič
Kris Ann Trimis
Kristina Rudinskas
Krystine Phelps
Lado Violeta
Lana Selby
Lander Hawes
Laura Clarke
Laura Geraghty
Laura Kisrwani
Laura Lea
Laura Smith
Laurence Hull
Laurence Laluyaux
Laurie Sheck &
   Jim Peck
Laury Leite
Leanne Radojkovich
Lee Harbour
Leon Frey & Natalie
   Winwood
Leonie Smith
Lesley Lawn
Lesli Green
Leslie Baillie
Leslie Benziger
Lewis Green
Liliana Lobato
Lillie Rosen
Lindsay Attree
Lindsay Brammer
Lindsey Ford
Linette Arthurton
   Bruno
Lisa Fransson
Lisa Simpson
Lisa Weizenegger
Liz Clifford
Liz Ketch
Lola Boorman
Lorna Bleach
Lorna Scott Fox
Lottie Smith
Louise Evans
Louise Smith
Luc Daley
Luc Verstraete
Lucas Elliott
Lucas J Medeiros
Lucia Rotheray
Lucile Lesage

Lucy Gorman
Lucy Moffatt
Luise von Flotow
Luke Williamson
Lydia Trethewey
Lydia Unsworth
Lynda Graham
Lynn Martin
Lynn Fung
M Manfre
Madeleine Kleinwort
Madeleine Maxwell
Madeline Teevan
Mads Pihl Rasmussen
Maeve Lambe
Mahan L Ellison &
   K Ashley Dickson
Malcolm and Rachel
   Alexander
Malgorzata Rokicka
Mandy Wight
Marcel Schlamowitz
Maria Ahnhem Farrar
Maria Hill
Maria Lomunno
Maria Losada
Maria Pia Tissot
Marie Cloutier
Marie Donnelly
Marike Dokter
Marina Castledine
Marina Galanti
Mario Sifuentez
Marja S Laaksonen
Marjorie Schulman
Mark Harris
Mark Sargent
Mark Sheets
Mark Sztyber
Mark Waters
Marlene Adkins
Martha Brenckle
Martha Nicholson
Martha Stevns
Martin Brown
Martin Nathan
Mary Brockson
Mary Byrne
Mary Carozza
Mary Heiss
Mary Lynch
Mary Morton
Mary Nash
Mary Wang

Mary Ellen Nagle
Matt Davies
Matt Greene
Matt Jones
Matt O'Connor
Matthew Adamson
Matthew Armstrong
Matthew Banash
Matthew Black
Matthew Eatough
Matthew Francis
Matthew Gill
Matthew Lowe
Matthew Warshauer
Matthew Woodman
Matty Ross
Maureen Cullen
Maurice Mengel
Max Cairnduff
Max Garrone
Max Longman
Max McCabe
Meaghan Delahunt
Meg Lovelock
Megan Oxholm
Megan Taylor
Megan Wittling
Melissa Apfelbaum
Melissa Beck
Melissa Quignon-
   Finch
Meredith Jones
Meredith Martin
Michael Bichko
Michael Dodd
Michael James
   Eastwood
Michael Gavin
Michael Holt
Michael Kuhn
Michael
   Schneiderman
Michael Shayer
Michael Carver
Michelle
   Lotherington
Mike Bittner
Mike Timms
Mike Turner
Milla Rautio
Milo Bettocchi
Mira Harrison
Miranda Gold
Miranda Persaud

Miriam McBride
Moray Teale
Morven Dooner
Myka Tucker-
   Abramson
Myles Nolan
N Tsolak
Namita Chakrabarty
Nan Craig
Nancy Jacobson
Nancy Oakes
Natalie & Richard
Nathalie Atkinson
Neferti Tadiar
Neil George
Nicholas Brown
Nicholas Jowett
Nick Chapman
Nick James
Nick Nelson &
   Rachel Eley
Nick Sidwell
Nick Twemlow
Nicola Hart
Nicola Meyer
Nicola Mira
Nicola Sandiford
Nicole Matteini
Nigel Fishburn
Nina Alexandersen
Nina Parish
Olga Alexandru
Olga Zilberbourg
Olivia Payne
Olivia Turner
Pamela Tao
Patricia Appleyard
Patricia Aronsson
Patrick McGuinness
Paul Cray
Paul Jones
Paul Munday
Paul Robinson
Paul Scott
Paula Edwards
Paula Enler Skyttberg
Pavlos Stavropoulos
Penelope Hewett
   Brown
Penny Simpson
Perlita Payne
Peter McBain
Peter McCambridge
Peter Rowland

Peter Vos
Peter Wells
Philip Carter
Philip Lewis
Philip Lom
Philip Warren
Philipp Jarke
Phoebe Harrison
Phoebe Lam
Phyllis Reeve
Pia Figge
Piet Van Bockstal
Pippa Tolfts
Polly Morris
PRAH Foundation
Rachael de Moravia
Rachael Williams
Rachel Carter
Rachel Matheson
Rachel Meacock
Rachel Swearingen
Rachel Van Riel
Rachel Watkins
Ramon Bloomberg
Rebecca Braun
Rebecca Carter
Rebecca Moss
Rebecca Parry
Rebecca Peer
Rebecca Roadman
Rebecca Rosenthal
Rebecca Schwarz
Rhiannon Armstrong
Rhodri Jones
Rich Sutherland
Richard Ashcroft
Richard Bauer
Richard Carter
Richard Gwyn
Richard Harrison
Richard Mansell
Richard Priest
Richard Shea
Richard Soundy
Rick Tucker
Rita O'Brien
Robert Gillett
Robert Hamilton
Robert Hannah
Robert Orton
Robin Taylor
Roger Newton
Roger Ramsden
Ronan Cormacain

Rory Williamson
Rosalind May
Rosalind Ramsay
Rosanna Foster
Rose Crichton
Rose Renshaw
Ross Trenzinger
Rowan Sullivan
Roxanne O'Del Ablett
Roz Simpson
Ruby Kane
Rupert Ziziros
Ruth Jordan
Ruth Morgan
Ruth Porter
S Italiano
Sabine Little
Sally Baker
Sally Warner
Sally Whitehill
Sally Hemsley
Sam Gordon
Sam Reese
Sam Scott Wood
Samuel Crosby
Santiago Sánchez
   Cordero
Sara Sherwood
Sarah Arboleda
Sarah Barnes
Sarah Booker
Sarah Edwards
Sarah Forster
Sarah Laycock
Sarah Lucas
Sarah Moss
Sarah Pybus
Sarah Watkins
Sarah Roff
Sarah Ryan
Scott Chiddister
Sez Kiss
Shannon Knapp
Sharon Mccammon
Shauna Gilligan
Shauna Rogers
Sheridan Marshall
Sherman Alexie
Sheryl Jermyn
Shira Lob
Sian Hannah
Silvia Naschenveng
Simon Pitney
Simon Robertson

Simon Clark
Simone Few
Sjón
SK Grout
Sophia Wickham
Sophie Morris
ST Dabbagh
Stacy Rodgers
Stefanie Schrank
Stefano Mula
Stella Francis
Stephan Eggum
Stephanie Lacava
Stephen Cunliffe
Stephen Pearsall
Stephen Pearsall
Steve Chapman
Steven & Gitte Evans
Stuart Wilkinson
Sue Craven
Susan Ferguson
Susan Higson
Susan Howard
Susan Winter
Susie Roberson
Suzanne Lee
Suzy Hounslow
Sylvie Zannier-Betts
Tamara Larsen
Tania Hershman
Tara Roman
Taylor Ffitch
Teresa Griffiths
Terry Kurgan
The Mighty Douche
   Softball Team
Thom Keep
Thomas Baker
Thomas Bell
Thomas Mitchell
Thomas van den Bout
Tiffany Lehr
Tim Kelly
Tim Scott
Tim Theroux
Timothy Cummins
Tina Rotherham-
   Winqvist
Toby Halsey
Toby Hyam
Toby Ryan
Tom Darby
Tom Doyle
Tom Franklin

Tom Gray
Tom Mooney
Tom Stafford
Tom Whatmore
Tony Bastow
Torna Russell-Hills
Tory Jeffay
Tracey Martin
Tracy Bauld
Tracy Lee-Newman
Trevor Wald
Tricia Durdey
Tricia Pillay
Val Challen
Valerie O'Riordan
Valerie Sirr
Vanessa Baird
Vanessa Dodd
Vanessa Nolan
Vanessa Rush
Vicki White
Vicky van der Luit
Victor Meadowcroft
Victoria Adams
Victoria Goodbody
Victoria Huggins
Victoria Maitland
Victoria Steeves
Vijay Pattisapu
Virginia Bond
Virginia Doster
Walter Smedley
Wendy Langridge
William
   Brockenborough
William Dennehy
William Franklin
William Richard
William Schwaber
Yoora Yi Tenen
Zachary Hope
Zara Rahman
Zoe Taylor
Zoe Thomas
Zoë Brasier